Secrets and Lies

REDEMPTION'S EDGE BOOK TWO

EXPANDED ANNIVERSARY EDITION

BOOKS BY JANET SKETCHLEY

The Redemption's Edge Series:

Heaven's Prey
Secrets and Lies
Without Proof

The Green Dory Inn Mysteries:

Unknown Enemy
Hidden Secrets
Bitter Truth
Deadly Burden

Daily Devotions:

A Year of Tenacity: 365 Daily Devotions

Tenacity at Christmas: 31 Daily Devotions for December

Readers Journals:

Reads to Remember:
A book-lover's journal to track your next 100 reads
(Available in two cover options, print only)

Secrets and Lies

REDEMPTION'S EDGE
BOOK TWO

EXPANDED ANNIVERSARY EDITION

JANET SKETCHLEY

Secrets and Lies, A Redemption's Edge Novel

First edition: Janet Sketchley, 2014
Expanded anniversary edition (Second edition): Janet Sketchley, 2024

© 2014, 2024 by Janet Sketchley www.janetsketchley.ca

ISBN 978-1-989581-14-8 (epub)

ISBN 978-1-989581-13-1 (print)

Edited by Angela Breidenbach.

Cover Design by Christina Fuselli, Fuselli Art & Design. Photography by Can Stock Photo Inc.

Published in Canada by Janet Sketchley.

FICTION/CHRISTIAN/SUSPENSE

DEDICATION

To Russell,
with love and gratitude.
You're a major source of the music in my life.
Come to think of it, you introduced me to my first Billy Joel
album,
Glass Houses, all those years ago.
And you make a fine pot of tea.

~~~

ABOUT THIS EXPANDED ANNIVERSARY EDITION

Carol and Paul's experiences in Toronto really started with an event in Calgary. This edition gives readers the full story, and I've taken the opportunity to streamline the prose.

Please note this book uses Canadian spellings. You'll see words like colour, neighbour, licence, and travelling, and they're not typos. You'll also see some hyphenated words like mid-fifties and mid-size. You'll also see Tim Hortons: a Canadian coffee chain, spelled without an apostrophe.

Prologue

"THOSE BROWNIES ARE for my movie night." In the apartment's galley-style kitchen, Carol Daniels stepped around her teenage son, Paul, and put away the cup she'd been drying.

He lifted another square of rich brown cake from the pan, balanced it on the stack already on his plate, and shot her a grin. "Jackie's always on a diet. I'm reducing the temptation."

"Right." Carol flicked him with her tea towel and grabbed a dish from the drainer.

A knock at the door said her friend from downstairs had arrived. "Want to hang around and see what movie she brought?"

Paul curled a protective hand over his food. "And risk sharing?"

He headed for his bedroom as she went to answer the door. The dog jostled past her, tail wagging. "Hey, Chance, I can't let her in if you're in the way."

She nudged the dog aside with her knee and spotted a white envelope on the carpet. Someone in the building must be doing another fundraiser. She picked it up, checked the peephole, and pulled open the door. "Don't trip over the welcoming committee."

While Jackie stooped to rub Chance's ears, Carol slit the envelope with her finger and pulled out a sheet of paper.

Your brother thinks he's safe in jail, but you and your son are easy targets. Especially the boy.

Tremors spread from her stomach. Rocked her whole body. She read the words again. And again. Studied the envelope. It bore her name in bold letters. "I—did you see anyone out there?"

"No. Why?" Jackie straightened. One look at Carol, and she reached for the note. "What's wrong?"

Carol held out the paper and wilted against the wall. Chance pressed his muzzle into her leg, whining softly.

Jackie took her arm and led her into the living room, then sat beside her on the couch. "You need to call the police."

"Maybe." Carol stood, stepped around the dog, and walked to the window. In the evening light, the traffic, pedestrians, and scraps of windblown litter on the street below looked the same as always.

What did she expect, a guy in a mask wearing a "villain" sign? Whoever he was, he'd left the note and was long gone. Another nut case.

Except this one sounded dangerous.

She turned to Jackie, speaking low so Paul wouldn't hear. "What can the police do? Every time there's something about Harry in the news, the crazies start calling. Even with our unlisted number. After the stunt that reporter pulled last week, they know where I live."

The memory sparked a slow burn in her cheeks. She roamed the cramped living room, tidying what was already tidy, straightening already-straight pictures on the walls. Forget the new job she'd applied for and her hopes of a higher salary to ease life for her and Paul.

Jackie's voice broke into her thoughts. "What about witness protection?"

"It's only been harassment until now, and we're not witnesses to anything. We're just related to a dangerous offender."

Carol darted into the kitchen and grabbed the pan of brownies. She carried them to the couch, plopped down beside her friend, and crammed the first one into her mouth whole. She forced herself to chew the second one slowly and concentrate on the taste, the texture.

Jackie waved off the food and drew her knees to her chest. "What are you going to do?"

The brownie went down in a lump that brought tears to Carol's eyes. "We have to move. Paul's all I have left."

"Where will you go?"

"Somewhere we can lose ourselves."

Chapter 1

Three months later

CAROL JOLTED UPRIGHT, eyes wide in the dark. She searched for familiar touchstones to pull her back to reality. The faint light outlining her bedroom curtains. The red digits on her clock radio, mocking her with the hours left until dawn. The two shadowed rectangles on her bureau—Paul's and Keith's school photos.

Her hands ached. It took a conscious act of will to release her two-fisted grip on the sheets.

Paul.

The dream's afterimages burned in her imagination. Her sixteen-year-old son, larger than life on a brightly-lit stage, arms raised to embrace the crowd's cheers, electric guitar slung low across his hips. An oversized brown leather jacket hung open over his faded tee shirt and jeans.

She knew that jacket. Butter-soft Italian calfskin, steeped in beer and Old Spice, nicked and scraped here and there and with a cigarette burn inside the left cuff.

Skip's jacket. Paul's father's.

In her dream, she'd stood beside her son but Paul only had eyes for his fans. An almost palpable energy radiated from his body—the same power trip that took Skip whenever he performed. With the same cost to those who loved him.

4

The cheering swelled. Paul swung his guitar in a move that knocked Carol off the stage.

She'd awakened from a panicked sense of free-fall. Her heart slowed now, each beat heavy, sodden. Hopeless.

She pushed sweaty bangs off her forehead. Breathe. Slowly. Deeply. Dreams died in the waking.

The dog stood like a shadow at her bedside. He gave another low whine and licked her arm.

"I'm okay, Chance."

She rolled over and buried her face in his shaggy fur. The scene played again in her mind. Shivering, she tightened her hold on the dog, anchoring in his comforting scent.

After a minute, she released him and slid out of bed, into floppy slippers and her old robe. She peered through a crack in the curtains. The street lay deserted.

In the short hallway, she pressed her fingertips against Paul's door. Light snores reached her through the wood. Her firstborn—the only one left to her since they'd lost his brother, Keith.

She fled for the kitchen, Chance at her heels. She flicked on the overhead light and turned on the radio to the all-night request show.

"Lookin' Out My Back Door"? An unusual pick for the middle of the night, but the whimsical song tugged her lips into a smile.

At least the bright tempo swept away the final shards of her dream. She grabbed the kettle and added enough water for tea. She had not moved halfway across the country to fall apart. This was a fresh start for her and Paul. Safe, anonymous, positive.

Once she'd plugged in the kettle, she snagged the wall phone. Her call went through on the third try. Lucky this time, for a change.

"Welcome to All-Request Oldies. What would you like to hear tonight?" On the radio, the music kept playing.

"Hi, Joey. It's Carol." She stretched the phone cord to reach the counter and poured boiling water into a blue-flowered porcelain cup.

"Carol!" He always sounded glad she called. As if she were a friend he hadn't heard from in years instead of a stranger who phoned once or twice a week. Part of the job, but he did it well. "What're you up to at this hour of the morning?"

She dipped the teabag, turning the water amber-gold. The scent of peppermint teased her nostrils. "Making myself a cup of tea." She kept her tone light. "Some nights I sleep better than others."

"I held off on playing Billy Joel in case you phoned."

She padded across the kitchen, careful not to spill her tea. "Am I that predictable?"

"Hey, I said 'in case.' One sec. Song's over. Don't go." Click. The hiss of dead air meant he'd parked the call and unmuted his station mic.

She slid a chair out from the table. Half-listening to Joey on the radio giving the next lineup of songs, she sank onto the neatly taped vinyl and eased her feet up onto its mate.

Chance rested his muzzle on her leg.

When the Beatles started singing "Blackbird," Joey's rich baritone came back on the phone. "You still with me?"

"Mm-hmm."

"Want to talk about it?"

"You've got work to do." The dream sounded silly now. Joey understood the usual ones of Paul in danger, but how could she explain why a band dream left her cold to the core, more... desolate? And shaken by aftershocks?

"I just bought us twelve minutes, so shoot."

She touched the cup's rim to her lips. Hot, but not painful. The spicy tea set her mouth tingling. "My son was playing in a band. Dressed like his father."

"His father's dead, isn't he? Are you afraid it's some kind of warning?"

"No—well, not about death this time. Maybe this is worse, because it's more likely to come true." The words froze her lips. "The boys never knew how big a rat Skip was. Paul built him into a musical legend."

Her fingertip connected the chips in the faded tabletop. "I shouldn't have called. I can't even think of a song to request."

"No worries. I know what you like by now. What kind of tea are you drinking?"

"Hmm? Oh, peppermint. It smells like freedom."

"Freedom's good. Tell you what, I'll wait fifteen minutes or so and play something to send you better dreams."

"Thanks, Joey. It's been good to hear a friendly voice."

"Trust me. You'll make it. I'll say a little prayer for you."

Ever since the first night in Toronto, when she'd found his show after a nightmare-fractured sleep, Joey'd been saying things would work out. So far, he was right.

She'd barely hung up the phone when doubt kicked in. She'd said too much. Shouldn't have mentioned Skip's name or that he'd been a musician.

Joey only knew her as Carol. No last name. With the extra details, he could find out who she was.

Fear tiptoed along her spine. If word leaked that she'd moved to Toronto, and if the note-sending psycho from Calgary heard...

She glanced down at the dog, asleep on the floor. Worst-case, what if the guy came looking for them? With over six million people in the Greater Toronto Area, only blind luck would let him find them.

Even so, she shouldn't have lowered her defences. From now on, she'd be more careful. She swallowed the last of her tea, rinsed her mug, and headed back to bed.

Warm but awake, she turned on her bedside radio and tried to drift away on the music.

Before long, Joey announced, "This next one's for Carol. Sleep well."

The haunting first notes of Billy Joel's "Through the Long Night" washed the tension from her muscles, and she smiled in the darkness. Her coping mechanisms might be odd, but they were safer than prayer.

Chapter 2

TUESDAY EVENING, PAUL Daniels hummed a Clapton tune as he passed a soft cloth over the guitar's glossy ebony-finished maple body. He polished them all with care, but this one he cherished—a Gibson Les Paul Custom, ticketed at almost six thousand dollars. Someday, he'd own an instrument like this.

The door chime sounded as he moved along the line of instruments. He turned and flashed a grin at the chunky teen who entered. "Hey, Barry, how's it going?"

His friend watched a black car pull away from the curb, then scruffed up his hair and untucked his shirt. "Better now. I'm glad Mom didn't decide to sit in on my lesson again today."

"After the performance you gave her last week? I'm surprised she let you come back." Paul stowed his cleaning supplies in a cupboard under the counter.

"Mr. Morelli convinced her I do better on my own. He can turn on the charm when he wants to." Barry rested his guitar case against his leg.

Paul shrugged. "He sure knows how to play the customers, but I've never seen that side of him in a lesson. Man, he can be fierce."

"That's because you're a prodigy. He's easier on me." Barry's eyebrows lifted, and his eyes narrowed the way they always did when he got an idea. "Morelli was so good with my mom, I'll bet he could even handle yours if she finds out about your work-for-lessons deal."

Ignoring the sudden catch in his breathing, Paul leaned his elbows on the counter. "It should be easier now that school's started. Homework's a great excuse."

"As long as you get it done."

"It'll get done."

Another student, Franca, emerged from the room at the rear of the store lugging a soft-sided guitar case, her face pale and pinched. As she passed the boys, she whispered to Barry, "Good luck. He's in a mood."

"You must be another prodigy. He knows there's nothing better to get out of me by pushing." Barry picked up his instrument and headed for the session room.

Alone in the storefront, Paul invented a few more chores for himself before taking his place behind the counter. He caught snatches of his friend's playing.

Barry didn't care about the music. Guitar was his latest way to spend his parents' money. Mr. Morelli must sense it. He sure didn't drive the boy as hard as he did Paul.

Franca was more like Paul. They knew what it meant to be taught by someone at Morelli's level. Especially Paul, who'd come begging for handouts.

Paul's hand strayed to his jeans pocket and pulled out a folded piece of paper. He'd been carrying it around all week, not sure what to do about it but not able to throw it away.

The words his mother muttered under her breath, and the savage way she crushed the letter and flung it into the kitchen garbage, had made him retrieve it after she went to bed that night. Feeling like a spy, he'd even replaced it with another crumpled sheet.

He let it fall open on the counter. The jagged handwriting greeted him like a secret friend.

Dear Carol, I'm truly sorry for the pain and shame I've caused you. I've changed, and I'd like to make a new start. I'm not asking you to visit or even phone, but could we write or e-mail once in awhile?

It was signed simply, *Harry.*

Paul peeled a sheet of memo paper from the pad beside the cash register, "Morelli's" in flowing black script across the top with the store contact information below. He chewed the end of his pen, one elbow flattening the letter. How to even begin? The man sure didn't qualify for *dear.*

Uncle Harry, I guess you can write me at the address on this page.

The letter had been forwarded from their old address in Calgary. Paul would be in enough trouble for writing at all without revealing where they lived.

He glanced around the store. Man, he'd been angry when Mom told him they were moving—all because of that jerk reporter. And she did the extreme makeover routine.

Lucky he hadn't been in the paparazzi shots, or he'd be using a dye bottle himself.

But to have lessons with Mr. Morelli made the move worth it all.

He returned to his letter.

It must be lonely there, so if you want to write that's fine. Mom doesn't know I'm answering you. In case you haven't heard, it's just me and her now. Keith died a couple years ago from a drug overdose. I'm sixteen, and I play guitar. I'm going to be a musician like my dad.

Paul signed his name on the bottom of the sheet, folded both pages, and stuck them in his pocket. He'd grab an envelope from home. Harry had printed the prison's mailing address beneath his name.

~~~

Patrick Stairs' fingers drummed the steering wheel as he waited for traffic to unsnarl. These extracurricular deliveries always made him tense. Lately, the man he knew simply as "Lear" had been piling them on. And adding other duties.

He cranked up the satellite radio until the bass notes vibrated in his bones, but it didn't loosen his cramped muscles.

The decision to work for the drug ring had been necessary at the time. He had no regrets. However, he no longer needed the extra funds.

Getting out was proving harder than getting in. Sour liquid oozed into his stomach. He popped an antacid.

Twenty minutes later, he eased the car into a parking space and wiped the damp from his palms. No point trying to find his calm centre. Three deep breaths, then he grabbed his briefcase and strode through the glass doors of the high-rise. In the mirror-finished elevator, he stared at the penthouse indicator and willed the cables to lift him faster.

The lawyer's trophy secretary greeted him by name. Before he could sit, she spoke briefly into the phone and waved him through to the inner office.

He pulled the heavy wooden door shut behind him. It latched with a metallic snick that always shivered his spine. Like the safety on a gun—but engaging or releasing?

Dropping into one of the twin burgundy leather chairs, Patrick slid the manila envelope across the wide teak desk. "The paperwork's all here."

The Honourable Z. C. Fontaine's hand pounced like a hawk on a mouse. He slit one end and riffled through the papers for the plain white envelope, quick fingers revealing an eagerness that didn't show on his face.

Patrick kept his own expression equally impassive. Mustn't let the clientele glimpse his contempt. He might be considered unreliable, a threat.

As much as he wanted out of this farce, he wanted out alive.

When he reached the sidewalk, he sucked a lungful of air, wishing for an hour at the gym to clear his head. But no, his project waited. He slammed the car door and double-checked her photo on his phone. Carol Daniels. Pretty. Blond. With no idea Lear had her in his sights.

She'd know soon enough. Patrick pitied anyone who had to deal with the drug lord. Including himself.

He keyed the Sticky Fingers Café into his GPS and pulled into the tide of moving vehicles. One more duty to fit into the margins between his investment career and Lear's deliveries.

When he braked for a red light, he tried to loosen his grip on the leather-wrapped wheel. Curse Lear and his string pulling. One day, the man would get what was coming. Patrick hoped he'd be there to see it.

The traffic lights turned green, and he gunned the engine. Objectively, this wasn't a difficult assignment. Take occasional meals at the café where the woman worked, and feed information to Lear. He could feign interest for the time it took to gain her trust.

Success meant release from Lear's clutches. Or so the drug lord had promised.

Acid sizzled in Patrick's stomach. The only promises Lear kept were threats.

Chapter 3

JOEY HILL HOOKED his sunglasses into the open collar of his shirt as he stepped into Total Service Automotive. The windows filtered out more sun than they let pass, giving the garage a subterranean feel. The taste of oil hung in the air. It was cool in here, but he'd rather take the September heat in the open.

At the service counter, his friend Ron greeted him and ran a broad, grease-stained fingertip along the day's work schedule. "Let's see. Oil change, tire rotation, and the chance to meet a lady. That's her over there."

The sole occupant in the waiting area was an attractive blonde, sitting with her back to the window and flipping through a *Readers' Digest.*

Not what he'd expected. "Thanks. I appreciate it."

Ron leaned nearer. "I hope you know what you're doing. Remember what I said about relationships. Tangle up with a woman who isn't a Christian, and she's more likely to weaken your faith than you are to help her find any."

Joey bounced his knuckles against the counter. "I told you, it's not like that. She's a regular caller to my radio show, and I wanted to meet her."

"Yeah, right."

"Then why did you tell me she made the appointment?"

Ron stretched out his palm for the car keys. "To thank you for the referral. Do yourself a favour, Joe. Don't do anything stupid."

"That's my new motto for life." Joey took a deep breath before he approached the cluster of chairs.

The blond woman frowned at the magazine and pushed up her dark-framed glasses as if taking a closer look.

"Excuse me... Carol?"

Her head jerked up. Cool blue eyes assessed him. "Do I know you?"

It was her voice, all right, but with a chill factor that didn't do much for his confidence. "Joey Hill. From All-Request Oldies?"

"Joey!" The lines around her mouth softened, but as he stepped closer they firmed again.

He dropped into the chair across from her, leaning back to show non-threatening body language, and tried to find a trace of the Carol he knew in the perfect features and confident hairstyle. He'd imagined her to be a little older, pale with worry-lines. The packaging didn't match what was inside.

After a minute, she smiled and lowered the magazine. "I thought you'd be different somehow."

"Yeah, I get that a lot. I sound taller on radio. Sorry to disappoint you."

"No! But you look normal." Her fingertips tapped the magazine in her lap. "I didn't mean that like it sounded. It's—you look as friendly as you are on the radio. I thought it was part of the show, that you'd be more formal and polished in real life."

He tipped an eyebrow. "You mean handsome."

"No, intimidating."

"Well, no worries about that. I can't even intimidate Ron, there, to give me a discount."

15

Carol glanced at Ron as he walked past them from the service bays. "He offered me a discount today because you referred me. That always seems backward. Shouldn't you reward the existing customer instead of the new one? Not that I'm complaining. And he was really good about fitting me into his Saturday schedule when I mentioned your name in the first place."

"I'm glad." Joey had arranged her discount to be added to his bill. Ron's prices were too low for wiggle room, and Carol and her son didn't sound like they had much extra money. Joey hadn't liked the thought of her driving to work each day in a car that could drop a wheel or something.

He tapped his fingers lightly on the armrest. "I'm spoiled working nights. I usually come in on a weekday. So, is Toronto starting to feel like home yet?"

"Getting there. My son adjusted faster than I did. Between school and friends, he's not around much."

"It must be tough being a single mom. Do you have a dad or a brother to be a role model for him, even long-distance?"

She looked down, fingers curling the magazine in her lap. "No. Just me."

"That's rough. But it sounds like you're doing everything you can."

A metallic clang came from the shop. Joey settled deeper into his chair. It was good to sit and chat in person instead of talking on the phone in his lonely sound studio at the station.

Next to the music, his callers were the best part of the job. Most conversations kept to the surface. Sports scores, movies, and of course singers and songs.

But the faceless contact with a friendly voice let a handful of regulars open up to him. That's when he felt they crossed the divide from acquaintances to friends, even if he wouldn't recognize them on the sidewalk. That's where he tried to make a difference through his words or with a listening ear.

He'd never felt this push to actually meet a radio friend before.

Now, he looked around the waiting area. At his shoes. His hands. At Carol. "So, here we are, able to talk for more than twelve minutes at a time, and we're quiet. I guess the best conversations only happen in the middle of the night."

She lifted one shoulder. As it came down, she seemed to draw into herself. "They haven't all been so good."

"Not the nightmares, no. But I've enjoyed our chats."

She nodded, her focus fixed on a point off to the side. "It's easier talking on the phone. Nobody can see you."

"I think lots of people feel that way."

Her brow drew into a slow furrow. The corners of her mouth pinched. "You set this up, didn't you?"

"You don't believe in coincidence?"

"No." The chill was back in her tone.

Heat tickled the back of Joey's neck. He hoped he wasn't blushing. "Ron thanked me for recommending him, so I asked him to book me in too."

He'd thought of going to the café where she worked, but surprising her in her own territory could have felt like an invasion. Neutral ground was safer, if maybe not safe enough.

He spread his hands. "I wanted to meet you. No agenda, no expectations. And no song line-up to keep on top of."

"And you didn't think to ask?"

"Would you have agreed to meet a person you only knew through the radio?"

Her hands curled the magazine in her lap as if she'd like to take a swipe at him. "So, what—"

The service bay door banged. Ron tromped toward them and dropped into the chair beside Carol's. "Ms. Daniels, I've got good news and not-so-good news."

17

Joey thought he heard a faint hiss of indrawn breath, but she revealed no other sign of stress.

Ron kept talking. "That knocking sound was nothing." He opened his fist and held out a pair of scuffed-up dice. "Some joker put these inside your tire rim."

She took the dice in her fingertips and frowned. "Skulls."

"Yeah, little cartoon skulls instead of pips. Weird."

Carol passed the dice to Joey. "I found a couple of these on the doorstep last week, around the same time the car started making such a racket."

He bounced them gently in his palm. "If you stepped on one, you'd take a nasty tumble. Do you have a lot of stairs?"

Her gaze locked with his, eyes wide. "He couldn't have found us. Wouldn't have done that to the car. It's a harmless prank."

He? Joey's heart stopped. "Are you in danger?"

"No. We're good." She turned to Ron. "You said there was bad news."

"You've got a rear strut leaking. It doesn't have to be done today, but I wouldn't want you to drive too far before having them replaced."

Carol's face looked stiff as wax and about the same colour. "Them?"

"They have to be done in pairs, front or rear."

Her tongue darted over her lips. "How much?"

Ron held out his clipboard and touched the work order near the bottom.

Carol scanned the paper. She seemed to shrink in on herself as if this new burden pulled her a little closer to breaking. Or as if she gathered resources to fight one more battle.

Her eyes glistened, and she blinked hard.

From the service area came the high-pitched, stuttering whine of a car's lug nuts being torqued off. Ron waited, studying his feet. No doubt, he'd been through this before. Carol probably had too.

Joey's battles had been different, but watching this one made him squirm. "Uh, Ron, Carol said you gave her a referral discount. If you do the work today, can it apply to that too?"

Carol watched him through lowered lids. Wondering if this was a con the two men had set up?

Ron's frown said more along the lines of *Do you have any idea how much this is going to cost you?*

Joey drew in a slow breath. The overnight stint at City Classics paid the pits after what he'd earned in his prime-time slot in Vancouver. But he'd seen Carol's reaction.

Holding Ron's gaze, he confirmed with the barest dip of his chin.

Ron bounced his palm against the knee of his jeans. "If I can get the parts, I can maybe squeeze it in before we close. It just means nobody's leaving early for their Saturday. Ms. Daniels, I can take you out to show you what I'm talking about. Like I said, it doesn't have to be done today. And if you want a second opinion, go ahead. But it does have to be done."

He unfolded from the seat and gestured for Carol to follow him into the service bays. "Stay close to me, and watch your step."

Joey sat and listened to the vague shop noises. He'd come to meet a friend. Only a friend. Until he figured out how to do life as a man of faith, he didn't dare complicate it with romance.

But he couldn't kid himself. The protective surge he'd felt for Carol just now—had felt when they talked before, for that matter—was more than friendship.

Chapter 4

TUESDAY MORNING BEFORE work, a loud knock at the basement apartment's front door interrupted Carol's solitude. Fingers dripping suds, she spun from the breakfast dishes and grabbed the nearby hand towel.

The doorbell rang.

"How fast do you think I can move?" She snatched her glasses from the table, shoving them into place as she headed through the living room. They never used this entrance. The kitchen opened directly onto the small parking lot.

The frosted glass window in the upper part of the door showed a single silhouette. Shoulders stiff, she opened the deadbolt and pulled inward as far as the security chain allowed. She peered around the door.

A man in a brown suede jacket stood on the step. He gave her time to study him, then asked, "Carol Daniels?"

"Who wants to know?" She drew back into the room. No photo-op here.

He extended an open leather wallet. "Detective Rick Garraway of the city police. Here's my badge. I'm with special investigations. That's why I'm not in uniform."

"Has something happened to my son?" Carol's legs wobbled. She clutched the edge of the door.

"It's okay, Mrs. Daniels. Nothing to do with your son, but I do need to talk to you." He extended his badge.

After a minute, she took it. It looked real, but she'd heard of scams like this. Suspicion replaced her fear. "What's this about?"

"May I come in, please?" He reached for his badge case.

"Wait while I call your office."

The detective's eyebrows lifted and he smiled. "Wise lady."

Gripping the badge, Carol shut and bolted the door. She ran for the phone.

When she let him in a few minutes later, Detective Garraway gave an approving smile. "You keep that up, and I won't worry so much."

She locked up behind him, then led him to the kitchen. If she had to have a stranger in her home, a cop at that, it would be on her terms, in the space where she felt most in control.

The detective hung his coat on a free peg. "May I sit down?"

At her nod, he drew a chair out from the table and sat as if settling behind his desk at work. He motioned for her to join him. "Mrs. Daniels—"

"Ms. My husband's out of my life. What's going on, Detective?"

Folding his hands on the tabletop, he leaned forward. "I'm here about your brother."

Carol positioned her glasses more firmly on her face. "I don't have a brother."

Patience settled over the detective's features. "I'm sure I'd say the same in your shoes. However, he's made enemies who may disagree. Since they can't get at him in prison, there's reason to believe they may target you."

His words hit like a tsunami. The threatening note in Calgary—the one that sent her running for cover.

Carol bit her lip and drew a deep breath through her nose, trying to slow her thumping heart. "I've had threats before. Mostly you can tell it's a crazy stage of grief. The victims' families know I wasn't involved."

She should tell him about the note, the horrifying message that still haunted her. *You and your son are easy targets. Especially the boy.*

Except he'd have to follow up. Try to find the culprit. If the writer learned that Toronto police were investigating, he'd know where to search. She couldn't risk him finding her—and Paul—first.

The detective steepled his fingers, palms apart, and stared down at his fingertips. "This is a little awkward. When your—ah, when Harry Silver was taken back into custody last June, certain details were kept out of the news.

"He asked for you to be warned, but the order must have ended up on a desk somewhere. I found out this week that you weren't contacted. On behalf of the law enforcement system, I apologize."

Carol sat straighter. "Warned about what?"

Garraway tapped his fingertips together. "This is not to be repeated. Silver turned himself in. Claimed he had a change of heart. Didn't even harm his hostage. The thing is, he confessed to a couple other crimes, including smuggling drugs."

"The dirty—" She couldn't stop the words that seared the air, but a cop would have heard them all before.

"Yes, I suppose he is, ma'am."

Heat rose in her neck. "You don't understand, Detective. I lost a son to drugs. With all the terrible things Harry did, he was pushing drugs too?"

"I believe his sole connection was transportation. He claims he was coerced, under the threat of harm against yourself and your family."

The detective leaned forward, forearms on the table. "The long and short of it is, Silver provided significant evidence against a major drug ring with branches throughout Canada. They cleaned up the one on the East Coast, and because one of the members got scared and started talking the gang didn't find out that Silver talked first. I'm investigating the connections here in Toronto."

He watched her, his eyes serious. "Ms. Daniels, until we haul this crew in, you and your son may be in danger. We've kept the lid on the rumours, but if these guys suspect Silver spilled on them, they'll want revenge. They made threats against you before, ma'am, when the stakes were lower. Relocating, and I notice you've changed your appearance from the description on file, will help. But there's no guarantee."

Garraway slid a white card across the table. "If you see any sign of danger, day or night, call my cell."

Carol fingered the card. This felt like a TV cop drama. A tiny corner of her heart was glad to see these creeps get what they deserved—or at least a portion of it. There was no price high enough for the life of her son and all the others.

How deep had Harry been in? If he'd been part of Keith getting into drugs...

She wouldn't go there. Not now. This new danger was enough.

~~~

The detective's visit made Carol late for work. She hit the cafe kitchen at top speed. No time to process what Garraway had said, no time to decide what to do. She forced her full attention onto the recipes and read each step twice. Waiting tables later, she repeated each customer's order aloud, wrote every detail on her pad. And made it through her shift with only minor mistakes.

Driving home, the same thing. Concentrate on traffic, on pedestrians. Don't listen to the fear scratching at the edge of thought.

Inside the apartment, she double-locked the door and leaned her forehead against it. Blessedly cool.

The dog snuffled and whined at her side, and she held out a hand for his welcome-home nuzzle. "I know you're hungry, Chance. Give me a minute."

She pushed away from the door and scooped food into his dish. No point trying to eat a meal herself, the way her nerves were jumping.

For once, she was glad Paul wasn't home yet. She had to think this through. Decide how to keep them both safe.

Garraway had said Harry's enemies threatened Carol and her family in the past. It sounded like this latest threat targeted her. Not her son. Did they think Harry cared more about his sister than his nephew? Especially now that the nephew wasn't a cute little kid?

Tension crept up her neck. Even if Paul wasn't on their radar, she was. Hurting his mother would hurt him. If they killed her—

A sob broke from her lips. She clamped them tight. She should have asked Garraway what kind of threats these goons made, but it didn't matter. She had to stay strong, stay alive, to guide her son into responsible adulthood.

By the time Paul arrived at ten, she'd made her decision.

She placed a mug of hot chocolate and some cookies on the table for him and brought a cup of strong black tea for herself. "Sit a minute. We need to talk."

"O-k-a-a-y." He dropped his backpack beside the door and eased into the chair in front of the snacks. "Thanks for this. What's up?"

Carol bit her lip. He'd fought the last move, but this was for his own good. "We have to find another place to live."

His outstretched hand froze inches from the cookie plate. "Our landlords love us. What gives?"

She shifted her tea to one side, watching the cup instead of meeting his eyes. "The Johnstones have been really good to us. I haven't told them yet. We have to leave Toronto."

"You are so not doing this to me again." Paul's palms slapped the table, and he pushed to his feet. His chair slammed to the floor behind him.

In the living room, Chance barked. The dog bounded into the kitchen.

Paul strode to the door, picked up his backpack, and came to stand in the middle of the floor. "Look, I know what happened in Calgary wasn't pretty. Jerk reporter, anyway, and you're better off without him. But you dragged me away from my friends, my school—no way am I doing that again with no reason."

The dog nosed at Paul's leg, then came to Carol's side.

She wound her fingers into his soft fur and counted to ten. "I'm sorry about Calgary. You don't know everything that went on. And there are reasons. If you'll sit down, we can discuss it like adults."

"Adults." He picked up his chair, replaced it at the table, and stood behind it, fingertips white against the brown vinyl padding. "So why do you want to mess me around this time?"

Carol hugged both palms against her cup, holding the eye contact. "A little respect would be good here. It's not all about you, you know." Except it was. That's why she had to do this. She sighed. "It's more fallout from your convict uncle."

Paul stood a minute, lips clamped tight. Then he dropped the pack and took a seat. He grabbed a cookie. "What now?"

"A detective came to the door this morning. To warn me Harry has enemies."

"Well, duh."

"Serious enemies. A drug ring. As if his own crimes weren't enough. They can't get at him in jail, so apparently we're the next best choice."

"He didn't—" Paul studied his cookie. He took a big bite. "I don't think he's to blame for Keith getting into drugs. At least I don't see how he could be. He wasn't that close to us." Carol shivered. "We can overcome people pointing and gossiping, judging us based on what he did. But we can't protect ourselves from organized crime."

She picked up her cup and held it to her lips like a shield, studying him over the rim. "I want to ask the detective to put is in witness protection."

Paul went completely still except for a narrowing of his eyes. The dog left her side and rested his muzzle on Paul's leg.

She waited. Couldn't he see? They had no choice.

He gulped his drink. "Did this detective have specifics? Exactly what sort of danger we're supposed to be in?"

"He didn't say. I was too surprised to ask more questions, but he left his card. I can phone him tomorrow."

"Sounds awfully vague to me. We're not worth bothering over, and Uncle Harry isn't either, for Pete's sake. I vote we stay. Chance can be our guard dog. Won't you, boy?"

Carol sat taller in her chair. "The detective thought it was worth bothering over. I don't want to move again either. This is a good place to live. You're in a good school, I like my job. We're making friends. But I can't risk anything happening to you, and if I died you'd be an orphan. You'd be moving anyway, because my will appoints Jackie as your legal guardian. You'd be living in Calgary."

His exhale bordered on a groan. "Mom, nobody's going to kill either of us. I'm not going to run if nobody's chasing me."

"You'll run if I say so. And I do. I'm phoning Detective Garraway in the morning."

"Do what you've gotta do. I'm not going with you."

The air left her lungs. She should be angry. Should force him to obey. But the set of his jaw, the tilt of his head, said he'd hold firm. "Paul, I'm your mother."

One corner of his mouth flickered. "I love you, Mom, but I'm not doing this again. You want to go, go. I'm staying."

Under the table, Carol clenched her fists until the nails bit her palms. She would *not* cry. Or beg. "Where would you live? You think *I'm* overprotective. What would you do, ask to move in with the Johnstones? Cecilia gets on your nerves just living upstairs."

"My friend Barry has a huge house, and he's an only child. His mom's kind of pushy too, but I wouldn't have to lose my friends."

Carol's scalp muscles constricted until her head felt ringed in fire. She squinted at her son. Her one reason to live. "I can't leave you behind."

Paul's shoulders lost their stiff posture. "Then we're staying. And we'll be careful."

Chapter 5

PACING HIS LIVING room, Patrick kept his tone level. "The woman is paranoid. It would help if I knew what I'm looking for."

Lear's mind games made it even more difficult to satisfy the man. Now, the drug lord chuckled, a cold sound like the satisfied mirth of death. "You're not looking for anything yet. Build a bridge. Impress her with your charm and financial smarts. You can do that, I trust."

Patrick unclenched his jaw. "I'm working on it."

"Good. In time, the lovely Ms. Daniels will hear from me. That money is mine, Pat, and if Silver won't tell me where it is, I'll get it through his sister. He should never have tried to hold out on me."

Back to gritting his teeth—Patrick had given up correcting Lear about his name. He picked up his after-dinner coffee and inhaled, letting the aroma soothe the edge of his nerves. "I have no idea what you're talking about."

"Typical. Her brother is Harry Silver. You've heard of him, at least?

"Yes." And he'd already discovered the family connection when he first researched Carol.

"Silver transported merchandise for me in the past."

Patrick's eyebrows lifted. No whiff of that on the internet.

Lear went on. "One of my teams broke him out of prison. Before we shipped him out of the country, he was supposed to tell my operative where to find a cache of money he'd hidden."

"But he's back in prison."

"Segregated, where I can't touch him. I still want the cash." Another cold chuckle. "He'll learn not to play games with me."

Patrick caught the undercurrent. He'd better not thwart the drug lord either. But what if he located the money first? Helped Carol find it? Delivered it to Lear as proof of his ability?

His reward might be release from Lear's grasp.

~~~

Carol stayed on high alert as the days passed, triple-checking the locks and watching for suspicious cars near the apartment. Paul wouldn't let her drive him to school—he said it embarrassed him. She hoped he'd be safe, wished she could pray he'd be safe. But that hadn't worked with Keith.

She found herself watching the café patrons, even the regulars. Detective Garraway had said her enemies wouldn't necessarily look the part.

One of Thursday evening's newcomers gave her a bad vibe. Thin face, a furtive look, and hard eyes that tracked her movements. She memorized his appearance. Just in case.

When he paid for his meal and left, the weight of her tension left with him. She circulated among the tables, refilling water, chatting with the remaining customers as the café emptied.

A well-dressed businessman sat alone in one of the booths. A recent part of the after-work crowd, with a reserved smile that made an oasis in the suppertime rush.

She paused at his table. "How's your meal, Mr. Stairs?"

He gave her a slow smile and finished chewing. "Patrick, please. I leave 'Mr. Stairs' at the office. The food is fine, as always." He glanced around the café. "Now that it's quiet, perhaps you'd join me for coffee?"

"Not while I'm on duty, but thanks anyway."

"When do you finish?"

"Seven."

"I can wait. My racquetball partner stood me up."

Carol studied him, trying to read his motives. She was adept at dismissing come-ons without offence, but Patrick didn't give any of the usual signals. He could have been discussing investment prospects.

"Did you want your dessert then too?"

"Please."

Just before seven, she topped up Patrick's coffee and brought tea for herself along with his dish of fresh fruit salad. It hadn't taken long to notice his obsession with healthy eating.

In the employee break room, she traded the frilled apron for a cherry-coloured cardigan and dashed a comb through her hair. As an afterthought, she paused to touch up her lipstick.

Patrick's face creased into a smile as she slid into the seat opposite him, but the light in his eyes didn't change. That's what it was. His smile never reached his eyes. The man was so—dispassionate. Maybe it gave his clients confidence that their investments were in safe hands.

He picked up his spoon. "Lily tells me you're the genius behind the caramel cheesecake I tried last week."

Occasionally, she'd seen him order a high-calorie dessert if he was with a heavy-eating client. "I'm doing most of the baking now. I only wait tables over supper. I'm glad you liked the cheesecake."

"Would you consider preparing some extras on the side?"

"Don't tell me you're a closet carbohydrate addict!"

His expression remained impassive. "I plan on hosting a semi-formal coffee and dessert evening for my clients. I usually frequent a gourmet bakery near my office, but your cheesecake was excellent."

Carol frowned. Her cakes were good but not exceptional. "If you tell me what you need, I'm sure Lily can work it into our baking rotation. I can prepare it the day of your event, and you can pick it up late afternoon."

"Unfortunately, I won't be free to do that. And I do require same-day goods. I should have phrased it more clearly. I'd like to engage your baking services on-site in my home the morning of the function. My kitchen is well-equipped with whatever you might need."

He sat forward, watching her, and mentioned a price.

She found herself nodding and asking for details. "I'm sure I can adjust my work schedule for the day." She took Patrick's card and shook his hand.

They left the café together and said goodbye on the sidewalk. Carol hurried to her car with a sense of anticipation. This was a win-win deal. Paid to indulge her love of baking without the temptation of eating the results. This would start filling the hole the move had made in her savings.

She was still shuffling recipes in her mind when she parked and let herself into the apartment. "Chance, don't trip me, you foolish dog. I know you're hungry, but I have to get in first."

When he was happily snuffling in his bowl and her own meal spun in the microwave, she flipped through the mail. Junk, junk, more junk. Bill. And a greeting card envelope with no return address.

She ripped it open and pulled out a card with a cartoon image of a treasure map. Inside, bright blue lettering wished

31

Good luck! Below it, tidy printing said *Thinking of you. A friend.*

Good luck for what? From whom?

The card and envelope landed in the recycling basket with the other unwanted paper. With a rebellious son, danger from a drug ring, and now a chance to earn extra cash, she didn't have headspace for games.

While she waited for Paul to come home, she pulled out her recipes and drew up a list of ingredients. Three assorted cheesecakes and a Black Forest. This should be fun.

When Paul let himself in near ten, she'd drawn up a solid plan of attack for Patrick's event.

A layer of her tension fell away as he re-locked the door, but she didn't let it all go. Yes, they were both safe for another day, but would their unseen enemies act on their threat? When? How?

Paul's backpack hit the floor with a thud, and he kicked his running shoes into the corner behind the door as he glanced at the open recipe books. "Hey, what's cooking?"

"Just plans, tonight."

When she explained, he shrugged. "Cool." He gave her a quick hug, grabbed his pack, and headed to his room.

Cool. She hadn't expected tears of joy, but a little conversation wouldn't have killed him.

At least he was home on time and talking to her, if only in passing. Probably had homework to do. He claimed his classes here weren't that different from Calgary, but he seemed to spend hours studying.

She remembered her own change when she was fourteen. Then, she'd switched cities, not provinces like Paul. Of course, she'd had her aunt to adjust to as well.

She snatched the phone from the wall cradle. Memory lane was a place where she didn't care to stroll.

It took five tries before speed dial one rang through to the radio station.

"Carol! Hey, thanks for the cookies. They were great!"

"I'm glad you liked them." She'd felt like a fool dropping them off at the station. Lest he get the wrong impression, she added, "I took a plate to my landlady too. We've added them to the menu at the café, and I wanted to practise."

"You're welcome to practise on me any time. I've got another couple of songs cued before I have to go, so what's new with you?"

"One of the café customers hired me to bake for a private party."

"That's great. Build up clientele, and you can open your own catering business."

"I couldn't." The words were out in an instant. "Even if I had the start-up capital, it'd be too risky. I have Paul to support."

"Don't you have any family at all? A relative who could stake you the money as a business partner?"

Who was left? Aunt Isobel, if the woman was still alive. Her estranged in-laws. Harry. "No." The word came out sharper than she'd planned. "Sorry. Consider me all alone."

"That's too bad. Let me tend to my duties here for a minute, and then you can tell me more about this catering job."

Seated at the kitchen table, Carol stared at the window and the darkness beyond. Harry used to try to push money on her, money instead of a relationship. At first, she'd refused because Skip didn't need more to waste. After he died, it was easier to simply depend on herself. If she earned it, she had control over how she spent it. When she found out what Harry was, she was glad she'd kept her distance.

Joey's voice in her ear made a welcome diversion. "So, this guy is one of your café regulars?"

"He comes for supper once or twice a week. Why?"

"Is he single?"

"What difference does it make?"

"A stranger invited you into his home. A wife would make it sound a little safer."

She tapped her fingers on the chipped tabletop. "He's a widower, but he wears his ring. Does that help?"

"I'm not trying to pry, Carol, but there are some sick people out there. It sounds fishy to me, like a rich guy looking for fun."

Carol's exhale came from memories more bitter than sweet. "I must have heard all the lines by now. Patrick's a gentleman. He didn't even try."

"Well, just in case, keep an eye on him."

He didn't sound worried so much as... defensive. Her spine pressed into the chairback. "Don't go possessive on me, Joey. I don't need a man. Been there, done that."

"I'm trying to be a friend. I can't help being male."

Her father. Her husband. Her rare dates since. The reporter in Calgary. Her brother. Especially her brother.

Carol dropped her forehead into her free palm. "I'm sorry. Most men in my life have been real—" She caught herself. Religious people didn't like those words. "Well, they were all, um, jerks."

"I see." He chuckled. "I've had my share of being an 'um, jerk' too, so maybe you're right. Don't hang up on me, though. I'm not the same man I was. Listen, I've got to get back to work. Meet me for a coffee or a walk on the weekend, *friend*?"

A smile twitched her lips. "Maybe. I'll call you tomorrow night after I've scoped Patrick's kitchen. Are you going to play me a song?"

"Billy Joel's coming up in about ten minutes. Enjoy!" The phone clicked, and Joey's voice migrated to the radio on the kitchen counter.

Carol gave her head a slow shake as she replaced the receiver. So maybe Joey was for real... what then? Her chest tightened. She knew how to be independent. Did she dare risk learning to trust?

Chapter 6

PAUL WATCHED TARA-LYNN draw a double line under the number she'd written. Her explanation made a lot more sense than their teacher's. "I get it now."

Tara-Lynn looked up, smiling. "I knew you would. We've got time. Why not do the next problem to make it stick?"

"Slave driver." He pulled the math textbook across the library table, frowned at the open pages, and began working out the answer.

Beside him, she jotted tidy numbers in her binder, her pencil moving twice as fast as his.

Ignoring the motion of her hand, the faint squeak of lead against paper, Paul followed the question to its end. He checked his answer against hers and gave an exaggerated sigh of relief.

The school librarian cleared her throat in warning.

He rolled his eyes and mimed wiping his brow.

Tara-Lynn grinned and closed her binder. "I'll do the rest at home."

"Thanks for giving up your lunch break to help me." He'd picked the most approachable of the class brains and made a desperate plea for help. Bonus for him she was female. Kind of cute too, now that he stopped to notice.

She stuck her pencil and eraser into her purse. "It's a heavy course load this year. Do you have a job?"

"A couple of evenings and most weekends. And I'm in a new band."

She studied him for a minute. "Don't tell me. Keyboard?"

"Lead guitar and vocals."

She tipped her head to one side and seemed to re-evaluate him. "Rock band?"

"Yeah. We cover a mix of current hits and old classic rock. Have you ever listened to the Beatles or the Eagles?"

She gave him a wry grin. "Mom's all about tenors and opera. I'm into Christian music, but I like some of the Beatles' stuff. Maybe I'll catch your act sometime."

"Maybe." If they ever landed a gig. Paul stuffed his books into his backpack and pushed away from the table.

Tara-Lynn rose too, hooked her purse over her shoulder, and picked up her binders. "Have you been playing long?"

"Every time I got my hands on a guitar. My dad was a musician. I've wanted to play for as long as I can remember."

They walked out into the hallway. Tara-Lynn's sleeve brushed Paul's arm as they stepped around a knot of students at a locker bank, and he eased away. Would she think he'd gotten close on purpose?

She tucked her hair behind her ear. "You said your dad *was*. Did he die?"

"Five years ago."

"That's hard. Mine's alive but out of the picture. He phones at Christmas and my birthday." She shifted her armload of books. "If I hurry, I can dump the math in my locker before English."

"Thanks again."

"See you later." She ducked into the right-hand corridor and hurried away.

Paul paused to watch her go. He liked the way her shiny light-brown hair brushed her shoulder blades, the way her jeans outlined the right amount of curve without being skin-tight. She was pretty, all right, but she didn't flaunt it like the blond rent-a-chick with the locker next to his.

Locker. Class. He put on a burst of speed and slid into the science lab before the door closed.

~~~

Shortly after eight that evening, the taxi Patrick had sent to collect Carol turned into an exclusive subdivision.

She tried to settle the butterflies in her stomach. So much for his stated concern that she'd be too tired after work to find her way. She took in the double driveways with their gleaming BMWs and Porsches. A car as old as hers wouldn't be welcome on their turf.

The houses stood tall and narrow, a runway of fashion models in designer brick and stonework, accessorized with immaculate lawns and shrubbery. Patrick's was a semi-formal affair of a bluish stone with pristine white trim.

The taxi driver opened Carol's door and followed her across the paving stones.

Patrick paid the driver and ushered her inside.

The home gave off an aura of serene beauty, like an art gallery. Patrick's easy patter soothed her as he led the way to a spacious kitchen. Finished in gleaming white with stainless steel appliances, it was saved from starkness by frosted glass cabinet doors and a faint blue motif in the ceramic tile-work.

She'd need to rent extra cake pans and pick up groceries, but working in this kitchen would be a dream. "Wouldn't it be easier for you if I baked at home and delivered?"

"I have a chef who comes in twice a month to prepare my dinners, and she has a penchant for expensive culinary gadgets. I'd like to see them get more use."

"I'll be happy to oblige. You're okay with me being here while you're out?"

"Perfectly. I'll send a taxi for you at seven. That way you can set up before I leave."

It had been hard to coax her boss into giving her a half-day off, but her usual midnight baking wouldn't work in someone else's home.

"I don't mind driving."

Patrick's offer of wine dismissed her protest. His silk shirt stretched taut against his shoulders as he reached for two cut crystal glasses. He fit so well in this beautiful home.

She swallowed her "no thanks" and nodded acceptance. Why not?

He carried their drinks into a sitting room—she couldn't think of a space this elegant as a living room—and set the tray on a glossy cherrywood coffee table. Then he sank into the embrace of a cream leather recliner and waved her toward the matching couch.

When she chose the wooden rocker, his mouth tightened.

She slid a palm across the satin-finished armrest. "Is this okay? I love rocking chairs. The motion's so soothing."

"Of course." Patrick picked up his glass and slid the tray nearer to her seat.

The effortlessness of his conversation and the gentle rock of her chair blended with the mellow wine. Carol relaxed in a glow of contentment.

To think Joey was suspicious of this man. He should see them now. She finished her drink and set the glass on the tray. What did it matter what Joey thought? But the spell weakened.

At Patrick's offer of a refill, she shook her head. "No thanks. I should be going. I've taken up too much of your time this evening. I don't imagine your work allows you much of it."

His slow smile was noncommittal. "It's sufficient for a single man. Please. Stay, if your son's not expecting you."

"I'd better go."

As he slid his cell from his pocket, a slender Siamese cat paraded in and positioned itself in front of the rocking chair like a guard.

Its stare turned Carol's admiration to unease.

"Patrick?"

He looked up, the question on his face changing to resignation as he saw the cat. He placed the phone on the table in front of him. "I know, Isis. Go find something else to do."

The cat's blue eyes glowed, irises narrowed in the equivalent of a scowl. A low rumble vibrated its throat.

The back of her neck prickled. "Patrick?"

Muttering a curse, he pushed up from his chair.

The cat swivelled one ear in his direction and crouched to spring. The unblinking blue eyes targeted Carol's face. The rumbling growl deepened to a snarl.

Carol bolted from the rocker. She caught at the door frame to steady herself, her feet sliding on the hardwood floor. She checked for pursuit, but the cat was sitting straight and tall in the rocking chair, staring at her.

Patrick stood frozen, one hand extended, whether to stop her or the maniac cat she couldn't be sure.

Lowering his arm, he shook his head and stepped toward her, ignoring the cat. "I am so sorry about this. Are you all right?"

She retreated.

He made no move to close the distance. "Can I get you another drink?"

"No thank you. I'm fine. But I'd like to go home."

"Of course. Shall we phone from the kitchen?"

He retrieved his cell from the coffee table, avoiding the cat. "Isis won't leave the chair until you've gone, but she'll fill the whole room with her attitude."

As soon as the taxi had been called, Carol headed for the front door. "Will the cat be around when I come to bake?"

"I can shut her away if you would feel better."

"I would. Why... does she do that often?"

Patrick focused on removing invisible flecks from the cuff of his silk shirt. "Isis considers humans to be lower life forms, with the exception of my wife. She and Rita had a special bond, and she is rather... protective. That rocker was Rita's favourite chair. I usually put it away before I have guests." He looked up, a rare flash of uncertainty in his eyes.

"I wish you'd said something! No wonder the cat hates me."

His forehead smoothed. "Thank you."

Carol reached for the doorknob as the taxi pulled into the drive. "I had another son, Keith. My one link with him now is a dog he brought home as a stray." She forced a laugh. "He named him Chance, said they'd both take the chance at a fresh start. But only one of them made it."

She fled to the taxi. Why had she told him? To let him know he wasn't alone?

Patrick followed with slower steps and paid the driver. He didn't meet her eyes, but there was a new warmth in his goodbye.

Chapter 7

CAROL ADDED A dollop of low-fat dressing to her salad, sprinkled grated cheese on top, and snapped the cover onto the plastic container. She uncapped a water bottle to fill it.

Paul sauntered into the kitchen. "Making lunch? You working Saturdays now?" Standing there in the doorway in his baggy sleep pants and rumpled tee shirt, he looked younger, less secretive.

"I'm going on a picnic with a friend. Grab me an apple, please?"

He took an apple from the fridge, inspected it, and tossed it to her. "Heads up!"

She made a clumsy catch and shot him a half-hearted glare. "Thanks, I think." She washed the apple and put it with the salad, then dropped a handful of cookies into a plastic bag.

"Save me some of those? Last time you gave too many away."

"The rest are for you and your friends, okay?"

"Great." He sat at the table and watched her pack the food into an oversized shoulder bag. "So, where are you going? Who with? How can I reach you if I need to? When will you be home?"

"Paul..." She took a step toward him. "Am I that bad?"

His smile didn't slip, but his jaw tightened.

Carol let a slow breath escape and pulled out another chair. A set of three in early duct tape, he called them. She touched his hand. "After losing your brother, I worry about what could happen. And now we have Harry's enemies hounding us."

Paul pushed away from the table and stood. "I'll believe those enemies when I see them. And I saw what Keith's choices cost him—and you. I have plans for my life. They don't include ruining it."

He stalked out. Seconds later, his bedroom door slammed.

Carol rested her forehead in her palm. He had no idea what it was like to be a parent. To worry. When he had children of his own, he'd understand why she tried so hard to protect him now.

She scrawled a quick note. *Centre Island Park. I'm sorry. Love, Mom.*

Glasses in place, she stuck her feet into running shoes and tossed on a jacket before heading out the door. Despite the hurry, she remembered to lock up.

~~~

Squinting in the late morning sun, Paul walked the half-block from his bus stop to Morelli's. Barry had razzed him about working on such a gorgeous Saturday, but their drummer had to work too. If they couldn't practise, what better place to be than the music store?

He pushed open the glass door and stepped inside, automatically glancing at "his" Les Paul Classic on the wall. The store was crowded today. Two teens stood checking out the guitars, and in the other corner a middle-aged man sat at one of the electric pianos, picking out a one-fingered tune.

A short line waited at the checkout, but his coworker Eric pointed toward the back.

Paul shrugged and ducked into the session room. It was empty, so he hung his jacket in the break room and tapped on the frame of the open office door.

His boss, wiry grey hair even more askew than usual, glanced up from his computer monitor. "Ah, Paul. Come in for a second. Eric will be needing you."

"It's getting busy." Paul approached the paper-strewn desk.

Mr. Morelli stuck his hand into one of the smaller piles and pulled out an envelope, which he scrutinized and passed to Paul. "This came for you."

Paul frowned, then focused on the return address. Kingston Penitentiary. No wonder the old man gave it such a funny look.

Sweat prickled his hairline. "My uncle, sir. He's in jail, and I guess he's lonely. Mom doesn't want him to know where we live. I should've asked you first."

Paul didn't know which he hated worse, sympathy or speculation, but Mr. Morelli's dark eyes showed compassion under the fierce grey brows. "Most unfortunate. He may write you at this address occasionally, but please instruct him not to call. You're here to work."

"I'm not ready to talk to him anyway. It's a long story. I'd better get out front. Eric's swamped."

At the old man's nod, Paul crammed the envelope into his pocket and fled.

Morelli was pretty open-minded, but thank God Harry hadn't put his name with the return address!

His palms went clammy at the thought of losing what he had here. There were other music stores, other teachers, but no other Morellis. The man had drawn more music out of Paul's soul in these few months than he could believe.

He slid behind the counter and signed into the other cash register. "May I help the next one in line?"

Eric brushed past to get guitar strings from the wall display. "You okay?"

"Yeah, fine." The envelope felt like a brick in his pocket as he bagged a guitar tuner for a customer and handed her the receipt.

Work kept the boys too busy to talk, which suited him. Eventually, Eric stopped shooting curious glances his way, and Paul relaxed into the Saturday rhythm.

He'd given Harry the address, but he hadn't really expected a response. Not to him. Harry wanted to write to Mom. She'd grown up with him, knew him before he turned into a monster. It'd never happen, but maybe Harry hoped she'd forgive him.

What would a dangerous offender have to say to a sixteen-year-old? Was he even allowed to communicate with someone underage?

Paul remembered how excited he and Keith had felt about their uncle's occasional visits. Being related to a famous racing driver was already cool, but to have the man sitting in their apartment telling stories, trying to be friends...

Harry hadn't come often. And he'd committed at least one murder while he was in town.

The store's welcome bell jingled and Paul jumped.

Beside him, Eric snickered. "Daydreaming?"

"Must have been."

Paul glanced at the entrance. He'd never seen Tara-Lynn here before.

She let the door close behind her and stared around at the instruments before her eyes met his. When he smiled, she did too, and she hurried toward him as if he were her one friend in a room of strangers.

"I was in the neighbourhood, and I thought I'd stop to see this amazing store you were telling me about."

Paul swept his right hand in a horizontal arc. "Here it is."

Eric laughed. "Show her around while it's quiet. I'm Eric, by the way."

His voice sounded deeper than normal, and Paul shot him a look. He knew Eric's taste in girls. Tara-Lynn didn't seem the type.

Paul led her to the far side of the store, where three electric pianos formed a triangle and portable keyboards stood propped against the wall. He pointed out the saxophones, trombones, and violins on display along the upper walls, and the recorders and tin whistles in the counter cabinet, then took her past music stands and a rack of music books to the line of guitars near the door.

Her gaze flitted from the polished guitar bodies to his face. "Which one's your favourite?"

Surprised, he touched the Les Paul. "Way out of my price range, but a guy can dream."

She grinned. "A guy can save too, when he has a job."

As he bent to pick up a customer's dropped tissue, he felt the envelope crackle in his pocket. "Most of what I earn goes into my lessons. Morelli's not cheap."

"Lessons. You *are* serious about your music."

"And I'd better get to work."

"Okay. Thanks for showing me around." Instead of leaving, Tara-Lynn began leafing through the sheet music.

Eric finished helping a customer and signed off his register. He grinned at Paul. "Later, dude. I think she likes you."

"See you." Paul watched him go, sold a package of clarinet reeds, and wondered about Harry's letter. Why was Tara-Lynn hanging around? All he needed was five minutes alone.

An older teen exited the session room, guitar case in hand. He noticed the girl at the music rack. "Hi, Tara-Lynn, what brings you in here?"

She spun around. "Jubal! How are you?"

"Great." He hefted his guitar case. "I come here for lessons. Mr. Morelli's a fantastic teacher."

"So I've heard."

"I've gotta get to work. See you later." Jubal headed for the door.

Tara-Lynn wandered toward Paul. "Jubal's good on bass."

"Is he ever. Where do you know him from?"

"Church. He plays in the worship team."

Paul must have looked blank, because she grinned. "It's like a band for praise music. Not your granny's style at all. You ought to check it out one Sunday."

"Yeah, in all my spare time."

Her cheeks went pink. "I'm sorry. I didn't mean to pressure you. If you like Jubal's playing, I thought you might—" She hitched her purse strap more firmly onto her shoulder. "Thanks for the tour, Paul. See you in class."

"Hey, I didn't mean it that way. It's work, and practice, and school. I barely have a second to sneeze. I'll see what I can do."

"It's okay. Bye."

Paul shook his head as the glass door closed behind her. Girls.

He pulled the letter from his pocket and stared at the bent envelope. Keeping it below counter-level although the storefront was empty, he tore it open.

Chapter 8

A CROWD OF waiting passengers clogged the approach to the island park's ferry dock. Young, old, many toting insulated picnic coolers.

Carol turned to Joey. "What do you think?"

He shrugged. "I guess we shouldn't be surprised. There aren't many warm Saturdays left by mid-September. The boat's big. This won't be as bad as it looks."

She fished in her pack for sunglasses and traded them for the plain frame she usually wore in public. "This sun is strong."

"Enjoy. We'll be shivering before long."

Something hard whacked her calves. "Ow!" She whirled around.

Inches from her own, a set of mocking eyes forced her backward.

Joey caught her arms, steadying her. "You okay?"

Now that she could see the stranger's full face, she couldn't look away. He'd been at Sticky Fingers—the guy with the creepy, hard stare.

With an insolent smile, the man hefted a skateboard as if to show what hit her. "Sorry."

He dropped the board on its wheels and sped away.

Cold crept through her limbs despite the hot sun.

Behind her, Joey squeezed her arms. "What happened?"

Had he been talking the whole while?

"Jerk whacked me with his skateboard." She twisted to examine her calves. A red line showed below her capris where the board had hit, but she wasn't bleeding. "I'm okay. Should have worn jeans."

Joey's brows crowded together. "He shouldn't be trying to ride in this crowd anyway. The way he looked at you—"

She pushed her sunglasses higher on her nose and inched deeper into the line for the ferry. "I don't know who he was, but he's gone now and he's not going to spoil our day."

"Carol—"

"Please. I don't want to talk about it."

"You're sure you're okay? We have a lot of walking ahead of us. Want to grab a coffee instead and do the island another day?"

She took a few quick steps to see how it felt. "I think walking might keep the bruises from stiffening up."

Joey surveyed the crowd that stretched ahead of them. "Looks like we'll be standing for awhile. Want to stroll a bit first? Next ferry might have a shorter line."

"We could do that."

They eased out of the crowd and followed the sidewalk away from the city centre, with Lake Ontario on their left. Huge willows swept branches down to touch the water. Ducks and Canada Geese bobbed on the surface.

The scrape of small wheels on concrete made Carol whirl.

Just a woman with a rolling carry-on case.

She tried to laugh it off, but she felt Joey's concern.

When he opened his mouth, she frowned and shook her head. If she told him she'd seen the creep before, he'd go protective on her. He'd ask more questions, and she'd end up revealing Garraway's warning about Harry's enemies.

She glanced at him as they circled around a girl pushing a baby stroller. It wasn't like telling him her fears was anything new. He was a great listener. But here, face-to-face, had a different dynamic than talking on the phone. And she did not want to tell him about her brother.

He nudged her arm. "How are the legs?"

"I'm good."

They passed boats moored near the water's edge and saw others out on the lake. Joey pointed ahead to a sign. "The water taxis go to the islands too. There's no line here. What do you say?"

An open boat glided toward the wooden platform. It would hold what, eight people? Ten?

She pulled the water bottle from her bag, popped the cap, and took a swallow. "I'm not a boat person."

A young man on the platform called out to them. "Great day to go to the islands! We haven't lost a passenger yet!" He reached to steady the craft as it came alongside.

The island ferries were huge. Filled with people. What if Skateboard Guy decided to get on with them? This way, he wouldn't know where they were.

She eyed the water taxi. "Okay, let's try this. Just don't make me sit on the edge."

"You sure?"

At her nod, he stepped off the sidewalk onto the platform. A few other passengers filed on board first. Joey paid—"You can get us ice cream later"—and the ticket seller helped them into the boat. It shifted a little under their feet but not as badly as she'd expected.

They found a free bench. Joey took the seat by the water and left Carol the inside.

The driver—pilot?—smiled at her passengers. "Welcome. It's a quick hop over to the islands. I'll drop you near the amusement park, and you can take the ferry back from any of its three stops. There are plenty of maps and signs to keep you from getting lost. Those of you wearing hats, you might want to take them off. If they blow overboard, they're history."

She revved the engine and left the landing platform behind.

Carol took a couple of deep breaths and tried to loosen her death grip on the bag in her lap. The cool breeze in her hair felt good. She grinned at Joey. "It's not so bad."

"Want to trade seats?"

"Don't push it, buddy."

The taxi picked up speed, threading among the other pleasure craft. It aimed directly at one of the returning ferries.

Carol's breath hissed in.

Joey's knee nudged hers. "Safest spot for her to pick. The ferry's moving. It'll be gone when we get there."

He was right. He had to be right. But that ferry was huge.

She couldn't look away. Sure enough, the water taxi cut across the ferry's wake, not even close to the bigger boat. She wilted on the bench.

Beside her, Joey whispered, "What if you close your eyes?"

"Whatever's coming, I have to see it."

As they approached the islands, carnival sounds floated out from the amusement park.

Carol and Joey stepped ashore and headed along the path with the other passengers. She swung her bag at her side. "That wasn't so bad. Want your ice cream now?"

He splayed a hand across his stomach. "And spoil my lunch?"

Most passengers from the water taxi headed toward the amusement park's happy voices and tinny music. Children squealed from the rides.

Joey grinned. "You survived the boat trip. Want to see if they've got a roller coaster?"

"Not on your life."

"Then let's explore."

A wide concrete roadway led them deeper into the park.

Carol's arms swung free at her sides. The open space allowed her and Joey to walk without touching, even when they met people coming in the other direction.

Joey made a good walking companion. He seemed to be soaking up the quiet too.

Clouds covered the sun now, and he wore his sunglasses hooked in his shirt collar. Even without their bulk, his nose wasn't as imposing side-on. It must be more broad than long.

Before they met, she'd pictured him as a tall, flashy, celebrity type, but his rich on-air tones deceived. His looks matched his character. Friendly and approachable. He knew how to listen, no matter how crazy she must have sounded at times.

She kicked at a pebble. "I don't know what I would have done some of those nights if you hadn't been there to talk to. I really appreciate it."

"We all need an ear once in awhile. I'm glad if it helped. Nobody was meant to handle life alone."

She'd always handled life alone, but the stakes kept getting higher. A shaft of sunlight speared through the woolly clouds. Light was good, light in the darkness. "Are all your callers as mixed up as I am? We could start calling you Dr. J."

He laughed. "It's lonely in the sound studio at night. I chat with a lot of the callers." He picked up a small twig from the path and tossed it aside. "I don't think of you as mixed up. I think you're a survivor."

Her foot scuffed hard on the concrete path. "What?"

"A survivor. You must be, to have lived through so much pain without breaking."

If he only knew it all. "I've come close."

"A lot of people are on the edge. I was, not too long ago. That's why I try to be sensitive when people need to talk. Do you ever think about God, Carol?"

"Not much." What good would it do?

Grassy lawns spread on both sides, dotted with mature trees. Across the grass to their right, picnic tables nestled beneath shade trees, water glinting beyond them. Joey pointed toward them. "How about lunch?"

"We just got here." But not as early as they'd planned. "Now that you mention it, I'm ready to eat."

They cut across the grass and followed the line of tables until they found an empty one. Joey brushed stray dirt and faded brown paint curls from the weathered tabletop, then dropped his backpack with an exaggerated sigh of relief.

When they spread out their lunches, he eyed her water bottle and salad with mock horror. "Where's the lady who loves to bake?"

Carol pulled the cookies from her bag and slid them across the rough boards.

"What have we here?" Nimble fingers unwound the twist tie and drew the bag nearer. "Mmm. Chocolate macadamia nut."

As she reached for her salad, Joey paused and bowed his head. She waited, not sure what to do.

He looked up with a smile. "Let's eat."

She forked a piece of tomato. "Don't you feel self-conscious praying in public?"

"Nope." Joey put down his sandwich and gave her that lopsided grin as he chewed.

He popped open his cola and took a quick swallow. "There's something about making a total idiot out of yourself in front of your whole world that breaks down the inhibitions. Back in Vancouver, I had this flashy crimson sports car. One night, I planted it through the dealer's showroom window. Told the police I returned it because of poor service."

Carol sat straighter on the bench. He didn't look like he was joking. "No way."

"My boss's daughter was with me. We were on our way home from a party, and in my... altered state of confidence it seemed a perfectly reasonable thing to do."

Impaired driving. Images filled her mind. A crumpled car wrapped around a utility pole, the police officer at her door in the pre-dawn, herself hugging her sobbing sons...

A touch on her forearm pulled her into the present.

Joey leaned across the table, eyes intent. "Hey, are you okay?"

He'd been sharing a personal story, and she'd zoned out. After all the times he'd listened to her. She squirmed on the wooden seat. "You were lucky. Driving drunk killed my husband."

The colour ebbed from his cheeks. "I had no idea. You told me about Keith, but—Carol, I didn't know."

"Don't worry about it. He was so far over the limit, they should have given him an award for voluntarily removing himself from the gene pool."

Joey fidgeted with his drink can, questions etching themselves between his brows.

She shrugged. "I didn't mean to sound harsh. It's just... Skip was a talented musician, but he was no good at life."

"Sounds like me before the crash. The life part, not the music. Too bad he ran out of chances." Joey spread his hands, palms up. "So now here I am, new job, new city, starting over. I'm not the same man I was in Vancouver."

"I'm sure the car dealers here are relieved." Her cheeks went hot.

Before she could apologize, Joey laughed.

They ate in silence until she asked, "Why did you tell me?"

"Because you seem like a lady with secrets—" He waved away her denial with his last piece of sandwich. "And I want to be totally open with you. I want you to know you don't have to hide with me."

Hiding was a way of life since her brother's arrest, and the letter threatening Paul in Calgary had sealed it. She had no other way now.

Joey looked toward the water. "There's more I have to tell you."

Uneasiness curled in her stomach. "Go on."

He took a slow drink before turning toward her, the pain in his eyes a tangible force.

Carol reached for his hand. "You don't have to do this."

His fingers curled around hers like a cry for help. She felt the willpower it took to speak. "It wasn't—" His voice died, even as his lips groped to form more words. He closed his eyes, swallowed hard, and looked down. "I went to jail."

A headache brewed in the base of her skull. She might have expected his news, after the stunt he'd pulled.

Joey let her hand fall to the table and stared out over the water.

She ran her fingers over the sun-warmed planks. The wood felt smooth as long as she went with the grain. "All I know is that you've been kind to me. I think you're a sensitive, caring person, and I can't imagine you the way you were before."

His smile looked like it came at a price.

Chapter 9

JOEY'S LAST BITE of sandwich went down like a rock. His throat muscles resisted every inch of the way. He swallowed again to try to ease the ache.

Carol's brows crept together, and she gave a sad sort of smile. "A friend of mine, he'd say you're a survivor. That you're making a new start."

"That deejay guy?"

"That's the one. He's a little flaky, but his advice is pretty good."

Giving her a mock glare, he stuffed the bag of cookies into his backpack. "Let's walk."

Carol put her things in her bag except the apple, which she polished on one leg of her capris. "You didn't have to tell me, but it doesn't change the Joey I know. Except I may never let you drive my car."

The hand holding the apple stilled. She shot him a troubled glance. Afraid she'd crossed a line?

Joey grinned and swung his pack at her, aiming to miss.

Her smile returned as she darted out of reach.

He shouldered his pack, and they wandered toward the road. "How are your legs?"

"Okay. Probably be stiff tomorrow." She crunched a bite out of her apple.

They crossed a footbridge toward a fountain. Ahead of them, an elderly couple rambled hand in hand. Joey pointed toward them. "Doesn't that warm your heart?"

"They're lucky."

The couple stopped at the fountain.

Joey and Carol kept walking, past a series of flower gardens. On another day, he'd have dawdled, absorbing the exuberant fall colours.

When they came into an open area, pedestrians strolled everywhere. He spotted people on rented bicycles, including a pair of girls on a two-seater.

The rest of his story burned in his chest. He had to tell her, but not here.

He angled away from the crowd.

Carol tossed her apple core into a plastic garbage can and fell in step beside him.

A narrow path led through a thin stand of trees toward the water. He pointed in that direction. "Want to check it out?"

Branches grazed their arms until they stepped onto a dirt trail at the island's edge. A graffiti-scrawled concrete barrier fenced them away from Lake Ontario.

Overhead, white gulls dipped and soared. Distant sailboats glided in slow motion, and nearer to shore a man stood on some kind of surfboard. A paddleboard maybe, since he used a long double-paddled pole to control it.

Confession time. Out with it. Now. While the path was mostly deserted. Ease into it gently. "What's your son up to today?"

"He's with his friends. They even do their homework together."

"Kids that age want their space. I'm glad he found a good group to hang out with."

Carol's lips thinned. "There's no sign of drugs. Believe me, I know the signs."

She'd told him about losing her son Keith. No wonder she hated even the mention of drugs.

Joey stopped and rested his elbows on the concrete barrier, staring at the line where water met sky.

She joined him. "Look at that guy on the board out there. I'd be petrified. Ever try it?"

"I said I was stupid, not crazy!"

"He seems to know what he's doing." A mix of frown and admiration on her face, she kept watch on the paddleboarder.

Joey's gaze traced the curve of her cheek, the tightness of her jaw, the tendons of her throat. She couldn't trust this experienced boarder to stay safe, couldn't trust her own son. Likely neither of them would let her down.

She trusted him a little.

He sucked air. If he thought about what he had to say, he'd never do it. "Carol, I—"

She yelled and spun around.

Whirling, he spotted a slim figure racing away with Carol's bag. He tapped her arm. "I'm on it."

The thief ran along the path and ducked sideways through an opening in the trees.

Joey pounded behind him, inching nearer.

They reached open ground. Both put on more speed. Joey had started cold, and a stitch knifed his left side. He growled and pushed harder, glaring at the back of the guy's head.

The guy checked behind. He missed a stride, caught himself, and lunged ahead.

Joey made a flying leap and crashed into the thief's ribs. Together, they slammed into a big green garbage can.

The container tipped. Rolled. They rode it to the ground.

His captive writhed and cursed, but Joey kept his fingers wrapped in the guy's shirt and shoved him against the grass. The garbage can rebounded off something and broadsided them.

This thief was a teen—maybe Carol's son's age.

Joey let go of the shirt and grabbed both wrists in case the boy had a knife. He planted a knee on his captive's thin chest while his own heaved for air. "I suggest—you give—the lady—back—her bag."

Footsteps thudded behind them. "Are you okay?"

"Yeah. Just—a little winded." He dragged a lungful of air. "I suppose we have to—report this. He'll be on the street by—nightfall anyway though."

Carol squatted beside him, staring at the boy on the ground. "Let him go. Please, Joey. He—Keith had hair like that—I—"

She twisted her bag from the boy's grip. "Whatever you're into, get out of it. While you're still alive. Don't do this to your family. Don't do it to yourself."

Joey drilled his captive with a stare. "You heard her." He lifted his knee from the boy's ribs, released the bony wrists, and jumped clear in case there *was* a knife in those pockets. "Get help if you—"

The kid was already racing across the park, limping slightly. Joey followed him with his eyes. *Jesus, reach him somehow.*

Carol stood a few paces away, her shoulders shaking.

Instinct said not to touch her, but he stepped nearer. "He's gone."

"Give me a minute. I'm sorry."

So much for a chance to clear his conscience. He didn't dare add to her load now.

"Hey!" Another boy jogged toward them.

Joey remembered seeing that green hoodie not far from where he and Carol had stood watching the water.

The newcomer slowed as he approached.

Carol palmed away her tears and turned to meet him.

The teen waved his phone at them. "Too bad he got away, but I have it on video. Just posted it online. Do you want me to send it to the police?"

Carol choked out something between a squeal and a whimper. Her face was dead white.

Joey grabbed her arm to keep her upright, but she was trembling so badly that he pulled her to his side. "Lean on me for a minute till you get your balance."

She flashed him a wild-eyed look. "I can't have my picture online."

He focused on the boy. "Could you take it down?"

"No way, dude, that was one sick tackle! Want to see?"

Joey tightened his arm around Carol's shoulder. Why couldn't things ever be simple? "Sure. I was kind of in the middle of it."

Watching himself barrel across the grass, leap through the air, and bring the thief down into the garbage can *was* pretty sweet. "Didn't know I had it in me. Could you start from the beginning? Maybe my friend isn't even on-screen."

The boy swiped his thumb across the small screen and Joey squinted to see how much detail there'd be. His stomach twisted. Carol's face showed, clear and startled. Beside him, her trembling increased.

He held the boy's gaze. "My friend doesn't want her picture splashed on the internet."

The boy's lips twisted down. "I tagged the local TV station. They give fifty bucks to the best amateur news video."

"Please." Carol sounded near tears again.

Joey pulled his wallet from his pocket and peeled out three twenties. "Here's sixty to take it down."

"No way, dude, I'm not taking your money. That's crazy."

"What if you blurred her out? Or cut the first bit and focused on the chase? That'd make a better video anyway."

The teen's brows came together. "I guess I could do that but, miss, it's no big deal. Really."

Joey glanced at Carol's taut jaw, her hopeless eyes, and levelled a stare at the boy. "It's a big deal in this case. Don't you see how scared she is? She's got an abusive ex with a restraining order that won't stop him. If he finds her again, he'll kill her."

The lie went down sour, but he had to do something.

At his side, Carol went completely still.

The teen stared from one to the other. "It's a big city. Even if facial recognition software found her in the video, he wouldn't know where to look after this."

Carol choked. "He doesn't know I'm in *this* big city."

The boy hesitated.

Joey pushed a little harder. "He's a cop."

"O-kay." The teen fiddled with his phone. "It's down. You'd better hope the station didn't already snag a copy. I'll edit it."

Carol released a long, shuddery breath.

Joey kept his arm around her as they waited.

The boy scowled at his phone and muttered under his breath. Then he looked up. "Got it. I chopped the part with you, miss, and uploaded the new version."

He focused on his phone, thumbs flying. Then he slid the phone into his pocket. "I messaged the station to say you made me cut you out—that you threatened to sue. They won't want to touch the first video now."

Carol stood a little taller, so Joey let his arm fall away. "Thank you." They both spoke at once.

Joey held out the bills again. "Take this. Please. You've done a good thing today."

"Nah, that's okay."

"Please. If you don't want to keep it, use it to make someone else's day. But I think you deserve a reward."

The boy shrugged. He curled his fingers around the bills and put them in his pocket. "Thanks, then. I hope the dirty cop gets what's coming to him." He loped through the trees toward the water.

Carol met Joey's eyes. "Thank you. For everything." A slow grin spread wide. "A cop?"

"That tipped it."

"I suppose. For the record, there's no abusive ex. I'm just me. Hiding. I don't want to talk about that either."

"Fair enough." How could Joey ever navigate this minefield to share his own destructive news?

Chapter 10

CAROL BUTTERED THE toast, filled both plates, and carried them to the table.

Paul inhaled deeply. "Mmm." He built a bacon and egg sandwich with his toast. "Sorry I was too tired to talk when I got in last night. How'd your picnic go?"

"It started fine. The park is beautiful. I'd like to go back."

"Started? What happened?" He took a huge bite of his sandwich.

"This kid grabbed my bag and ran off. My friend Joey chased him down, but it kind of spoiled the day. You should have seen his tackle." And his skill talking the second kid into cutting out her part of the video.

Paul wiped a dribble of yolk from the corner of his mouth. "Wow. This guy's a hero. You meet him at work?"

"No, he's a deejay with City Classics FM. He does the overnight request show, and we've talked when I call to ask for a song. Then, I met him when I got the car fixed."

"And you worry about me getting into trouble? That's like dating a guy you met in a chat room."

"No, it's not. For starters, I knew he was male. You don't know who a person is online. And we're friends, not dating."

"And you just happened to meet him at the garage?"

Carol carried her empty mug to the counter. She pulled the tea cozy off the pot. No, Joey shouldn't have set that up, but her instincts said she could trust him. "He's a nice guy. Besides, he doesn't know where we live."

"If you say so." Paul attacked his hash browns.

The phone rang. She set down the teapot and checked the caller ID. No name, but it looked like a local number. Probably one of Paul's friends. "Hello?"

"Ms. Daniels." A male voice, light, casual. Deadly.

Her fingers froze to the phone.

"Welcome to Toronto. I trust you received my card in the mail."

Card? She didn't dare breathe.

The caller chuckled. "Good luck. Treasure map. I thought you'd appreciate it. About yesterday—I hope your experiences at the ferry terminal and on the island haven't damaged your appreciation for my city. And I ask you not to disappear again. The more effort it takes to find you, the less pleasant it will be when I do."

Disappear. The letter writer from Calgary.

Carol's lungs emptied. She pressed her free hand flat on the counter-top to keep from falling. *Brave. Be brave.*

How dare this creep threaten her son? She cleared her throat. Pushed the words out. Angry. "Do I know you?"

"Not yet. Your brother did some work for me before his, ah, disgrace. Now that you're here, it's only right that I personally oversee your quest."

Brother. Work. The rest of what he said didn't stick.

The band around her lungs eased. She brought her palm to her forehead. Not the Calgary sicko. Harry's drug lord. Little shivers slithered down her spine. Bad, but not her worst fear.

This was the sort of bottom-dweller responsible for Keith's death. She bit her lips to hold back a tide of hatred.

"Remember, Ms. Daniels, I have eyes everywhere. I'll be in touch." Click.

The dial tone droned in her ear. She hung up and braced both hands against the edge of the counter. Her mind tingled with cold—the cold of decay, of evil. Of fear.

"Mom?" Paul's chair scraped. He squeezed her shoulder. "What is it?"

"I don't know." She groped for her tea, then shuffled to the table.

He sat opposite her. "Who called?"

Carol's first swallow of tea burned all the way down. So did the second. "He said he'd be watching me and he'll call again." Another swallow of tea. "It sounded like a threat."

"Who was it?"

"That drug lord the detective warned me about."

She jumped up and ran to the phone. "Would you get my purse? It's by my bureau." Shaky fingers grabbed a pen from the cup and jotted the number off the call display.

Paul plopped her purse onto the counter. "It'll take more cash than this to buy him off."

His wry grin twisted her heart. She flipped through her wallet and pulled out the detective's card.

Garraway answered on the second ring.

She set her shoulders and willed her voice not to shake. "This is Carol Daniels. I think that drug lord just called."

It sounded silly, like a little girl crying about a monster in the closet. She braced for a parent-like admonition to calm down and forget about it.

"Are you in danger, Ms. Daniels?"

"Not yet." She shouldn't have called.

"Tell me everything. Take as much time as you need."

Her muscles loosened a bit. "It was a Toronto area code. He didn't give a name."

Paul put his arm around her.

Blinking back tears, she let herself rest against her son as she gave the phone number. The caller's words burned in her mind and she repeated them verbatim. Describing the voice was harder.

Detective Garraway asked, "Do you know what he meant by this quest?"

"I have no idea, Detective. What do I do now?"

"Try not to worry, and don't take any chances. When he calls again, we'll get a better idea what we're dealing with."

"I'm not answering any more calls I don't recognize."

"For now, you're best to answer, Ms. Daniels. You don't want him knocking on your door."

~~~

Joey's feet drummed a steady rhythm as he jogged in the small park near his apartment. Fresh air and motion always cleared his thoughts and made him feel more balanced.

Yesterday with Carol was great. The walking, the company. Until that kid grabbed her bag and the other guy took that video. He'd never seen anyone so terrified. He'd had to help. But did he have to lie?

Starting another lap around the park, he wiped the sweat from his forehead with the back of his hand. It wasn't the lying. He'd already confessed it, knew God had forgiven him. Again.

It was how fast he'd done it, this instinctive need to protect Carol at any cost. He gulped a lungful of air. Good thing he hadn't seen his buddy Ron at church this morning. Ron from the repair shop, who'd warned him about getting into a relationship with a woman who didn't share his faith.

He increased his speed despite the burn in his legs. He wasn't looking for a relationship. Not yet. Not until he'd figured out who he was in this new life. Carol wasn't looking either. But she needed a friend, and even without this uber-protective streak he could hardly cut her off.

One foot skidded on the gravel path. He took three quick steps to keep from falling.

His phone rang. Pulling it from his pocket, he slowed to a walk and tried to control his breathing. "Hello?"

"My dear Mr. Hill. I saw you on the news last night. It seems you're a hero."

Joey took the phone from his ear and read the call display. *Unknown.* He usually checked first and didn't answer those.

"Who is this?"

"You did business with associates of mine on the West Coast, before you ran afoul of the law. I opened a file on you when you moved into my territory." Amusement laced the stranger's tone.

Joey's lungs seized. He hunched over and braced a hand on one thigh, trying to coax his airways to work. "How did you get this number?"

"That's not important."

"Well, add me to your do-not-call list. I'm clean now. You don't have anything I want."

"My silence, perhaps."

Sweat trickled from Joey's forehead along the bridge of his nose and dropped off the end. He stared at the damp spot on the gravel for a ten-count before he straightened up. He was breathing again, but his brain wasn't kicking in.

The other man chuckled. "Does the lovely Ms. Daniels know your dark secret?"

Joey's heart clenched. "Does she need to?"

"My thoughts exactly. You did such a fine job building her trust yesterday. I arranged that little incident to unsettle her, and your heroics played very nicely into my plans. Who better than you to keep an eye on her for me now? Which of course you couldn't do if she knew all."

A young couple walked toward Joey with a German Shepherd on a leash.

He lowered his voice. "What do you want with Carol?"

"That needn't concern you at this point. Continue to gain her trust. Should she confide in you, encourage her to cooperate with me. I'll be in touch." Click.

Joey stared around the park. The couple with the dog walked hand in hand. A mother and two children sat on a bench, the children's feet swinging in the air. Another jogger circled the perimeter. A typical Sunday afternoon.

Except for the words he'd just heard. The sweat from his run flash-chilled against his skin.

Chapter 11

ON MONDAY MORNING, Carol clung to the welcome illusion of security in the café kitchen and told herself Paul would be safe at school. He'd refused to stay home, and despite her fear she knew he was right. They couldn't hide in the apartment waiting for another threatening call.

By late afternoon, the day's baking was complete except for sticky cinnamon buns and carrot cakes waiting to be iced. At a tap on her shoulder, she shut off the mixer.

Lily, the café owner, wore the tiny vertical frown line between her eyebrows that meant someone had crossed a boundary. "Can you take the phone? He says it's urgent."

Heat washed Carol's body, followed by cold. The wall clock said four thirty. Paul was out of school, but he wouldn't call except for an emergency. What now? Or was it Detective Garraway? Or yesterday's caller?

She followed Lily's rapid march to the counter phone, half wanting to run ahead, half to drag her feet. "Hello?"

"Carol? It's Joey. Hey, you sound tense. What's wrong?"

She sagged against the counter. "I can't take personal calls at work."

"I don't have your home number. Can I see you tonight? We need to talk."

A wizened elderly lady came to the counter. While Lily boxed a half-dozen butter tarts, the lady stared at Carol. She lowered her voice. "I've got to go."

"What about tonight?"

"Where?" *Not my apartment.* But yesterday's caller knew her unlisted number. Maybe knew where she lived. And Joey wasn't a threat.

"How about my place? Visitor parking's in front of the building. I'm in 617. Let me give you my phone number."

She'd picked him up for the picnic. She could find the place again. Grabbing a paper napkin from the counter dispenser, she pulled a pen from her pocket. "Shoot."

When she hung up and turned toward the kitchen, Lily intercepted her. "Is everything okay?"

"I think so. I need to finish my icing."

Lily's blend of practical businesswoman and motherly hostess always left her unsure of how much guard to let down. The café owner would sympathize about the threatening phone call, but how much patience would she spare for the jumpy after-effects?

Carol ducked through the swinging kitchen doors.

On the way home from the park on Saturday, Joey had been upset about lying to convince the boy to cut out her part of that video. He'd told her he couldn't do it again. What if one of the reporters from wherever the boy sent the video identified Joey and asked for more details? Would his conscience make him talk?

~~~

Carol stepped out of Sticky Fingers and scanned the street before hurrying to her car, keys bunched in her fist. No sign of trouble. Paranoid maybe, but the mystery caller said he was watching her. Would she know him if she saw him?

She stopped at home to feed the dog and change out of her work clothes. Nothing amiss, and no sign of Paul. She'd grabbed the mail and tossed it on the table. Now, a heavy cream envelope caught her attention among the ad flyers.

It looked like a wedding invitation. For her landlords, maybe? The letter carrier must have put it in the wrong box.

Jackie's loopy handwriting surprised her, scrawled beside a scratched-through Calgary address. The original typed label named Mrs. Carol Daniels and family.

Who did she know who'd be getting married? She barely glanced at the embossed silver wedding bells before opening the card. *Amy Silver and Gilles Renaud.*

Her reserved little cousin Amy would be in her mid-twenties now.

Carol tapped a fingernail against the invitation. When she married Skip, Aunt Isobel had cut all ties. There'd been no further contact.

Morbid curiosity made her wonder how Amy had turned out living under Isobel's thumb, but she had no intention of stepping back into her aunt's sights.

She grabbed a pen and ticked the *will not be attending* box on the reply card.

Before heading out, she left Paul a note with Joey's number. She'd probably be home before her son anyway. Joey had to be on the air at ten.

Joey buzzed her into the building and met her when the elevator opened onto his floor. Part of her wanted to punch the door-close button and retreat. Whatever his urgent talk, surely he wouldn't launch into it here?

She adjusted her glasses. "Didn't think I could follow the numbers?"

"Simply being hospitable. The kettle's on, if you'd like tea."

"Would I ever."

He held the door to his apartment. "Regular or peppermint?"

"Oh, mint, please." He'd told her he didn't drink herbal teas. He must have bought this for her.

He hung her windbreaker in a tiny but neat closet and led her past a kitchen alcove to the living room. "Make yourself at home. I'll see to our drinks."

A brown cloth sofa and chair made a vee at one corner of a leather-look square ottoman, facing a mid-size TV. A hardcover Bible lay on the ottoman—a Study Bible? There was a test?—beside a library bar-coded Dean Koontz paperback.

An oak entertainment centre hugged one wall, with a bulky stereo that must be wirelessly linked to the speakers mounted in the room corners. Carol dropped her purse beside the sofa and browsed the CDs, hundreds of them in alphabetical order by artist. The eclectic mix made her smile. Plenty of classic rock like Joey played on his show, but classical too, jazz, contemporary.

Some of the non-rock names she recognized. Louis Armstrong, Diana Krall, Johnny Reid... her gaze flicked to the bottom right. The man even had Zamfir's pan pipes. Six Billy Joel CDs sat with the J's.

The CD changer display showed four disks loaded but paused. What had he been listening to?

"What do you think of my setup?"

She spun, half guilty as if she'd actually opened the tray to peek.

Joey set a plate of cookies and two music note patterned coasters on the ottoman. "Downloads take up a lot less space, but my music collection is all I've kept from my old life. Minus a certain segment of songs and plus what I've added since."

He left the room and returned carrying two porcelain mugs to go on the coasters. "When the player goes, I'll have to convert to digital like the rest of the world."

He opened the CD tray, lifted one out, then selected random play. Piano notes danced into the beginning of "Vienna," and he grinned. "You don't mind Billy Joel?"

Carol returned his smile, eyeing the disk in his hands. "What's that one?"

"Not Billy." He slid a case from the A's. "Todd Agnew. One of my newer favourites. The lyrics might bother you."

"Explicit?" She tried to be matter-of-fact, not to let her disappointment show. Lots of people liked crude lyrics, but Joey didn't seem the type.

"Christian."

A giggle tickled her throat. "You mean like hymns?"

"Mostly songs about God, and us, and how much we need Him. But he covers a few hymns like you've never heard them, sister. Rock and blues."

He snapped the case shut and re-shelved it. "I can't tell you how much God means to me." Smiling, he spread his hands. "So don't worry about a sermon. Let's eat."

Carol sat at the end of the sofa nearest the ottoman and chair.

Joey eased into the chair. He held out the plate of large chewy-looking golden cookies. "White chocolate macadamia nut. Not as good as yours."

She took one, then settled into the couch with her mint tea. "You didn't have to buy special tea just for me."

He raised his coffee in salute. "Hospitality. I was going to pick up cake from the deli, but I thought you'd get suspicious."

Her fingers tightened on the mug handle. "Should I be suspicious?"

"Nope." He finished his cookie and reached for a second. "Help yourself or I'll have a stomach ache."

The CD changer shifted into the driving beat of "You May be Right."

Instead of taking another cookie, Carol kept time with her fingertips against the side of her mug. "So what did you want to talk about?"

His moustache twitched. "Too bad our day out came to such a crazy end. Did you see my picture in the paper? They must have lifted it from the video."

"No, but I told Paul what happened. Most of it, anyway. Thanks again for... covering for me."

"You know I can't lie for you again. And I can't hide you from the police if they identify me from that video clip and need a statement."

"Don't worry. They know where to find us."

His shoulders lost their stiff set. "I was afraid you or Paul were into something illegal."

Carol shook her head. She had enough secrets without people imagining more.

Joey extended a hand, palm up. "I'm caught, here. Friends don't pry, but they don't let their friends struggle alone. I want to help."

"It's nothing. I had a bad experience with a reporter before I moved here. I thought we were dating, but he was chasing a story." Let it go at that. No point telling him about Sunday's terrifying phone call.

She inhaled a deep draft of mint. "There's trouble in my family. It all blew up in my face, and I ran. I guess Saturday it all came back at me and I panicked. I have a new life here, and I'm not going to let another reporter dig it all up again." Or let that creep from Calgary find Paul.

Joey drained his mug and set it on the ottoman. "About your brother?"

Hot tea splashed Carol's chest, soaking her cotton blouse. She was halfway to her feet when Joey dashed from the room.

He brought her a soft blue bath towel. "I'm sorry. Here."

Pressing the towel against herself like a shield, she stared at him.

Joey dropped into his chair, hands folding and unfolding between his knees. Waiting.

She picked up her mug and drank what she hadn't spilled, then clutched it to her chest on top of the towel. "How did you find out?"

His hands folded and stilled. "Searching online last night. And a bit more today. They have some awful, tabloid-type photos."

"That was the supposed boyfriend." She shivered at the memory.

Joey took her mug. "I'll get you a refill. Close your eyes and listen to the music."

She did, but she trained an ear on the kitchen too.

He ran water, singing along to "Uptown Girl." The microwave pinged.

Soon, he came back with her mug. "Fresh tea. I am so sorry, Carol, I didn't think you'd do that."

She pinned him with a flat stare. "As far as I'm concerned, I don't have a brother. I don't want to talk about him."

Joey's mouth tightened. Sadness washed his features. "The past is past. But I care."

"He didn't touch *me*, if that's what you're asking. I wouldn't be alive." She drew her fingers through her hair. "He only took blondes. I had dark hair until I came here."

"There were good shots online too. You looked lovely. Not that you don't now, I mean—" His mouth snapped shut, and he went to stare out the window.

She took a sip of tea. It burned and soothed at the same time. "The last cookie is calling you."

Joey turned. He shrugged when he saw her waving the plate, but he eased into his seat. And he took the cookie. "If your, ah, non-brother is in jail, and the miserable excuse for a reporter's in Calgary, what's got you so scared?"

"I'm not—okay, I am. A man phoned on Sunday. On our unlisted number. I found out recently that Harry was running drugs. So this drug boss wished me luck on a quest and said he's been watching me." A gulp of tea resisted the trembles. "I don't know anything about a quest. And I don't think he'll believe that."

The last words came out in a whisper. Her grip on the tea mug made her fingers ache.

Joey circled the ottoman to sit beside her, then pried the empty mug free and set it down. His hands cradled hers. "Could Harry have hidden something? Money? Evidence? Drugs?"

"I haven't spoken to him in years. I don't have a clue what he might have hidden, or where. Paul refuses to move again, and the man on the phone said he'd find us wherever we went."

Joey's grip tightened. "This guy doesn't sound like he's playing."

"He enjoyed scaring me. I could tell by his voice."

"Could Harry tell you what the man wants? If he got you into this, he owes it to you to get you out."

She nibbled her lower lip. The detective had said Harry asked them to warn her about the drug lord. Did her ex-brother actually care, or was this part of his crazy plot to reopen communication between them? A sigh pushed from the depths of her lungs. "I wish I knew what was going on."

"Would you feel better if someone else asked for you? I could contact the prison, if you gave me a written note to prove I'm legit."

She pulled her hands free. "No thanks. But that's really sweet. I told you the police know where to find me? This is why. The detective I talked to said to wait for more instructions. If I have to talk to Harry, I will. But as a very last resort."

The care in Joey's eyes and the worried twist to his mouth warmed her heart. She stood. "I should go."

Billy Joel was singing "The Stranger." Joey picked up the remote and clicked off. "I'll walk you to your car."

Chapter 12

PATRICK'S TAXI COLLECTED Carol early Tuesday morning. She hadn't slept well, between anticipating today and dissecting last evening with Joey. Why did he have to go digging for information?

Most people who knew about Harry either avoided her or tried to pump for gory details. Joey seemed more concerned about her. But so had the two-faced reporter in Calgary.

She squirmed against the taxi's upholstery, inventorying the boxes again in her head. Patrick's insistence on providing transportation rankled. Her little Toyota had its dents and scrapes, but it got the job done. Even if it wasn't as fancy as most of the vehicles in his elite subdivision.

Maybe the taxi sprang from a misguided form of chivalry. With the amount he was paying for this catering job, she could put up with a quirk or two.

The cabbie pulled into Patrick's driveway and popped the trunk. He took the heavier box and followed her to the door.

Patrick let them in, immaculate as ever in a charcoal suit and periwinkle silk shirt. After paying the driver, he hefted the second box and led the way to the kitchen. "It's a beautiful morning. You'll have the sun in the kitchen."

And the oven. Good thing she'd chosen short sleeves. She set her box on the counter and surveyed the gleaming space. "This will be a great place to work."

"As I said, I'm glad to see it get more use. If there's anything you can't find, you may need to search. There's no logic to how my chef stores my gadgets."

"Is your cat around?"

Patrick avoided her eyes. "It's difficult to view a creature that independent as mine. She's shut in the bedroom. I have a meeting in the area. I'll stop here before I go to the office."

Carol busied herself setting out recipes and ingredients. When she heard the front door close, she stopped and drew a breath. "This should be fun."

She donned her apron and scanned the kitchen. Patrick had everything else. There must be a radio or mini television here somewhere. She spotted a slim under-cabinet console and tuned it to Joey's station. He'd be home now, or out for a morning run, but she liked their daytime line-up.

Patrick returned around eleven. Cheesecakes and chocolate cake layers rested on cooling racks, and Carol was ready to assemble the Black Forest.

He stepped into the kitchen and surveyed the work in progress. "Everything looks wonderful. It smells even better."

"Thanks. This kitchen is a dream."

"Would I be intruding to make coffee?"

"Of course not. Is the radio okay?"

"It's fine. Quieter than I usually hear. I often close the door. It's a small price for good food."

He filled a small kettle and plugged it into an outlet at the far end of the counter from where she stood measuring whipping cream into a bowl. As she added sugar and vanilla, he poured coffee beans into a grinder.

When the whirring clatter died, she asked, "What time is your gathering tonight?" The rich aroma of fresh-ground coffee danced in her nostrils.

"Eight." Patrick spooned coffee into a mid-size French press.

"I'll help you set up before I go." He was paying too much for simple baking.

"Thank you." He poured boiling water into the press, stirred it, and set the cover in place. "I'll come back for my coffee shortly."

After he left, she closed the kitchen door as a sound barrier and set the mixer on high to whip the cream.

She was ringing the bottom cake layer with a chocolate icing dam when Patrick returned.

He'd traded his shoes for suede slippers and removed his suit jacket. He still wore his tie.

She focused on sprinkling kirsch on the cake and mounding cherry filling behind the dam. This was how he unwound? She'd stick with leggings and oversized sweatshirts.

Patrick took a clean china mug from the cupboard and filled it with coffee before settling at one of the high stools at the central island. "I've never seen this done before. You don't mind if I watch?"

"Not at all." She placed the second cake layer gently atop the first and built its chocolate rim, then sprinkled more kirsch and piled the remaining cherries in the centre.

As she swirled whipped cream around the sides of the cake, he said, "Would you join me for lunch when you're finished? Chinese, perhaps?"

Her grip tightened on the spatula. Joey's warning echoed in her mind. "No thank you. I arranged to be late, but my boss expects me at the café."

Patrick raised his left hand, long fingers extended to display his wedding ring. "I wasn't making advances. I've lost my wife, but I continue to honour her memory."

She hoped she wasn't blushing. *See, Joey?* But she'd been suspicious too. Poor man, living alone in this luxurious shell. "How long ago?"

"Three years in December."

"I'm sorry."

His nod acknowledged the husky layer of sympathy she hadn't been able to control.

"People who haven't grieved don't understand." Carol put the remaining baking dishes into the dishwasher, added a soap pod, and set it running. Patrick had one of the whisper-quiet ones, not like the monster at the café.

She picked up the vegetable peeler and unwrapped a square of chocolate to shave onto the Black Forest. "Losing my son Keith was hell."

"I can imagine."

She focused on letting the chocolate curls fall evenly over the cake top. "He was only twelve. I never knew how he got into drugs." Skip was gone by then, and she'd thought they were doing okay.

Tears blurred her sight. "We got him help, and he tried— he really did. That's when he brought home a stray dog, Chance."

She glanced at Patrick, then away, and pulled a tissue from her pocket. "He stayed clean for a month. Then, one night I got the call at work. He died before I reached him."

Shoulders trembling, she turned from the cake, away from Patrick. Tears soaked the wadded tissue pressed to her eyes. This was old grief. Not a sharp, sobbing outburst but deeper, a reservoir whose flow was harder to contain once the retaining wall cracked.

Patrick's seat legs scraped.

She braced herself, but he didn't touch her.

A cupboard door rattled, followed by the sound of liquid poured into a cup. "Cream or sugar?"

"I don't want a drink, thanks." Her throat squeezed the words into a tortured whisper.

"Coffee is the universal neutral ground. The cake will wait." No sympathy in his tone, simply a quiet command that eased a few degrees of her tension.

"One milk then, please. No sugar." Tears still leaked, but the toaster and bread maker on the other side of the kitchen grew less blurry.

Patrick handed her a coffee mug. "Come with me."

Again, the calm authority soothed her, and her legs unlocked to follow him. In the sitting room, the rocking chair was gone from its corner, but she wouldn't intrude again now that she knew its history. She wedged into a corner of the couch, her mind deliberately blank.

Patrick took the matching chair, a safe distance away. "I open the French doors from here to the dining room for dessert gatherings. The clients are free to mingle. Naturally, Isis remains shut away."

Carol swallowed an experimental sip of coffee. Her throat ached, but the muscles moved. A second swallow went down with less pain, the third almost normally. She stared into the milky brown liquid. Too soon to thank him. That would reopen the wound.

She listened as he described his expected guests, their surface interplay and manoeuvring. He seemed to have a good insight into what made them tick. That must be helpful in his work. He sketched a gently amusing view, neither condescending nor judgmental, yet not seeming to count himself among them.

Professional distance would keep these clients from being friends, perhaps, but did this man open up enough to have friends?

Right now, his reserve let her piece together her composure, but she hoped he had a safe place to be himself. She didn't know what she'd have done some nights without Joey at the other end of the phone.

Patrick finished his coffee and went to open the doors to the dining room. "I'll set up while you finish the cakes. We'll leave them in the kitchen until this evening, and the servers can slice them when they arrive to do the final preparations."

Carol carried her mug to the kitchen. She couldn't dwell on gratitude for what he'd just done. Instead, she put the final chocolate curls on the Black Forest and the chocolate cheesecake, then spread caramel sauce and pecans on one vanilla cheesecake and raspberry puree on the other. Carefully, she transferred them to the large stainless-steel fridge.

He could house a big family. Had he and his wife dreamed of children?

Suit jacket in place, Patrick reappeared while she was cleaning up. "I need to get to the office. If you're nearly finished, I'll wait and set the alarm."

Forget alarms, the cat would keep her from entering uninvited. She gave the counters a final wipe-down. "As soon as I unload the dishwasher."

"I'll phone a taxi." He handed her an envelope. "Your cheque."

She wiped the last moisture from the cake pans and stacked them in the box. The ingredients already filled its mate. "Thank you. By the way, I didn't tell my boss why I needed the morning off. Please don't mention this to her. I know you weren't able to pick the cakes up from Sticky Fingers, and we don't deliver, but Lily might see this as a conflict of interest. I hope your event goes well tonight."

"I'm sure it will. It's unfortunate you have to finish a shift at the café now after the early start."

Packing finished, she perched on one of the high stools. "I'll make it."

"No doubt. I imagine it's hard being the sole provider."

"Plenty of people do it." At least she didn't have Skip's spending habits to worry about anymore.

Patrick leaned one hip against the counter and studied her. "One thing troubles me. You said you had no family, yet you have a brother."

Her hands clenched in her lap. "I had a brother. We don't talk about it."

"It took time to place you, but I remember the news articles."

"So you know why I disowned him."

Patrick's sea-green eyes could have cut glass. "He'll get what he deserves. He was a wealthy man when he was arrested. Did all the money go to his victims?"

A chill swept through her, and she scolded herself. A person who handled investments all day was bound to see the financial angle in everything. "As far as I know. His lawyer was livid. Harry insisted on disposing of all his assets and dividing the money among his victims' families before the courts could set damages."

"Why?"

"The lawyer seemed to think it was to minimize legal fees. It certainly wasn't out of the goodness of his twisted heart." She adjusted her glasses, thinking aloud. "He gave it all away. Unless he had a secret stash—"

Drug running. He might have kept that money untraceable. Is that what the drug lord meant by a quest? Did he think she was after hidden money?

Harry had sent her their mother's things and sold everything else. If he left money in a safe-deposit box or storage, it would still be there. She'd have to tell Detective Garraway.

Patrick stood patiently, his eyebrows raised in invitation. Carol shrugged. "I wouldn't touch it, even if it did exist."

"If Silver has money, he'll never be free to use it. I share your scruples, but you have a son to think about. It might be worth your asking." He spread his hands. "This is my line of work. I could help maximize for... Paul's?... future. Under the circumstances, and as a friend, I'd waive the fees."

"I appreciate the thought, Patrick, but he's out of my life and he's staying there."

The taxi's horn sounded in the drive. Carol slid off her stool and grabbed her purse and the nearer box. "This was supposed to be a fresh start, and suddenly everyone's after me about my jerk brother."

"Are you in trouble?"

Heat crept into her cheeks. She didn't know Patrick well enough to worry him about the mystery caller. "I'm fine. A friend asked me about him yesterday, and now you. I guess the timing upset me."

"Forgive me, how close a friend?"

The serious look in his eyes stopped her. "A good friend. I trust him."

Holding the other box, he made no move for the door. "May I ask his name?"

"Why?"

"I have well-placed contacts in the city. Would you let me reassure myself that he's legitimate?"

"I appreciate your concern, but he's not a con artist. He's a deejay at City Classics FM. They would have checked him out before they hired him."

"Anyone who knows you're Silver's sister is bound to wonder if he shared his wealth. Some may want you to share it with them."

His cool tone raised the hairs on her neck. This man could be her paranoid twin. "Joey's not like that. He knows I don't have anything to spare." But he had offered to contact Harry about this mysterious quest.

The taxi horn sounded, longer this time.

"I have to go, and you're late for work." Carol fled. She'd have paid her own fare home if he hadn't been behind her with the second box.

Chapter 13

PAUL HELD THE violin bow up to the light. At one end, the normally cream-coloured hairs were a slushy grey. "You're right, it does need help." He smiled at the little girl on the other side of the counter, then met her mother's eyes. "Put rubbing alcohol on a washcloth and run it over the hairs. You'll get the worst of this out."

He looked at the girl. "And no more touching. Fingers are what made it dirty." He winked.

She glanced at her fingers. "They're not grey."

Beside him at the other cash register, Eric chuckled.

Paul tried to keep his face straight. "No, but the oil sticks to the bow hair, and that's what does it."

She checked her fingers again, probably for drops of oil this time, as her mother thanked Paul and put the bow into the violin case. As they left the store, the girl turned to wave.

Eric elbowed him in the ribs. "I wish I had what you've got, man. The girls all like you, even at that age. And you ignore them. Maybe I should try that. Let me think... no."

Paul straightened the stack of sale flyers on the counter, then glanced toward the session room where Jubal was taking his lesson. Eric's shift finished in five minutes. Paul would be alone when the older teen came out. Wednesday nights were slow so they'd be able to talk.

His hand went to Harry's letter in his back pocket. What would Jubal think?

He watched his coworker sign off the other register. "Have a good night, Eric. Leave the girls alone."

Eric shot him a wicked grin on the way out.

Paul leaned his elbows on the glass countertop. He'd read the letter four or five times and still couldn't get his head around it. The man deserved a reply, he guessed, but he didn't know what to say.

How could a killer like Harry speak of God and forgiveness? The letter sounded sincere, and maybe it was nice to think that even someone so terrible could start again.

Thinking about it hurt his brain. Did he even want Harry forgiven? Shouldn't the man pay for his crimes?

Forgive and forget. Would God do that after what Harry did? What did that make God? Amazingly strong or pathetically weak?

Paul checked his watch. He hoped talking to a friend who understood God would help, but he couldn't tell Tara-Lynn about Harry. It wasn't fear of driving her away. He didn't have time for a love life. How could he speak to a girl about what his uncle had done to those women?

Jubal seemed to have it all together, and if he went to Tara-Lynn's church he should know God. Good thing Jubal took lessons twice a week. If Paul had to wait until Saturday, he'd go nuts.

The letter weighed on his mind, but how to bring it up? Start by asking about God, then forgiveness. Build up to it.

The shop bell jingled as a customer entered, spiking Paul's anxiety. Why couldn't this guy have come ten minutes ago, instead of when Jubal was about to come out?

He tried for a calm tone. "May I help you?"

The man took off his faded Blue Jays cap, revealing salt and pepper hair cut in a mullet. Grey pouches under his eyes spoke of too many late nights in smoky rooms. "Your boss is expecting me. The name's Donnie Leyland."

"He's almost finished a lesson, sir. Should be less than five minutes."

"Thanks." Steel-grey eyes studied him. "Are you the Daniels boy?"

Paul's fingers tightened on the edge of the counter. Mom's mystery caller wouldn't have given a name. Just in case, he memorized the man's features. "Paul."

The visitor stuck out his hand to shake. "Call me Donnie. I used to play with your dad."

Throwing away his suspicions, Paul clasped the man's hand. "Cool. It's good to meet you."

The session room door opened. Jubal stepped out, followed by Mr. Morelli.

Morelli's face creased into a huge smile. "Boys, this is my good friend, Donnie Leyland. He's a superb studio musician, and he's played with more famous names than I can count."

Donnie hiked one shoulder in a casual shrug and nodded to Jubal.

Jubal raised the end of his guitar case in salute. "Wish I could stay, but I've got to get to work." He grinned at Paul and carried his instrument out to the street.

Paul frowned at the closing door and tried to bury his rising desperation.

Mr. Morelli tapped his arm. "Paul, will you join us in the session room? If a customer comes in, we'll hear the bell." He led the visitor out of the display area.

By the time Paul locked his till and followed, the two men were comfortably settled in chairs. He took the seat Morelli indicated, trying not to stare at the musician who'd not just known but played with his father.

Neither man minded staring at him though.

He looked down at his interlaced fingers.

Mr. Morelli handed him a guitar. "I was bragging to my friend about my star pupil. When he learned you were Skip Daniels' son, he asked to hear you play. The arrangement you passed last week would suit well to begin."

Star pupil? Most ranted-at, more like.

With each rant, Morelli tugged at his wiry grey hair until Paul expected handfuls to come out. Come to think of it, his teacher's hair looked pretty wild now. Jubal's lesson must have been rough.

Morelli's black eyes twinkled in an expressionless face. "Don't disappoint him."

Paul slid forward in his seat and rested the guitar on his leg, one hand cradling the neck, the other resting against the strings. He closed his eyes, feeling the instrument, letting it grow into an extension of his hands.

He breathed in through his nose, remembering the musical score. Although rock was his thing, the lessons included complex classical pieces and theory. Mr. Morelli insisted on a broad foundation.

Ignoring the two men, he warmed up with simple chords and fingering, then segued into the difficult classical number that had caused so much damage to his teacher's hair. His fingers stumbled at the beginning, but he'd nailed this one last week and his confidence grew.

Then he played a tricky exercise he'd been perfecting for a month and eased into a classic Beatles song.

Another guitar joined his.

He muffed the beat, recovered, and flashed Donnie Leyland a grin. "Sweet harmony."

Donnie inclined his head gravely and concentrated on his playing.

Paul hadn't heard this counter-melody before. He tried to memorize it with one ear while keeping up the main tune.

They ended in a crescendo of strumming and laughter.

The shop bell sounded. Mr. Morelli pressed Paul's shoulder. "I'll see to it."

Paul peered at Donnie through sweaty bangs. "That was fun. Could you show me again?"

The older musician studied him through narrowed lids. "Son, you've got everything he had. Maybe more."

In the storefront, Paul heard his boss talking with the customer. "When did you play with Dad?"

"I was with the band for about four years. Left a couple years before he died."

"Why did you leave?"

Donnie rested his arms on the guitar body. "Skipper was too high-maintenance. The guy was good, but knowing it ruined him. And he didn't want to be a musician—he wanted to be a star. Spent more energy chasing women than perfecting his music."

Paul didn't look away. If this man wanted to make him flinch, it wasn't going to happen. "Did my mother know?"

"Skip wasn't subtle. How is she?"

"Mom? She took it hard when my younger brother died, but she's doing okay."

"I read about that. I'm sorry."

Donnie played a complicated riff that seemed to take his full attention, then raised his head. "If you want to play this thing, I mean really play it, you've got to serve the gift. It's hard work, but it's the best. If you just want to follow in your father's footsteps, don't waste your time. It's too much grief, and there's easier ways to meet women."

Paul's splayed fingers tapped a gentle rhythm on the guitar body. "This comes first. Right now, a girlfriend would be a distraction."

Donnie's greying eyebrows rose. "You sure didn't get that from your father. Let me run through that harmony for you again, and then the maestro and I have some catching up to do."

As they positioned their instruments, the older musician paused. "I'd prefer you didn't mention me to your mother."

~~~

By Thursday's supper rush, Carol had replenished the café display case. She put on a clean serving apron and tucked a fresh order pad in her pocket.

She'd enjoyed baking at Patrick's—until the talk at the end. A catering business would be fun, but it was a risk she couldn't afford to take. Maybe once Paul finished his education. In the meantime, Patrick's fee would add to the college fund.

She checked her reflection for flour smudges before heading into the dining area. Heavy semicircles under her eyes taunted her about last night's dreams. Thank God for Joey on the other end of the phone.

Most tables were occupied, and a friendly buzz of conversation filled the café. She took orders, chatting with the regulars. Lily encouraged a home-style atmosphere at Sticky Fingers, and it made for a happy place to work.

It didn't feel as safe since the anonymous phone call, but who could suspect elderly Miss Calhoun, who came the nights she wasn't serving at the soup kitchen? Or the Termolis, with their photos of a gorgeous baby grandson? Estella sat alone tonight, but her eyes sparkled. "My Leo gets out of the hospital tomorrow."

Carol pressed her hand. "I'm so glad."

When she brought the Italian woman's bill, she set a takeout container on the table too. "Fresh cinnamon rolls, one for Leo and one for you. A welcome-home treat."

As she stepped away, Patrick entered. He slid into a nearby booth, holding a rolled-up newspaper.

She pulled her order pad from her apron and went to his table. "How was your dessert evening?"

"My guests were most complimentary. Thank you again for Tuesday."

"It was a pleasure. Lily has a wonderful home-style beef stew for the special tonight if you feel like comfort food. That wind is raw."

"That sounds perfect. I don't often eat red meat, but on a night like this it won't kill me."

Health-conscious, self-controlled, rich, and gorgeous. Too bad he couldn't get over his wife's death and be happy again. He'd make someone else happy too.

The remaining tables filled, and a few satisfied patrons ventured out into the cold. More than one regular asked for coffee or tea refills to put off the inevitable.

By the time she brought Patrick's coffee and fruit cup, the pace had slowed.

His green eyes seemed cooler than usual. "Have you spoken to your friend Joey recently?"

"Last night. Why?"

He unrolled a local tabloid and flattened it on the table.

She frowned. Patrick was a *National Post* person if she'd ever met one, or maybe *Globe and Mail*. Why would he even pick this up?

"Toronto Deejay's Drug Conviction Exposed." The headline seared her brain.

It couldn't be Joey. It couldn't.

Popular overnight radio personality, Joey Hill of City Classics FM, hasn't always been as clean as he'd like us to think.

Carol gripped the table edge to hide her tremors as she read. The article sensationalized Joey's disastrous car stunt and public humiliation. And his jail term.

She let out a shaky breath. Tears stung her eyes. She didn't dare look at Patrick.

He cleared his throat. "I'm sorry to bring bad news. I hoped you'd already seen this. It's best to know the truth."

"I knew about the accident and that he'd been in jail."

"Not about the drugs?"

Her glare burned past the tears. "No."

Patrick's smooth features didn't change. "I didn't want to be right about this, Carol. But I do want to see you safe. A man with drug connections, asking about..." His gaze darted sideways and he dropped his voice "...about Silver."

Carol crossed her arms tightly across her chest. To signal distance, or to keep her heart from ripping out? "Joey is my friend."

"You might want to rethink that."

Retorts boiled on her tongue. She clenched her teeth. Sticky Fingers was no place for a shouting scene, and she needed her job. Finally, she hissed, "I should have known better than to trust either one of you. Not Joey and not you, with your smug I-told-you-so."

She stormed into the kitchen, fury hammering in her veins, and soaked a towel in cold water to press against her eyes. The mother of all migraines brewed in her skull, but it was better than hysterical sobs.

Behind her, Lily asked, "Are you okay?"

"Headache. I can make it until seven. Just give me a minute."

"Take your time. I'll do up Mr. Stairs' bill and the Uxleys'. Everyone else is finished."

"Thanks, Lily." Carol kept her forehead and eyes buried in the cool towel for a count of one hundred deep breaths. Then she tossed the towel in the laundry and swallowed two painkillers from her purse.

She checked the mirror and smoothed her hair. How could she be screaming on the inside without it showing?

When she peered through the window in the kitchen door, Patrick had gone.

Tray in hand, she began clearing tables. Mindless work, anything to keep from thinking.

The re-rolled tabloid lay at Patrick's place alongside a folded page torn from his notebook. Opened, it read simply *I'm sorry. If you need to talk, please call.* Below the text lay the precisely drawn digits of his phone number.

He'd left a twenty-dollar tip for an eighteen-dollar meal. Carol folded the money and stuffed it into Lily's collection can for the children's hospital. The note and tabloid landed in the recycle bin.

Chapter 14

CAROL LAY ON her back in the darkened bedroom, eyes closed. Even the glow from her bedside clock hurt. She tried to concentrate on the radio's soft music. The painkillers blunted the pain, but her head throbbed too much to let her escape into sleep.

Patrick's smug expression swam in her memory. He'd been right about Joey, and his satisfaction still burned her. Why couldn't people mind their own business?

From the kitchen, a muffled thump and footsteps told her Paul had come home. Her mother senses could relax now, but sleep stayed out of reach.

Almost ten o'clock. She should shut off the radio or change channels. Instead, morbid curiosity pinned her to the bed until the opening theme to Joey's show.

She drew the covers up to her chin. Would he even mention the article? Surely, he'd heard about it even if he hadn't seen it.

"Welcome to the Thursday edition of All-Request Oldies. I'm your host, Joey Hill."

Was his voice strained, or was that her imagination? "Listeners in the Greater Toronto Area may be wondering who I really am, thanks to the diligence of a local tabloid."

He did sound strained. She pressed her lips into a satisfied line.

"I guess you can call me an example of 'before and after.' The *after* is the guy you've been spending your evenings with at City Classics FM. For those who haven't heard, the *before* was a swelled-headed celebrity with a drug problem who wrecked his career and landed in jail.

"In hindsight, I should have been more open about my past, but who wants to start over with his old reputation hovering over his head? I hope—I pray, if I can say that on the air—you'll forgive me and accept me as I am."

Carol rolled onto her side, knees tucking up into a fetal position.

Joey's laugh sounded forced. "Enough talk. Let's get to the music you love. Tonight, the first request goes out to a mixed-up deejay whose initials are J.H."

Wordless voices and a light drumbeat. She recognized it just as Ringo Starr began to sing. The "No No Song." Her mouth twitched into a smile in spite of herself. *The floor's not a good place to wake up, is it, Joey?*

When the dreams woke her at two, she made herself a cup of peppermint tea. The light didn't hurt her eyes as badly, so she wrapped up in a blanket. She thought she'd lose herself in a graveyard shift movie with Cary Grant, until she realized it was *Charade*. A widow in danger, threats about a missing fortune, and a friendly stranger who might be a villain in disguise? Not tonight.

Shuffling to her room with her tea, she wished she could afford cable or internet.

In the morning, her muscles ached like she'd been wrestling an elephant. Even her soul felt bruised. But as hard as it was to crawl out of bed, she wanted a few minutes with Paul before he left for school.

He glanced up from his cereal bowl when she walked into the kitchen. "You look terrible. What's wrong?"

She put on the water for coffee. "Migraine last night. It's going to be a long day."

"Call in sick. You never miss a shift."

Staying home would give her too much time to think. "I took Tuesday morning for my catering project. Plus, Friday baking stocks the café up for the weekend. I need to be there."

"Not if you scare the customers." Paul stood and carried his bowl to the sink.

When he left, she locked the door behind him. The apartment felt empty despite the dog shadowing her steps.

How to fill the hours before work? She needed to keep Joey out of her head. Save herself from a mental rant that made less sense each time she rehashed it.

When she left the apartment two hours later, the bathroom sparkled and both beds had fresh linens.

The day's baking took extra concentration. Her eyes brimmed as she mixed a batch of white chocolate macadamia nut cookies for the weekend customers. She should never have trusted Joey.

When her shift ended without Patrick coming in, she let out an audible sigh of relief. He often showed up on Fridays, even if just for coffee and a fruit cup.

Thoughts of Patrick pushed another hot button. He hadn't had to go out of his way to let her know about Joey's past. Or to be so smug about it.

Maybe his perfect appearance matched perfect behaviour, but the world she knew was full of broken people.

Why did Joey's down side have to be drugs? She couldn't handle that, not after losing Keith.

Her heart lay like a deflated balloon. In all their conversations, would it have killed him to tell her about his past?

When she reached the apartment, a hungry dog met her at the door.

No sign of Paul. If he stayed home once in awhile, she'd have someone to talk to beside a late-night disc jockey. Their place wasn't much, but she did the best she could. Paul had too much of Skip in him, if he always had to be out.

She fed Chance and reheated a plate of leftovers. When Joey's show began, she was ready.

He opened the program by thanking the kind listeners who'd phoned to encourage him the night before.

It took six tries on speed dial one—she'd delete that after this call—to get through.

"Welcome to All-Request Oldies. What can I play for you tonight?" His voice was back to the rich baritone she used to find so comforting.

Her glare should have burned the radio, but the song played uninterrupted. "I called to say our visit to Kensington Market tomorrow is off."

"You could have just stood me up. I deserve it. I didn't think I'd hear from you again."

"How could you deceive me like that?"

Joey's groan sounded near tears. "I tried to tell you in the park, but I couldn't."

She remembered his struggle, how she'd sympathized. Anger coalesced and burned like a new-formed star. "You tricked me."

"By the time I realized what drugs had done to your family, I was afraid to break your trust."

"Well, that worked fine." Carol slammed the phone into its cradle and stalked away even though he was in a sound booth halfway across the city.

Too upset to focus on TV or a magazine, she went back to the kitchen to make tea. The radio was playing John Denver's

"I'm Sorry." She hit the power button, but the song finished in her mind.

Let him be sorry. Instead of a drink, she'd give the apartment a good vacuuming. Her landlords lived upstairs, but they were hard of hearing. And Paul didn't have to be in until eleven on Fridays.

By Sunday afternoon, the apartment and the car were spotless.

Paul kept himself scarce. Saturday, he'd gone out to get help for a writing project. Today, he was out again, supposedly studying with Barry.

Worry teased her stomach. Her son seemed evasive lately, but she couldn't pin it down. At least he was clean of drugs. Her searches came up empty, and he showed none of the behavioural clues.

She unwrapped a square of margarine and plopped it into the mixing bowl to make peanut butter cookies. Some parents would jump on her for invading her child's privacy. She'd bet they'd never lost one to drugs.

The phone rang, and she tensed. *Unknown name.* Her teeth caught her lower lip as she hissed in a quick breath. Heart hammering, she pressed the receiver to her ear. "H-hello?"

"Ms. Daniels, you sound distressed. Can I help?"

"You can stop calling and leave me alone." She clapped a hand to her mouth. Making him angry was not a good idea.

He chuckled, low and satisfied. "Not yet. I have a little job for you first."

"Job?" The word came out in a squeak.

"For now, I simply wanted to express my sympathy about your friend Joey's past. An unfortunate end to a promising relationship. I'll be in touch about the job." Click.

Carol swore at the phone and slammed it into the cradle. Arrogant creep, jerking her around like this. Tormenting her with how closely he was watching. How could he know she and Joey were friends, let alone know the tabloid news ended the friendship?

One of his spies must have been at Sticky Fingers when Patrick did his big reveal.

Except the place had been nearly empty. Surely, none of the regulars would be involved.

She'd phoned Joey Friday night. Had they tapped her phone? Or wasn't there new technology that let people listen through glass? After dark, with the light on in the kitchen, she wouldn't see anyone outside the window.

She checked it now. No one around. She felt itchy as if someone had been watching—and as if his eyes had left a dirty residue.

This caller knew too much. And he had a job for her. Dread settled deep in her bones.

She hurried out of the kitchen for her purse with the detective's card. Behind her, the phone shrilled.

She froze. Forced her stiff legs to carry her into the kitchen. Please, not the drug lord again.

Calling back with "Incidentally..." would probably appeal to the sadistic creep. Holding her breath, she checked the call display.

"P. Stairs." She'd given Patrick her number when they made the catering agreement. Odd that he'd have kept it afterwards.

His satisfaction as he unfolded the tabloid filled her mind.

Guilt pierced her resentment. She shouldn't have been rude to him, but apologies would have to wait. She spun on her heel and went for her purse. Behind her, the phone rang three more times before it stopped.

She brought the detective's business card to the kitchen and keyed the number into the phone. One of these days, she'd convince her landlords to move into the new century and get a cordless.

"Garraway speaking."

His calm tone dropped her tension down a notch. "Detective, it's Carol Daniels. I'm sorry to bother you on the weekend again, but I've had another threatening call."

"No worries, Ms. Daniels. It goes with the badge. By the way, I've come up negative on any hint of a safety-deposit box for Silver. We're following up with his former contacts, but nobody's too eager to talk to us. I understand you're not on speaking terms, but we may have to ask you to contact him, depending on what this caller says to you. Did he give you more information?"

"He said he has a job for me. That he'd tell me later. He also mentioned a falling-out I had this week with a friend. The only way he could know about that is if he's tapping my phone or somehow listening to my conversations."

Garraway snorted. "He wants you to know he's watching. That's a standard intimidation technique. I'll have a tech team come by and check your phone line. Stay alert. And let me know when he contacts you about this job."

"Unless he's listening now and realizes I've already talked to the police. Maybe he'll quit calling."

"In our dreams, Ms. Daniels. In our dreams. Goodbye, now. Don't let him spoil the rest of your weekend."

Carol hung up and roamed through the apartment, peering out the windows. Nothing suspicious in sight, but would she know what to look for? She scrubbed her palms against her leggings. Curse Harry for dragging her into this—whatever *this* was.

~~~

Patrick's phone buzzed like an angry hornet in his pocket. He dropped his magazine and jumped from the chair as if stung. Lear must think he'd sweated long enough. That was the drug boss's style. Hang up on the end of a bad report and let the minion stew.

Maybe he could have patched things up after Thursday's debacle with Lear none the wiser, but the network's eyes were everywhere. He didn't want Lear to think he was holding out on him. And he needed to keep this assignment. If he could bring Lear the money...

He thumbed the call pickup. "Yes?"

A volley of obscenities hit his ear. He held the device away until the tirade slowed, then continued as if the drug lord hadn't spoken. "I couldn't do what you wanted with that deejay around. Isolating Carol from her friends makes her rely more on me."

"I was using him too, you fool. Did you think you were the solo player in this particular chapter of my game?"

He ignored the insult. "Yes, I did. Had I known..." He'd have done the same. He needed to be the one to produce the cash. Needed to get out of this mire.

"Give me one good reason not to pull the plug on this." Lear's voice grated dangerously low.

Patrick pulled at his collar, craving air. "Setbacks happen. Scare her, and she'll run to me. Don't worry."

"I never worry. I act." Click.

Shoving the phone into his pocket, Patrick rested his forehead against the cool strength of the wall. What a mess.

Chapter 15

CAROL PULLED INTO her parking spot behind the apartment and stepped out of her car. Chill fingers of wind drew shivers along the back of her neck. Time for a thicker jacket.

She could hardly wait to put her feet up. Mondays at the café meant extra baking to replenish from Saturday and Sunday, and her muscles ached from her weekend cleaning binge at home. Her heart ached too. She ignored it.

Her key turned with no resistance as if the door were already unlocked. How often did she have to warn her son to take their safety seriously?

She'd locked the door that morning. She always double-checked. Paul must have come home early and forgotten to re-lock it.

She ducked inside and flicked the light switch. Rap music blared from the kitchen radio. She shut the door and hung her coat on a peg. Paul's leather jacket wasn't there, so he'd gone out again. Without locking up. He'd hear about this.

She glared at the radio. They left it on all day as company for Chance, but her station played oldies. Not rap. The angry lyrics hammered at her ears. Frowning, she hung her purse on the nearest chair and reset the channel. And lowered the volume.

Dirty dishes in the sink said Paul had been home for supper. He hadn't tidied up as well as usual. Must have been in a hurry to catch the bus. Maybe that explained the unlocked door, but it didn't explain the rap. Paul was a rocker like Skip.

"Chance, you crazy dog, I don't know how you did this..." The dog hadn't come running when the door opened. The noise must have scared him.

The phone rang. Patrick? He hadn't called again on Sunday, nor stopped at the café this evening.

She needed to apologize, but she didn't want to have to make the first move. Let it come out casually as if the scene at Sticky Fingers had been no big deal. Neither of them liked awkward displays of emotion.

Caller ID showed an unfamiliar number. Her bones chilled.

"It's one of Paul's friends." But she didn't believe her own words. She grabbed her purse from the chair and unzipped it, rummaging one-handed for her wallet while she forced the other hand to pick up the phone.

"Hello?" Got the wallet. She wedged it between her stomach and the counter to fish out Garraway's card without dropping the phone. Whatever the creep said, she needed to hear it clearly and relay it to the police.

"Ms. Daniels."

She'd only heard the voice twice, but there was no mistaking it. The hairs frosted on the back of her neck.

"It's unfortunate about the dog. I didn't know my representative was afraid of them." Click.

The detective's card slipped from her fingers.

"Chance?"

She bolted for the living room, afraid of what she'd find. "Chance?" No sign of him. She rounded the corner into the

105

hallway too fast and banged her elbow on the wall. The pain made her run faster.

Nothing in the bathroom. She threw open Paul's door. No dog. She reached her own bedroom and stopped in the doorway. Chance lay sprawled in the middle of her bed, a dark stain spreading from his head.

Her breath caught in her throat and erupted in a scream. When the sound didn't wake the dog, another scream formed.

She pressed her hand over trembling lips. She wanted to gather the dog, blanket and all, and race to the vet. The rational part of her brain made her stop and scan the scene. The boys' photos, everything else, stood untouched.

A sob pushed from her mouth, and she fled for the kitchen. She grabbed the detective's card from the floor and punched in his cell number.

"Garraway."

Hot tears flooded her eyes. "It's Carol Daniels. My apartment—they've been here—they killed my dog. I—" She caught her lip between her teeth to stop the sobs.

"I'm on my way. Are you safe?"

"I think so."

"Don't touch anything. Fifteen minutes. I'll be there."

Carol slumped against the wall. She needed tea. Her stomach heaved. Maybe she needed to throw up.

She walked unsteadily across the kitchen and collapsed into the nearest chair. What evidence had she already ruined, running through the apartment, resetting the radio? Touching the phone, but there'd been no choice.

Thank God Paul had gone before that creep came in.

Her heart stopped. The unlocked door. The mess not cleaned up. What if they took Paul?

Approaching sirens wailed, then cut off.

She bolted out the kitchen door and around to the street.

Two black-and-whites stood in front of the house. The flashing lights died before she reached them.

One of the officers jogged to meet her. "Ms. Daniels? Why didn't you wait inside?"

"My son. I think they took my son."

In the dimming light, the officer didn't look old enough to wear a badge. "Where's Detective Garraway?"

"Try to be calm, Ms. Daniels. He's on his way. I'm Constable Holland. This is Constable Groves."

The female officer who joined them matched his height but had ten years on him.

An unmarked car pulled up across the street. Garraway sprinted over.

Constable Holland spoke first. "They may have her son."

Garraway focused on Carol. "What makes you think that?"

"The door was unlocked. He didn't clean up like he usually does. If he was here when they came—"

Garraway's features hardened, but the hand he rested on Carol's shoulder was gentle. "Let's go inside, and you can tell us what happened."

Legs trembling, she led the police up the driveway to the rear door. "This is the way I came in."

The officers scanned the kitchen. Groves pulled a chair away from the table and gestured to Carol to sit.

Her knees wobbled, but she glanced at Garraway. "I won't mess up any clues?"

"It's okay. When you're ready, give us as many details as you can."

She sank onto the seat and tried to remember the first minutes after she'd come home. The phone call burned sharp in her mind, and the image of Chance on her bed. Fear for Paul clouded the rest.

Detective Garraway sent the other two to search the apartment. He looked smaller in jeans and a sweatshirt, but his eyes said he was on duty.

He opened his notebook. "Ms. Daniels, the caller apologized for the dog?"

"Maybe to make me look for him." If she'd walked into her room with no warning...

"Possibly. The call's timing sends a message that he knows your movements. You'd just arrived."

A shiver traced Carol's spine.

Garraway tapped his pen against his paper. "He didn't mention your son?"

"No."

"So it's possible Paul left on his own. I'm betting that's the case. If these people wanted to use him as leverage, they'd let you know they had him."

It made sense, but she didn't dare hope. She could kill Harry for dragging them into this.

Constable Holland returned. "Sir, the dog's alive."

A hiccuping sob burst from Carol's lips. She slumped forward onto the table, face pillowed on her folded arms, and let the tears flow.

A hand squeezed her shoulder. "Tell me where you keep the fixings, and I'll make you a coffee. You've had a nasty shock."

She looked up into Garraway's compassionate brown eyes. "Can you get him to a vet? He was my son's—" A fresh wave of tears drowned her words.

Holland brought her the tissue box from the counter. "We'll take care of him, don't worry."

Garraway asked, "Do you know where your son might be?"

Carol's lips twisted and the tears came harder. Garraway meant Paul. He wouldn't know this was old grief for Keith.

She tried to swallow the pain. "There's a list of numbers taped inside the cupboard door beside the phone. His cell's on top."

Garraway studied her for a minute. He strode across the room and picked up the phone. "I'm likely to startle him, but not half as much as if you try to talk to him right now."

He keyed in the number and waited. "Paul Daniels? Detective Rick Garraway calling. There's been a break-in at your apartment. I'm here with your mother. Are you all right?" He flashed a thumbs-up to Carol.

Her eyes welled again. She gave Garraway a wobbly smile.

A loud knock came at the door. It pushed open, and Carol's landlords rushed in.

Garraway, on the phone with Paul, frowned at the intrusion.

Basil Johnstone frowned back, as his wife dashed across the room. "Carol, dear, we just came home. What happened?"

"Someone broke in while I was at work. They hurt Chance."

"Well, of all the nasty things!" The woman sat at the table and took Carol's hand. "Will he pull through?"

Holland spoke from behind Carol. "I hope so, ma'am. We'll get him checked out."

Carol dabbed her eyes with a tissue. "Officer, this is Cecelia Johnstone, and her husband Basil. They're my landlords."

Garraway finished his call and turned to them. "Detective Rick Garraway. This is Constable Holland, and Constable Groves is around here somewhere."

"Here, sir." Groves stepped into the kitchen. "Everything seems in order, except the painting over the sofa is upside down."

"See if you can get any prints." Garraway rubbed a hand across his forehead. "Ms. Daniels, your son is on his way. He says he hasn't been home since he left this morning. The intruder must have done your radio."

"And helped himself to my food!" She pointed to the sink. "I thought Paul came home for supper."

Garraway hooked his fingers on the top of the refrigerator door and pulled it open. "We'll check the handle for prints. Do you see anything missing?"

"The milk jug was almost full this morning, and that plate in the sink had chicken legs. He ate half the cookies too. The dirty, no-good—"

Cecelia squeezed her hand.

Basil stood in the doorway, shaking his head. "Why would he break in and attack the dog, then instead of thievery or wrecking the place, fix himself supper?"

Garraway shrugged. "Holland, you take the dog to the vet and go back to your patrol. Groves and I will finish up here."

"Yes, sir." The young officer ducked out of the kitchen and returned carrying the pink blanket, Chance's head barely visible in the crook of his arm. "Don't worry, Ms. Daniels."

"Where are you taking him?"

"I'll check with Dispatch, and we'll let you know when he's settled."

Basil opened the door for Holland and closed it behind him. "How did they get in?"

Constable Groves turned from inspecting the sink area. "Back door. Minimal signs of tampering. Looks like it was forced by a pro."

Cecelia clucked her tongue. "You'll lock the dead bolts tonight, won't you, Carol?"

Garraway scanned his notes. "If the dog was in fact unplanned, the other actions seem more like pranks, to taunt you about the caller's ability to breach your safety."

Cecilia's fingers tightened on Carol's hand. "What caller?"

"A man called when I got home—"

The door opened. Paul burst in and ran to his mother. "Are you okay? How's Chance?"

Carol clung to him, fighting tears. She'd wanted a fresh start here, not to put them both in danger. If anything happened to Paul—

She looked at the detective. "You have to stop him."

Garraway nodded. "That's the plan. Don't worry about the dog, son. He's in good hands."

Cecelia stood. "We'll be upstairs. Carol, dear, you and Paul come up for tea when you're done."

Basil drew his keys from his pocket. "I'm going to the hardware store right now for new locks. I'll put them in myself. We'll all sleep better tonight."

Garraway wore a doubtful expression, and Carol silently agreed.

He took down the landlords' contact information. "As the property owners, you'll be kept informed."

After the older couple left, the detective tapped his pen against his notepad. "We thought they took Paul tonight. If they think you're stalling, that could be a real possibility. Whatever instructions they give you, play along. And talk to me."

Groves came into the kitchen and checked the fridge and radio for fingerprints.

Garraway said, "Get the cookie jar too."

"Yes, sir. The other rooms are clear of bugs."

"We'll move out and let you finish up in here." Garraway motioned toward the living room.

Once Carol and Paul settled on the couch, the detective dropped into the chair facing them. "Groves is with investigations, not our street force. Good thing I couldn't send her earlier today. We'd have had to sweep again anyway."

He flipped through the pages of his notebook. "They didn't go after you or Paul. That means they don't know Silver's already talked. Part of this is to put pressure on him, but I don't like the sound of this quest or job the caller keeps talking about. When they give you any more clues, I need you to contact Silver and see if he can shed any light on this."

Carol bit her lip.

Paul stared at his knees and looked like he wished he was invisible.

Garraway continued. "I've asked for extra patrols in the area. If you see trouble, either of you, call me right away. We're not ready to close the net on this operation yet, but we have to keep you safe."

He gave Paul one of his cards.

Paul nodded, his jaw tight.

Her son's too-old eyes reawakened Carol's anger. She reached across the middle couch cushion and squeezed his hand. Somehow, she'd win this fight and give them both the fresh start they so desperately needed.

Chapter 16

PAUL FINGERED THE detective's card in his pocket and watched the police walk out the door. What kind of person would attack an innocent mutt? It wasn't like Chance would have jumped at him. More likely the dog had tried to make friends.

The apartment felt hollow without Chance. Would he be okay?

As if that was Paul's biggest problem now. If Mom contacted her brother, she'd find out they'd been writing. She'd be furious. What if Harry told her about the band?

His stomach twisted. Mom looked so pale, so drained. With the break-in, and almost losing Chance, the last thing she needed was to find out he was playing guitar. Not that he wanted the fireworks it'd bring either.

It all came down to whether a convicted killer could keep a secret.

He wrapped his mother in a hug. "Mrs. Johnstone will start the tea before those officers fasten their seat belts."

"She's worried about us."

"And curious."

"I guess. Would you run up and tell her I have to stay here in case the vet calls?"

113

"Go have a cup of tea, Mom. I have homework anyway, and I can take a message."

"I'm not leaving you by yourself."

And this was why he kept his secrets.

Why couldn't she give him some space, have a little faith in him? He tried to keep his voice level. "You heard Detective Garraway. Extra patrols, and the creeps have to give us time to get what they want. I'll be fine."

Her chin quivered, then firmed. "I need to stay home."

"All right." He jammed his feet into his running shoes and went outside.

He came back with the landlady, a steaming teapot, and a plate of fresh banana muffins.

Mom needed the company, and if he didn't get his math finished there'd be trouble in class tomorrow. He hung up his jacket, poured a glass of milk and snagged a couple muffins, then headed for his room.

It felt weird opening the door and going in. Like his space had been violated.

The guy would have prowled everywhere, even if he didn't make a mess. The officer checking for bugs had been in here too.

Paul closed his door and set the snack on the edge of his desk. He opened the closet and reached past sweatshirts and jeans to squeeze the left parka sleeve. The rolled magazine buckled inside.

It stank, having to leave his stash at Barry's place. After Keith, Mom got too good at finding hiding places. Keeping even one or two issues was risky.

He settled at his desk with his homework, one hand massaging a cramp from his neck. Math came so much easier in the library with Tara-Lynn. He should have asked for her phone number. A bit of help might get him to sleep before midnight.

A male voice joined the women's in the kitchen. Mr. Johnstone must be here with the new door locks.

Paul turned on his radio to mask the conversation. His station played heavier rock than his mom's. Tonight, it chased away the uncomfortable sense that lingered after the intruder.

He left it on when he finally crawled into bed.

In the morning, his head ached and his eyes felt gritty.

Mom looked worse. Had she slept at all? He sniffed. She was drinking coffee, and she'd made a full pot instead of using the single-cup thing. Not a good sign. He poured himself a cup too.

Her lips pulled into a thin smile. "Can you meet me at the café or go to Barry's after school?"

Paul's shirt collar seemed to tighten. He tugged at it. "I'd be okay coming in here alone, but I'll be late."

His conscience squirmed. "Maybe you should get Mr. Johnstone to walk through the place with you after work."

The coffee mug shook in her grip. "Invade my home, nearly kill my dog, and eat my food? That creep better hope he's not here when I get home!"

"Mom!" Paul drained his cup and put it in the sink. He slid into his jacket. "I gotta go, but listen. You're always worried about me. Well, I don't want to lose you either."

He barely caught the bus. It already felt like a long day.

Math came before lunch today, so at noon Paul and Tara-Lynn headed for their table in the school library to tackle the new assignment. He'd be glad not to face this one after work tonight.

After school, he had an hour to cram for a science test before heading to the store. It made sense to clear his head first, so he walked Tara-Lynn to the bus stop. Okay, forty-five minutes to study.

115

When he pushed open the door to Morelli's and stepped into the shop, school and home stress fell away. He loved this place. The instruments, the lessons, his Einstein-haired boss. Here, and practising with the band, he could be himself and let the music run free in his soul.

Greeting the clerk he'd relieve in ten minutes, he cut through the showroom. He stowed his backpack and jacket in the tiny break area and called hello to Mr. Morelli in the office.

"Paul, I have another letter for you."

Frowning, he stepped into the office. "From the same place?" He'd mailed his reply on Sunday. Today was Tuesday. No matter how bored Harry might be, Canada Post never gave that kind of turnaround service.

The envelope bore the penitentiary's return address, though. And a hand-scrawled note. *Personal—Urgent.*

Paul raised his eyebrows and shrugged at his boss. "Sorry, sir. I guess I should see what it's about." In the doorway, he turned. "He's not in for theft, Mr. Morelli. And he won't show up here."

Morelli spread his hands. "I'm sorry one so young must carry secrets like this and bear his family's shame. If you need support, I'm here."

"Thank you." Paul hurried to the break room, tearing open the envelope as he walked. When he unfolded the letter, smaller rectangles fell out. He retrieved two photos from the floor. Mom, outside Sticky Fingers, and him, here at the store.

If Mom ever saw this... He stuffed the photos into the envelope and shook open the letter. Halfway down the page he realized he hadn't taken in a word. He checked the clock. Five minutes. He sat at the tiny table and began again.

Dear Paul, these pictures came in the mail today. Certain people want money that I've hidden. This is their way of threatening you if I don't cooperate. It was to be their payment for arranging my escape. Even though I'm back inside, they want what's due.

If they haven't contacted your mother yet, they will. Tell her to look in the desk I sent. She'll remember how to open the secret drawer. Neither of you are safe until that money is gone.

She'll be angry about you talking to me, but she needs to know. If it would keep you out of trouble, tell the police and have them talk to her. My enemies have eyes here, and if I'm seen running to the warden, everything will hit the fan.

After Keith, I know you won't want to cooperate with drug dealers, but please don't mess with these people. Playing the hero will cost your mom a second son.

Paul winced. The man knew how to get his point across. Standing, he skimmed the last lines.

You and your mom look well. I pray for you daily.

He stuffed the letter into his pocket and left the break room feeling sick. Dirty money and drug dealers. An uncle with a past like Harry's, praying for him.

~~~

By the start of the supper rush, Carol's eyes burned like desert sand. She'd run on adrenaline and coffee all day, and nearly ruined a batch of cookies at that. She ducked into the washroom and splashed cold water on her face. They were short-staffed today. Going home wasn't an option.

Home. Were her enemies in the apartment now, setting up more pranks to scare her? Would Basil and Cecilia install a security system if she begged?

117

Would it matter if they did? The apartment wasn't safe. Nowhere was. Running hadn't helped. She had to trust Detective Garraway to do his job.

She frowned into the mirror as she refreshed her lipstick. She had to stand her ground. Like she'd done as a teen, battling her aunt's restrictions and rules. Aunt Isobel had always wedged hands on hips and put the younger Carol's choices down to wilful stubbornness.

Life with her aunt and cousin hadn't made good memories, but that was probably as much Carol's fault as Isobel's. Two strong natures battled until they couldn't agree on the colour of the sky. Arranging an early marriage by conceiving Skip's child had seemed like a perfect escape.

Carol donned a clean apron and picked up an order pad. She'd grown up fast with a baby at seventeen. Too bad Skip never did.

Pinning on a smile, she pushed through the swing doors into the dining area.

Friendly chatter hummed around the handful of occupied tables. The street door opened. Estella and Leo Termoli scurried in, shedding drops of rain.

Carol's heart lit up, and a few of the regulars called out happy hellos. She poured two glasses of ice water and carried them to the couple's usual table.

"Mr. Termoli, you shouldn't be out on a night like this, but it's wonderful to see you. How are you feeling?"

He flashed a shy grin. "Don't know what all the fuss is about. I'm too dried-up to die." His wife beamed, patting his hand.

Carol set the clinking glasses in front of them. "Better not overdo it on the water, then. I'll come back once you're settled." She pressed his shoulder before moving to take an order from the family at the next table.

Over the next twenty minutes, more customers trickled into the café despite the autumn rain. As Carol carried meals to the group of university students in a corner booth, Patrick stepped through the door and propped a dripping umbrella beside the coat rack. His reserved demeanour seemed unchanged by last week's tabloid upset.

She returned his smile, willing her arms to hold the loaded tray steady. The stacked plates clinked mildly, but the tremor passed.

Too bad the weather hadn't kept him away tonight. Now, she had to face him with a throbbing head and nerves on edge.

Chapter 17

CAROL TOOK HER time serving the four university students in the corner booth. She owed Patrick an apology, but she wasn't going to fawn over him.

Finally, flipping to a fresh page on the order pad, she moved to his table. "I'm glad I didn't chase you away. Sorry about last week. You were trying to help."

Cool green eyes met hers with no trace of resentment. "Consider it forgiven. I regret being the one to bring bad news."

Heat crept up her neck. "Tonight's soup is chunky chicken vegetable, if you're feeling the dampness."

"Perfect. Thank you."

Waiting tables kept her moving and awake. The rain kept the crowd down, a blessing on a night when they were short a server.

When she brought Patrick his coffee and a fruit cup, he said, "You seem troubled."

The nearest tables were empty, but she lowered her voice anyway. "Someone broke into my apartment yesterday. I was awake most of the night." And listened to Joey's show but didn't call.

His brows came together. "Were you at home?"

"A man called as soon as I got in. Like he knew I'd been out when it happened. He's been threatening me. This time, his creeps attacked our dog. Keith's dog." Her voice broke.

Patrick's face set as still as marble. "Was the dog badly hurt?"

"He took a nasty blow to the head. The vet wants to keep him longer for observation, but I'm picking him up tomorrow."

"Allow me to pay the bill. It's not charity. I know what the dog means to you, and I can afford to keep him at the vet's long enough for a proper assessment." His lips twisted. "Consider it my vote of friendship."

She blinked scratchy eyelids. "That's very generous, Patrick, but he'll be happier at home."

"Will you at least consider it? You don't want to lose him."

"Thank you." Carol left him to his coffee and set to work clearing the corner table. One of the students had left a folded paper with his tip. She opened it.

You looked worried tonight. We prayed for you before we left. God loves you, and He can help.

Sliding the note into her pocket, she scanned the café. Was it that obvious? Patrick met her eyes and smiled, but the few other diners didn't glance her way.

God loves you. Right. *He can help.* Right. Like He helped with Keith.

Maybe it wasn't fair to blame God for Keith. Carol stacked spaghetti-streaked plates and piled the cutlery on top. But couldn't God have kept her son alive until help came? Or given her a premonition to go home?

She carried her load into the kitchen and returned with a tray for the rest and a hot wet cloth to wipe the tabletop. These boys were sweet to care about her. Maybe she could slip them a few cookies next week.

They came every Tuesday, sometimes with others, laughing and carrying on but not troublesome or loud. They always seemed to have fun. Not her idea of Christians at all.

Her shift ended at seven. She hurried from the kitchen, zipping her jacket.

Patrick hadn't left his table. He rose to meet her. "Will your son be home?"

"No. Why?"

"I was thinking of you walking into your apartment unprotected. May I offer moral support? Just to confirm it's safe?"

"I'll be fine, but thank you." For once, she'd been glad to hear Paul was going to be late. Surely, they wouldn't come back the very next night, but if they did and he was home alone...

If they'd returned, what would she find?

She nibbled her upper lip. "On second thought, I'd appreciate the company. If you're sure you don't mind."

"I wouldn't have offered if I did." Patrick slid his phone from his pocket and swiped a finger across the screen. "In case we get separated in traffic, what's your address?"

He walked her to her car under cover of his umbrella, then hurried to his own.

As she threaded through the streets to her apartment, she wondered how Patrick would see the neighbourhood. The homes were simple but well maintained, and more expensive than her dented Toyota would lead him to expect.

The Johnstones were her friend Jackie's ex-in-laws—"outlaws" Jackie called them now—and they'd given her a break on rent at Jackie's plea. It was still a stretch financially, but it put Paul into a safer, better school.

Signalling, Carol pulled into the driveway and parked behind the house. No sign of trouble. But there hadn't been yesterday until she went inside.

Patrick had left his car on the street. He walked along the driveway toward her.

As they approached the door, a light came on above them and hinges squeaked. "Carol? Is that you, dear?"

"Yes, Cecilia. I brought a friend with me to make sure it's safe."

"Basil could have come down."

"No need to drag him out in the rain—it's not good for his joints. I'll see you tomorrow."

"Good night, dear."

The shiny new key unlocked both deadbolt and door handle.

Patrick rested a hand on her arm. "Allow me, just in case."

She reached for the light switch and let him pass, then stepped into the kitchen. Everything looked fine. She inhaled. Everything smelled fine. The radio played quietly. She hadn't needed to leave it on with Chance gone, but the thought of coming home to silence was too much.

Patrick stood his umbrella on the boot tray and took off his shoes. "Shall I do a proper check?"

"We'll go together." At least after her weekend cleaning frenzy she didn't have to worry what he'd see.

They hung their dripping coats on the pegs and went into the living room. Patrick glanced around. "Nice Monet."

"Thanks. It's only a print."

"If you'd owned an original, your intruders would have left a bare patch on the wall." He started down the hallway. "Your landlady sounds protective."

"They've been very good to me. They weren't sure about taking a single mother and teenager, but now they treat us like family. Paul has no grandparents, so that's a bonus."

Both bedrooms and the bathroom checked out. Carol felt her tension slip from her shoulders. She led the way to the kitchen. "Thank you for this. I didn't realize how nervous I was. Do you have time for another coffee?"

He checked his watch. "I don't want to intrude."

"I need a tea anyway."

"In that case, yes, please." He pulled a chair from the table as she filled the kettle.

"I'm sorry for the duct tape. It's—"

"Please don't compare our homes. The chair is sturdy, and your neighbourhood seems safe. That's what's important."

"Thanks." She set two floral porcelain mugs on a tray and filled a plate with peanut butter cookies. Patrick might not want one, but her nerves said she did. She spooned coffee into the single-cup filter and dropped a mint teabag into her cup. No-name coffee for a man who ground his own beans. But it was all she had.

"I like living here. Cecilia mothers me too much, but that's a small price." When she'd made their drinks, she picked up the tray. "I've spent most of the day in a kitchen. The living room's more comfortable."

She settled on one end of the couch, feet tucked up beside her for warmth. She couldn't put on her scruffy slippers with Patrick here. She took a cookie and rested her tea mug on her leg.

He sipped his coffee. "You've made this a cozy space."

"I try. My mother was a genius at creating atmosphere with no budget. It's amazing what paint, fabric, and thrift store finds can do."

"That accent table and mirror didn't come from a thrift store."

"Neither did the bookcase or the desk in Paul's room. They were Mom's. Gran'papa was a carpenter."

Remembered sawdust and sunshine drew a wistful smile. "We didn't visit often. They were French Catholics, and Mom married an English Protestant."

"Ah, the dark ages."

Carol's happy childhood had been church-free except on those visits. Until her mother "found Jesus" at a tent meeting and it tore their family apart.

She bit into her cookie. Peanut butter muddied the taste of her tea but tonight, she needed both sugar and mint.

Patrick twisted to study the Monet above their heads. "Rita and I viewed some of his originals in Paris. The *Water Garden* is amazing."

"No one can take away the special memories." Not that she had a lot of those herself.

"Speaking of taking, did they steal anything?"

Pushing her bangs off her forehead, she stifled a sigh. "No theft, no vandalism. They turned the painting upside-down on its wire, changed my radio, and helped themselves to my food. Pranks, except for Chance—and the phone call."

A crease formed between Patrick's eyebrows. "Do you remember what I said about unscrupulous people wondering if Silver shared his wealth?"

"If he hid anything, I wouldn't know where to look. I haven't spoken to him since he was arrested. The first time."

Patrick tapped his fingers on one leg. "Silver won't be out of your life while this man is threatening you."

"It may have nothing to do with Harry." Although Detective Garraway thought it did.

"I could be your go-between. Contact Silver so you don't have to, ask him about any money an enemy would be after. Find its location for you."

"No. But thank you."

His lips thinned. "You don't trust me."

"Trust isn't easy." Joey's lopsided grin sprang to mind. She looked down at the last of her tea.

"You can't trust indiscriminately, but there are a number of respected citizens who can vouch for my integrity. I'm what's known as a safe bet."

"It's not really about trust, Patrick, and I'm not questioning your integrity." She met his gaze. "I appreciate your kindness, but I can't let anyone else wear my danger."

"You have a son. I have no one." He raised his hands as she opened her mouth to protest. "But why would it come to that? I collect the sack of gold, if there is one, your caller asks for it, and I give it to him. Mission accomplished. He leaves you alone. Your danger is in defying him."

The last mouthful of tea went down cold. She set her mug on the tray and rose. "Let me think about it."

Patrick stood too. "I've taken more of your evening than I intended. Thank you for the coffee and conversation."

Over her protests, he carried the tray to the kitchen.

A gentleman, even if somewhat reserved. Classic looks, nice build, financially secure. She caught herself eyeing the graceful line of his hips with the same detached appreciation she'd feel for a fine sculpture and shook her head.

The outside door opened as he shrugged into his coat, and Paul stepped in, dripping rain.

Carol introduced them, and the assessing once-over Paul gave her guest made her smile. Testosterone and defence of territory. *Welcome to manhood, son.*

Paul hung his jacket on a peg but stayed in the kitchen, setting out hot chocolate powder and a mug, while Patrick fastened his coat.

Umbrella in hand, Patrick leaned nearer, speaking low. "Please consider what I said. I find myself... concerned... for you." An unreadable light flickered in his eyes. Tight lines bracketed his lips.

Carol double-locked the door behind him. Even though locks hadn't stopped the intruders the last time.

Chapter 18

ANOTHER BAD NIGHT left Carol longing to crawl back under the covers once Paul left for school.

Her nightmares hadn't stopped at playing out her fears for Paul. Harry and Joey, even Patrick, stalked through swirling mists, buffeted by gusts of windblown money. She'd seen Keith again, but he turned into Chance as a faceless man bashed his head with a length of chain.

Peppermint tea at three a.m. did nothing, nor did baking the banana muffins she and Paul ate for breakfast four hours later.

Listening to Joey's show hadn't helped either, although she liked the songs. He even played Billy Joel, "out of habit," he said. That made her pick up the phone, but she'd hung up before completing the call.

Alone in the apartment that morning, she finished the breakfast dishes and started a load of laundry. Twenty minutes before the vet's office opened, she put on her glasses, grabbed her purse, and headed for the car.

Chance greeted her with loving brown doggy eyes and a limp hand-lick that made up for the vet bill. A stubbly patch on the left side of his head surrounded an ugly, stitched-up cut. The swelling caused the wound to look worse than it truly was, but the sight made her cry.

She dropped to her knees and buried her face in his fur. "I thought I'd lost you too."

He whimpered, twisting to lick her cheek.

Once she got him home, she left him conducting a slow but thorough investigation of the apartment and headed for work. Cecilia had offered to check on him a few times today, which meant Carol wouldn't be worrying.

She arrived at the café early, mentally running through today's baking line-up.

The sight of Joey at one of the tables stopped her in her tracks. How dare he show up here?

His smile didn't stretch as wide as usual, and his posture seemed stiff. Bracing for potential fallout?

Lily called out from the cash, "Morning, Carol. Wow, you don't look so good. Do you need me to call in a replacement?"

The same concern echoed in Joey's face.

Carol cut him a glare. "I'll make it." She headed straight for the kitchen even though it meant passing his table. No way would she be childish and take the long way around the room to avoid him.

He caught her jacket sleeve. "Carol, please. I've been worried about you."

"Let me go." She tried to pull free without disturbing the handful of other customers. Lily had her back to the scene.

"Please," he repeated. "Is everything okay?"

Her glare should have iced his coffee. "I'm fine."

His moustache twitched. "No offence, but you don't look it."

"Save your concern for someone who trusts you."

Red tinged his ears. "Maybe I'm just missing our conversations, but I've had this terrible feeling things have gotten worse. They have, haven't they?"

"Pray. You said it works."

"I have been." His eyes were settled and dark-rimmed, but they glowed with the same sincerity that fooled her before. "Since Monday. What happened?"

"Someone broke into my apartment and tried to kill my dog. Happy now?"

He released her sleeve to take her hand, his fingers warm and gentle. "Is he okay?"

"Almost."

"Any clues?"

"It's that drug boss I told you about. He phoned as soon as I got home. To taunt me."

Carol shivered, gaze locked on Joey's, remembering her visit to his apartment. He'd asked if Harry had hidden anything, offered to be her go-between. He'd concealed his own history with drugs...

She bit her lip. "I have to get to work. We're out of your cookies."

"First thing I asked, even though I came for brunch." Joey released her hand and gripped the edge of the table. "The man who called you called me too."

"What?" Carol glanced at Lily and lowered her voice. "Why?"

Red crept up his neck. "He recognized me from that video of us in the park and knew about my conviction out West." Joey sank a little in his seat. "He threatened to tell you about that if I didn't cooperate."

Carol shifted her weight to her back foot and crossed her arms tightly across her chest. Pain brewed in her skull. "Cooperate with what?"

"For now, to stay close to you. I wanted to build a friendship anyway. No way would I do anything to hurt you—"

"Except deceive me." And ask if he could be her link with Harry.

"If I refused, he'd get someone else to do his dirty work. This way I could warn you. Then that tabloid story made it a moot point. He accused me of setting it up. Said he'd find me another assignment."

His jawline hardened. "Next time, I'll go to the police."

Carol shifted her purse strap higher on her shoulder. "When you offered to talk to Harry for me, was that for Creepy Voice?"

"His voice *is* creepy. Terrifying. And as suspicious as it sounds, that was my own bright idea."

She drilled him with a stare. "So this could be the truth or it could be damage control."

Palms up and fingers spread, Joey rested his hands on the table. "I have no proof. Would you tell your detective? I'll answer whatever questions he wants to ask."

"I will." And tell Garraway about her own suspicions.

"If you need to talk, call me. I promise not to think you've forgiven me. And I'll be praying for you."

Carol forced a smile. "Thanks." She hurried into the kitchen, heart pounding.

On her break, she told Lily she needed to check with the police about the break-in. It wasn't exactly a lie, and it gave her an excuse to make the call. She didn't want to bother Garraway later on his off hours.

Judging by his harried tone, now wasn't a good choice either. "Should I call later, Detective? It's not an emergency."

"You've caught me now, so shoot."

The cafe was nearly empty, but she kept her voice low. "Before the break-in, a friend asked me if this drug dealer could be after something of Harry's. He offered to contact Harry about it so I wouldn't have to."

"Why didn't you report it at the time?"

"I thought I could trust him, but I found out he has a history with drugs. Now, he says my anonymous caller wanted him to keep close to me but that the contact offer was his own idea."

"Give me his name, and we'll check it out. Don't get your hopes up, but if he's working with them we can let him play intermediary for you. Makes your part easier, and gives us more evidence."

She told him where Joey lived and worked. If he'd been using her, let him pay. And if the police proved his innocence...

Later, while she ate her lunch, her mind chewed on the possibilities. Innocent or guilty? Which did she want him to be?

~~~

"Would Paul Daniels please report to the office?"

The secretary's voice over the intercom made Paul jump even though he'd been expecting it. Curious stares prickled his spine as he gathered his books and excused himself to his teacher. "I'll be back if I can."

Detective Garraway, in street clothes, met him at the office door. "Your vice-principal said we could use his office."

Two visitors' chairs took most of the space between the desk and the wall. Paul dropped his books on one and sat in the other.

Garraway adjusted the privacy blinds before taking a seat behind the desk. His smile looked tired. "I told your vice-principal this was about your apartment vandals. Is it?"

Paul had phoned as soon as he got to school but hadn't said why. "Promise you won't let Mom know this came from me."

The detective blew out a breath that could have been a groan. "As long as it's not pertinent to the investigation. Or putting you in danger."

"They sent my uncle a photo of Mom."

"Recent?"

"Yes."

Garraway nodded. "To let him know they can get at her."

"That's what he said."

Garraway tilted his head and narrowed his eyes. "Why is he talking to you?"

What if Harry's letters broke some sort of prison code?

Paul stared back. "Mom won't even say his name. If she finds out I wrote him, she'll freak. But he said he's changed, and I wanted to know if it's for real."

"We'd all like to know that, son. Until this investigation wraps up, he needs to keep quiet. Then he'll have his chance to talk."

Paul unzipped his binder and slid the photo of his mom from Harry's envelope. He pushed it across the desk at the detective.

Garraway frowned at the picture, then locked Paul's gaze. "Just the one? You're not a target too?"

Paul studied the scuffed desktop. Silence stretched. At last, he mumbled, "Don't tell Mom. She's already on my case."

"Taken at school?"

"A place I don't want her to know about. I have a job, and she'd make me quit."

Garraway fiddled with the red mesh pen holder on the desk. "Paul, I'll do my best not to get you in deep with your mother, but show me the picture."

Careful to keep the letter hidden, he retrieved the second shot. He didn't know what to do about the money, but that was not up for discussion. The detective might want to turn it over to the drug lord.

No way would Paul let scum like that get their hands on more money to hook other innocent kids like his brother. If he disposed of it himself, they'd have to leave his family alone.

He handed over the photo. "This is stupid. I work in a music store, and Mom doesn't want me playing guitar."

Garraway scanned the picture. "Sounds safer than a lot of things you could be doing, but I'm sure she has her reasons. Where's the store? I need to be able to find you."

Paul told him, and Garraway made a note. "I won't show this to your mom, but I'll let her know about the threat."

The detective tucked the photos into his pocket. "You could ask your uncle if he knows what's behind these phone calls, but I won't play you against your mother. When they give her more information, she'll need to contact him herself. Is there anything else you want to tell me?"

Want? Paul shook his head. Good choice of words. "Thanks for meeting me here instead of the apartment, Detective."

"You're welcome. I'm sorry things are mixed up at home. You two are strong. You'll get through this. Try to stay on the same side." Garraway replaced the pen holder in its original spot and stood. "We should have this settled soon."

"I hope so." Paul zipped up his binder and gathered his books. A distant buzz made him grin at the detective. "Class is over. Thanks for the reprieve."

Garraway clapped his shoulder. "It's about time you caught a break." He held the door and motioned Paul to go ahead.

The hallway teemed with students in end-of-day cheer. Paul dumped his books in his locker and ducked into the crowd.

The band had practice at Barry's, but he had time to find Tara-Lynn and say goodbye. Maybe even walk her to the bus stop and risk Barry's comments.

He liked Tara-Lynn, but he wished people wouldn't joke about them being an item. He wasn't giving up his music for her or anyone else, and she deserved a guy who'd put her first.

She smiled at him from a circle of giggling friends and he thought better of stopping. "See you tomorrow, Tara-Lynn."

Her friends giggled harder. She returned his wave, but her smile dimmed. Had she wanted him to interrupt? Girls!

Spotting Barry and Nicole, he angled toward them.

A scowl replaced Barry's usual carefree attitude. "Sleazy trick they pulled for tomorrow afternoon, isn't it?"

Paul shrugged. "What did you expect? They want us to go to the assembly." It sounded juvenile, taking attendance before and after, but who'd stick around otherwise?

"Let's find a way to blow it off. Having a deejay do the drug talk is new, but we've heard it all before."

Paul stared at his shoes. "This guy's a friend of my mom." Or was. Maybe that's why she'd acted so stressed even before the break-in. "I want to hear what he has to say."

Barry snickered. "And she worries about *your* friends."

Chapter 19

FRIDAY MORNING, CAROL washed and dried an apple and added it to her son's lunch, careful not to crush the cookies she'd already placed in the bag. Her eyes burned. She'd never been so glad to reach the end of the week, and she still faced eight hours on her feet before the day was done.

Not that time off would help her rest, not with these anonymous phone calls pressing on her. Say Harry did have a hidden stash of evidence or money or valuables, and this guy wanted it. Why tell her where it was?

Detective Garraway thought Harry had a level of concern for her safety, but she knew better. Her ex-brother didn't care about anyone but himself.

Paul rushed through the kitchen and grabbed his leather jacket from the hook by the door. "Thanks for my lunch. I'm late." He stuffed it in his backpack, put on his shoes, and darted out the door.

Releasing a lonely sigh, Carol locked up behind him. "I love you too. Have a good day. Thanks for thinking about mine."

She chopped carrot sticks for her own lunch, to go with the salad and homemade muffin waiting on the counter, then tucked everything into the fridge until she was ready to leave. She'd washed the dishes and settled with a second cup of tea when the phone rang.

Grumbling, she pushed to her feet and crossed to the wall phone. She'd buy her own cordless phone before much longer. This was crazy.

Unknown name. Different number, but the man always used a new number.

The hovering sense of doom thickened. Landed on her shoulders. Her hand fought gravity to lift the receiver. "Hello?"

"Good morning, Ms. Daniels. For your weekend assignment, it's time to pay your brother's debt."

Trembling started in her arms. Spread to her body, her legs. She braced herself against the kitchen counter.

There was no way to prepare for that voice. Or for the malice behind it. "I don't know what you're talking about."

"His hidden money."

She glanced at the window. No one there. Instinct screamed at her to run, but he'd find her again. Her free hand ached from its grip on the edge of the countertop. "I don't know about any money. I have no idea—"

"Then why did you come here?"

"To get away from Calgary. Toronto's a good place to hide." *Right, tell the drug lord your secrets.* But he seemed to know them already.

The caller chuckled. "Not if you're hiding from me. Very well. I'll play along. You don't know about the money."

"I don't."

"Your dear brother promised me money and neglected to pay it."

"I—"

"Obviously, Silver can't access it himself, but he hasn't communicated the location with me. I want that money, Ms. Daniels."

The threat in his tone curled around Carol's throat. And tightened.

"I—"

"If you truly don't know its whereabouts, you'd better hope he tells you."

"I don't even know how to contact him." Pressure built in her chest. Why couldn't this creep terrorize Harry instead?

"He's written to you in the past."

"Your spies didn't tell you I tore up every letter?"

"They did say you didn't write back."

Chill slid down her spine. How closely were these people watching her? "I didn't save his address."

"My dear Ms. Daniels, surely you have the intelligence to look up an address. If not, your son can do it for you. He seems like a bright young man."

"Leave my son out of this. I'll—I'll get what you want. Just give me time."

"Time. I can loan you some. Use it wisely." Click.

Carol sagged against the counter, staring at the phone in her hand.

Silence. The dial tone kicked in. She shook her head and replaced the handset in the cradle. Her heart pounded, and her lungs fought for air.

Sadistic creep, with his "borrowed time" threat. Worse than that, he'd mentioned Paul. If he touched her son, she'd—what? What could she do to protect her son?

She brushed away tears. She'd protect her son by finding this money. Even if it meant talking to the one who'd gotten her into this mess.

Fingers shaking, she punched Garraway's number into the phone. When he answered, she poured out the latest threat and her fears for Paul. "You're sure you can't get one of the wardens to ask Harry about this? Or phone him yourself?"

"Ms. Daniels, he can't be seen to be cooperating with us. Even an incoming call would be too risky. There are watchers everywhere. Your safety depends on this."

"Could I write and ask Harry to phone you? It'd be faster than waiting for another letter, and we need this settled."

Garraway's chuckle warmed her, where the drug lord's had brought fear. "Faster, and it keeps you from speaking with him directly. Give him my cell number. I'll have the prison address for you in a second. Here goes."

She wrote it on the back of the detective's card. "Thank you."

"We've increased vigilance around your home since the break-in, and you can reach me if you need to. There's no point trying to trace these calls, since he always uses a new number. Try not to worry, Ms. Daniels. You've bought yourself time by needing to contact Silver. They know you're cooperating, so you should have nothing to fear."

Had the detective emphasized the word "should"? How could she not be afraid with such an evil man "personally overseeing" a search she hadn't even begun?

~~~

Paul strolled into math class empty-handed, his open leather jacket not giving him the calm he tried to project. A few kids were missing, but most slouched in their seats, chatting. He'd bet he was the only one who'd rather have a regular class, complete with homework, than this dumb assembly.

His life stank. Hiding his music. Letters from prison. Scary phone calls at home. The break-in. Chance could have died. Now, he had to endure "the talk" again. And the memories.

The math teacher surveyed the class. "You know the drill. Keep it to a dull roar, and please be polite to our guest. Drug abuse is an ongoing issue. We need people like Mr. Hill to share their stories."

All around Paul, students groaned.

The teacher waved her hands for quiet. "At least he's a deejay. That should count for something, right? Celebrity? Music? Work with me, here. It could be worse. I could have set a test for this afternoon."

A student called from the back of the room. "Are you going?"

The teacher's chin lifted. "I am. And not just to watch the exits."

As the students straggled out, Tara-Lynn caught up to Paul. "Hi."

"Hi, yourself. How was lunch?"

"Good." She walked beside him until they funnelled into the auditorium.

Paul flopped down in a chair. "It's more comfortable than math, anyway."

She settled her purse on her lap. "I hope this guy is interesting."

The boy on his other side pulled out his phone and started a game.

Paul stared at the stage. "Yeah."

Tara-Lynn nudged him. "Hey, it can't be that bad."

"I could give the talk. My brother died of an overdose." He stared straight ahead. "I found him."

"Oh, Paul! How long ago?"

"Two years this month."

She leaned nearer, gripping his forearm through the leather jacket.

The school principal stepped behind the podium. "Thank you for coming this afternoon. Please give your full attention to our guest as he tells us the truth behind the recent tabloid scandal and about his arrest and jail term. Let's welcome local radio personality from City Classics FM, Mr. Joey Hill."

Applause filled the air, although most kids Paul knew listened to harder-edged rock than an oldies station would play. Deejays were cool. That was enough.

A shortish, ordinary-looking man walked onto the stage. He shook the principal's hand and faced the students with a smile Paul suspected would look strained if he were closer.

"Thank you for giving up the joy of your classes. I hope you don't get extra homework for this."

A collective groan made Joey shake his head. The principal raised a hand in salute and left the stage.

Joey planted himself behind the podium and lowered the microphone. He scanned the audience for a long minute before speaking. "My name is Joey Hill, and I failed life."

At least he was honest. And alive to tell about it. Paul blinked away the image of Keith's dead body soaked in blood-streaked vomit. He shivered.

Tara-Lynn squeezed his arm. "The teacher won't make you stay if you explain."

"She'd send me to study hall." The memories would follow. "I'll be okay."

He concentrated on the man on stage. What did Mom see in him?

Joey was still talking. "Some of my friends blew it in high school, but I guess I had to wait for a larger audience."

A kid behind Paul snickered.

"I got into radio right out of broadcast school. By my late twenties, I had a high-profile spot with a classic rock station in Vancouver. I had it all. And I lost it. My weekends were like some of yours. Parties, girls, drugs. The highs were why I lived. But the highs are a lie. When you crash, you're lower than ever. So you have to do it again, but more. It's a cycle you can't break. It's hell on earth."

Keith had said he wanted to quit. That he was scared he'd die. Paul hadn't believed him. What if Keith really had tried? Did it feel better to see him as a victim instead of a loser?

Troubled by the passion in the man's voice, Paul slid lower in his seat.

"If you're on drugs, I'm living proof you can get off. And you need to get off, fast. I'm lucky I lived to go to jail. The drugs could have killed me. Or a stupid stunt could have."

He spread his arms. "You have no idea the humiliation. Police cars, reporters in my face, doing time as a public example." He scanned the room.

"I made it somehow. For me it was because I was so desperate I turned to God. Don't worry, I'm not here to preach. But I can't pretend I had any strength of my own to pull me through. I'll be telling that story Sunday night at Grace Community church, seven p.m."

Tara-Lynn elbowed Paul. "Cool!"

Joey paced a small oval as if considering his next words. He returned to the microphone. "I got out of jail early on good behaviour. Part of my release was an agreement to speak to kids like yourselves and warn them about drugs. Once I met my quota, I had to get away.

"So I came here. I do a syndicated late-night phone-in show on City Classics FM. Great station, terrible slot for a former daytime star. And I was lucky to get it. Hey, I'm lucky to be alive."

It sounded like this guy was winding down. Paul listened to the rustling around him. The boy beside him shut off his game and stowed his phone.

Joey leaned against the podium. "If you're into drugs, think about what I said. Get help. If you're thinking about trying them, save yourself the risk.

"Here's another thought for you to chew on. I built a new life. Did my best to forget the mess I made. Made friends, even one special friend. Didn't know how to tell her about my past, so I didn't. When that gossip rag finally spilled my story, I was almost relieved. The tension of hiding was tearing me up."

Paul glared at him. *What about her tension now, buddy?*

"Well, I lost the lady. Maybe worse in the bigger picture, I realized I'd lost the opportunity to let others learn from my mistakes. Hear me, young people. I don't know you. Some of you are in good space. Some need help. Some deal drugs. Some are clean.

"I do know each and every one of us messes up. If you need help, get it. If your friend needs help, give support and don't judge. Share your own story when it's needed. Whatever it is, you can bet you're not the only person to go in that direction."

Joey stuck his hands in his pockets. "Thank you for listening. I'll hang around for awhile if there are any questions."

With a ripple of polite applause, the students surged from their seats, most toward the exits.

Paul checked his watch. Final class started in fifteen minutes. Plenty of time for the smokers and snack fiends to satisfy their cravings. A short line of kids straggled toward the stage to meet the speaker.

You couldn't go by appearances, but Paul figured not all had questions about the talk. Three curvy girls in designer jeans seemed more star-struck than impacted by the message. Another one, pale and hanging back, he knew by reputation. Did Amber truly want help? If Joey was genuine, could he help her find it?

Tara-Lynn nudged him. "I want to talk to him. Come with me?" Her eyes sparkled, but her voice shook.

"Okay." He bent nearer. "Um, you're not in any kind of drug trouble, are you?"

Her delicate brows drew together, then she smiled. "You sound worried. Thanks. I'm kind of into writing, and I liked what he said about letting our stories help others."

She glanced toward the stage. "I want to ask if he'd let me interview him, but I've only had a couple things published in our church newsletter. I'm not exactly Ms. Freelance Journalist."

Paul jammed his fists into his jacket pockets. It took guts for Joey to come here today and lay his soul bare. Did he have enough to face Carol's son?

Did the son have enough to introduce himself?

Chapter 20

PAUL AND TARA-LYNN walked down the auditorium's central aisle until they reached the knot of students waiting to speak to Joey.

The pale girl, Amber, stood apart from the others, off to the side.

Paul tried for his friendliest smile. She looked like she needed reassuring, but what could he say?

Fidgeting with her purse strap, Tara-Lynn stepped nearer to Amber. "Maybe I should have tried harder to get you to quit."

How'd a girl like Tara-Lynn get involved with a druggie? Paul kept his eyes down and his ears open.

Amber's toes tapped against the stained carpet. "It wouldn't have mattered." Resentment tinted her voice. "Life is good for you. Today? Joey? He's been where I am, and he found a way out."

Her words made Paul look up.

Tara-Lynn frowned. "You're not the only one with problems."

"I get what she means." Faced with twin stares, his first thought was to duck and cover. Instead, he told Tara-Lynn, "You and I have problems, but not this sort. We don't understand."

He focused on Amber. "My brother died of an overdose after he swore he'd quit. I thought he was a fake. That he wasn't trying hard enough. I had no idea."

Amber's mouth tightened. "That's what I meant. Drugs are different."

Tara-Lynn spoke softly. "I'd still like to be your friend."

Regret for Keith stung Paul's heart. "I couldn't help my brother, but I'll try to help you."

Amber studied him for a long moment, then nodded.

"I have a new number." Tara-Lynn pulled a notepad from her purse.

After adding his home and cell numbers beneath her tidy printing, Paul tore off the sheet for Amber. "Try my home first unless it's really late. I'm on pay-as-you-go for cell. Seriously though, call. Any time."

They chatted about what Joey had said until it was Amber's turn. When she left them, the weight of her problem stayed with Paul.

Trying to shake it off, he asked, "So, what does a math whiz write about in a church newsletter?"

"Budget updates." Tara-Lynn's lips twitched in a brief grin. "No, I did an article on the after-school play group where I volunteer, and one on the youth group's park ministry project last summer."

"Park ministry?" He watched Amber speak to Joey. The man's smile went from friendly to intent as he listened, his focus never leaving her face.

"Games and stories for kids at the local playground."

It took a minute to get his brain in gear. Kids. Park ministry. Focus on what Tara-Lynn was saying. Not on Amber.

A twitch of Tara-Lynn's lips said she'd caught him zoning out. She cut her eyes in Amber's direction. "We were friends before this started. I hope he can help her."

Then she pushed on as if to keep from hearing the soft conversation. "Snacks too. We set up for a couple hours each morning in one spot and another in the afternoon, and just have fun with them."

"No preaching?"

She cut him a look. "How many little kids do you know who'd sit for a sermon? We tell them a story when they're having their snack. Sometimes it's from the Bible, sometimes about kids like them who trust God. What we want to do is let them know Jesus loves them and cares about their problems."

No point debating that with her. Why risk their friendship? "You sure like kids, don't you?"

"Maybe it's because I never had a little brother or sister."

He grunted. "Pluses and minuses to that one."

"I'm sorry about your brother."

"It's hard to remember the good years after what he put us through in the end."

Joey said goodbye to Amber and watched her walk away. She stopped near the exit. Waiting for them?

After a minute, he turned to Paul and Tara-Lynn. His expression said his thoughts remained with Amber. "Hi."

Tara-Lynn stepped forward. "She needs you more than we do, if there's more to say. We can go."

"Thank you. But the school counsellor will have all the contacts she needs. My job now is to pray for her." Joey's smile included them both. "But that's not why you stuck around in here on a sunny day."

In the lengthening pause, Paul took Tara-Lynn's hand. "My friend is a writer, and she wants to interview you."

"Well... who do you write for, miss?"

"My name's Tara-Lynn Kierans, and I've only written articles for my church newsletter, but people need to hear positive stories about God changing lives and if the local papers won't take it there are Christian ones that might—"

Joey's moustache twitched. "Slow down, you've convinced me. It'll make a pleasant alternative to the smear story about me the other week."

A blush lingered on Tara-Lynn's cheeks, but the change in her breathing said she'd conquered her nerves. "I'd actually like to do two stories. One for the mainstream press on your positive example, and one giving your faith story. Kind of like your two talks."

"Sounds good. Come Sunday night, take notes, and we'll get together next week." He pulled a business card from his pocket. "You can leave a message for me at the station, or I'm on-air after ten on weeknights if you phone the request line."

She tucked the card into her purse. "Thanks."

"Thank *you*. I've had a fair bit of media coverage since I blew it, but this may be the first positive exposure."

Tara-Lynn glanced toward the door. "We'd better get to class. Thank you, Mr. Hill."

"Joey." He shook her hand and reached for Paul's, clearly anticipating an introduction.

Paul matched his grip and drilled him with a stare. "I'm Carol's son."

Joey's handshake stiffened. He nodded slowly. "Paul. This is the third school I've visited this week. I had to hit yours eventually."

He released Paul's hand. "Is your mom okay? I keep thinking about that mysterious caller and the break-in."

Paul felt Tara-Lynn's stare. He hadn't told her any of this. "We're handling it. How could you hide your past from her? You must have known she'd freak."

Joey plowed both hands through his hair, leaving a jumbled mess. "It's hardly the first thing I say when I meet someone—'Hello, I'm a former drug addict.' When I found out about your brother, I couldn't bring myself to tell her." His shoulders sagged. "I like to think I helped a little before the end."

"And then undid it all."

Pain flickered in his eyes. "Guilty. I've regretted it ever since. Before you leave—will you come with Tara-Lynn for the interview? I'd rather not be alone with a student."

"Why me?"

"You got her into it."

"I'll go with her Sunday night too." Let him think it was for moral support. Paul wanted to know if the guy was for real.

Joey seemed decent. If it wasn't for Mom, Paul might like him.

Chapter 21

CAROL SURRENDERED TO a jaw-cracking yawn as she let herself into the apartment that evening. A cup of peppermint tea and a candlelit bubble bath would be the perfect end to her workweek.

She liked her job, and baking there meant she did less— and ate less—at home. Eight hours on her feet took a toll though, especially when the café was busy like today.

Chance's toenails clicked on the linoleum as she locked the door, and she held out her hand. "Hey, boy, you're looking better."

Laughter drifted from the television. She headed for the living room. "I'm home. How was your day?"

Odd, to find Paul home on a Friday night. He sat on the couch, feet up on the coffee table, arm deep in a bag of sea salt and pepper potato chips. "Good, I guess. What about yours?"

"Okay. Did you have supper?"

He waggled the near-empty chip bag. "I was going to wait for you, but I got hungry. Hey, I brought in the mail. You got a letter marked urgent from our old address. It's on the table."

Carol's heart thumped, then slowed as her mind caught up. The drug king knew how to find her here. He wouldn't use her Calgary address. And the hater who scared her out of town couldn't find her this way.

Irony would have it be a letter from her brother now that she had to write him. Not that she wanted to read what Harry had to say.

A sigh pushed from the bottom of her lungs. "I'd better check it out. And I'll heat up the last of the chili."

Returning to the kitchen, she made a mental note to do a chicken pot pie and a batch of meatballs on the weekend. Coming home to cook supper didn't appeal at all.

The envelope had *Urgent personal message, please forward* scrawled in a strong, vibrant hand. Postmarked Halifax like the wedding invitation. After all these years, why would her cousin Amy want to reconnect?

She slit the envelope and pulled out a single sheet of paper folded around a long-distance phone card and a photo of a smiling young couple. The man's eyes held a daredevil glint, and the woman radiated happiness. Carol studied her, the long straight hair and petite stature, looking for hints of the child she once knew.

Turning over the photo confirmed her guess. The same confident handwriting from the envelope read *Amy and Gilles*. She set the picture and card on the counter and frowned at the letter.

Dear Mrs. Daniels, please forgive the intrusion, but I must speak with you about Amy's and my wedding. I assume since your reply came postmarked Toronto that you have moved, but I am unable to find you to make direct contact. Please use the enclosed calling card to reach me at the number listed below. Should Amy answer, do not identify yourself but ask for me.

Yours sincerely, Gilles Renaud.

Carol scooped two bowls of chili from the casserole dish and set them in the microwave, then picked up the phone and punched the numbers.

On the third ring, a man answered.

"Hello, this is Carol Daniels."

"Yes, one moment please." Muffled voices drifted over the line before he returned. "Sorry, Mrs. Daniels, I asked Amy to excuse us. Thank you for calling. Would you please reconsider attending our wedding? For Amy's sake? My mother insists we go home to Montreal for the ceremony, and she's invited half the city. Amy has no one."

"Please, call me Carol. What do you mean, Amy has no one? What about her mother, her friends?"

"Amy's mother died seven years ago. When we met, Amy was starting a new position and had no close friends."

The mix of love and confidence in Gilles' voice melted Carol's reserve despite her better judgment. Amy needed someone like this after Aunt Isobel. Too bad the girl had lost her mother, though. Carol knew how that felt.

She stretched the phone cord so she could sit at the table. "I'll have to think about it."

"Let me pay for your flights and accommodation. As part of my gift to my bride."

Carol muffled a sigh. If this young man was half as sweet as he sounded, Amy had done well indeed. "It means that much to you?"

"When she smiles, my Amy is the most beautiful woman in the world."

"It would mean accepting your travel offer. I'm sorry, but finances are too tight after our move."

Part of his wedding gift. Carol massaged her forehead. How was she going to pay for a gift?

"Fantastic! I'll make the arrangements first thing tomorrow. For how many people?"

"My son and myself. He's sixteen."

"Can you come early and reconnect with Amy? She says it's been a long time."

Lily might give her a day off, but Paul had school. "We need to be here all week."

"In the future then, now that we've found you. What's your email address? I'll send your reservations."

Carol hesitated, but her enemies already knew where to find her. "I don't have email. Could you mail what I need? My son's name is Paul, for his ticket." She gave him the address, then ended the call.

She stirred the chili and gave it a couple more minutes in the microwave.

Paul sauntered into the kitchen. "What was that about?"

"We're invited to my cousin's wedding in Montreal in November."

He flipped pages on the wall calendar. "When?"

"The first Saturday and Sunday. Does it matter?"

"I guess not, if I plan ahead. Montreal? You going to drive?"

"Her fiancé must have money to burn. He's flying us."

"Sweet. I didn't know you had any cousins."

"I haven't seen her since I married your father. I used to live with her and her mother. Aunt Isobel was a real barracuda. I couldn't wait to get away."

She darted a guilty glance at her son. Did he feel that way about her?

Paul stopped the microwave before it beeped, then carried their bowls to the table.

The phone rang as Carol plugged in the kettle. When she saw a strange number on the caller ID, her adrenaline spiked.

Not twice in one day! "Hello?" Her voice came out shaky, and she gripped the counter edge for support.

"Hi, is Paul in please?" A girl, young and maybe nervous herself.

Carol's fear evaporated. "One second." She covered the mouthpiece. "It's for you."

He took the receiver. "Hello."

Carol set out spoons and glasses. Paul had never mentioned a girl, but if he had Skip's style she'd better expect a string of them.

Expecting was one thing, letting go another.

She glanced at her son as she picked up the water jug from the counter.

Phone cord wound around his forearm, he circled on the short length remaining. Something in the tilt of his head and his concentration said this wasn't just any girl.

He grimaced. "Tomorrow, I'm doing stuff till around six. Yeah, that's where I'll be. Okay, see you then."

He hung up and turned to Carol. "My friend Tara-Lynn. We have another friend who needs a distraction, so we're gonna do a movie."

"She sounds nice."

"It's not like that. But she is."

It felt good to sit down. Carol chewed slowly, letting the tension leach from her body. She watched Paul stir extra pepper into his bowl. "How was school?"

"Same old thing. We got the drug awareness lecture today." He got up and popped bread into the toaster.

Her throat tightened in mid-swallow. She reached for her water glass and took a drink. "Does it make a difference?"

"Today's might have. The speaker stuck around to talk afterwards, and one girl said if he could get off drugs, maybe she could too."

Carol's eyes burned. Keith had tried. He really had. But his efforts, the support system, her desperate prayers, nothing saved him. She hoped this girl made it. "If they'd only listen and not mess around in the first place."

"They're crazy to start, but once they're hooked..." Paul buttered his toast and carried it to the table. "Mom, I thought I understood Keith but I didn't. Maybe you can't unless you've been there."

He scooped up a mound of chili with a triangle of toast and crammed it into his mouth. "I like it better this way without the mushrooms."

"I know, but it's my turn next time. You can pick them out."

His nose wrinkled. "Still taste 'em. This guy who did the talk, he's been clean for a couple years now. He lost everything. Had to start over again in his thirties. With a record. He did what I guess I'd do, kept quiet and tried to put it behind him."

"What else could you do?"

"He said he should have been making something positive out of his mistakes by telling others. Now, he's doing that. I think that's why the kids listened."

Paul took another toast-scoop of chili. "Tara-Lynn's going to interview him, after we hear him Sunday night. He wasn't allowed to talk about faith at school, but he said God made a big difference. She's into that stuff, so she'll know if he's legit."

Carol slid her empty bowl aside and drew her tea mug nearer. "Interview him?"

"She wants to be a writer."

Not all journalists were vultures. Yet her positive impression of the girl paled. And what might Paul have said about his brother? Or hers? "Don't give her anything to write about you."

He rolled his eyes. "What's to say?"

"Paul."

"I know—we're hiding. Except the bad guys know where to find us. But I wouldn't talk about Uncle Harry anyway. I'm not gonna tell a girl what he did."

She laid a gentle hand on her son's. "Do you think about it a lot?"

He shook his head. "I'm over it. I don't get him though." He wiped the dregs of chili from his bowl with a corner of toast.

Carol scowled at her tea. What was there to understand? The man was a monster.

The phone rang. Paul jumped up to get it. "Hello? Sure, one second." He stretched the cord across the kitchen and passed the receiver to Carol. "Detective Garraway."

Pulse rising, she took the phone. "Hello."

"Ms. Daniels, Rick Garraway here. I received information you should know about."

"What now?"

"Our friends sent Silver photos of you and Paul."

Her focus locked on Paul as he cleared the table. "What does this mean?"

"They're showing him they can get at you, so he'd better tell you where to find his money. We didn't spot any bugs, but they may still be listening to this call. You can't be too careful with this bunch."

It took a couple of tries to get her voice working. "So why did you call?"

"We have nothing to hide. They know you don't know where the money is, and that the Department doesn't know where to find them. I wanted to give you the update and to encourage you to get that letter off to Silver as soon as possible. If they hear you now, they won't have to ask later."

Thoughts whirled in her head, connecting the dots the detective hadn't marked. His serious tone warned her not to

155

blow this. No mention of drugs or Harry's evidence. Stick to the demand for the money.

"It's on my list. First thing tomorrow."

"Ms. Daniels, when you hear from Silver, don't try to grab the money and run. If we can't find you, these thugs might. Unless we get a break tracking them, you have to give them what they want. Your lives are more important."

"Why don't they ask him where it is?" And leave her and Paul out of it.

"It's one thing to send anonymous photos, but we're watching now. Any phone call or letter from him, we'd know where it went. They could have done it that way in the beginning, but they obviously assumed, like I would have, that you came here to get the money."

Carol felt another headache brewing. "I didn't know it existed. Toronto was home once. It's not my fault my ex-brother lived here too."

"Good night, Ms. Daniels. Will you mail that letter right away? I wish you'd been able to do it today. We want you out of danger as soon as possible."

"I will. Good night." She crossed the kitchen and hung up the phone.

Paul poured himself another glass of water. "What's up?"

"Garraway said they might be listening to our calls."

"They checked the place for bugs."

"Maybe there are other ways. Could they tap an outside wire?" She shrugged. "If they were listening, now they know I don't have the information yet. The creep called this morning after you left for school. He says Harry has money hidden and I have to find it. Now, I have to write Harry and hope he'll tell us where it is."

Paul's mouth pinched. "We can't give them more money. They'll ruin more lives. Like Keith's. And ours."

Heaviness built in her stomach. "We don't have a choice. But I hope Garraway's investigation lands them all in prison."

"So you're writing to Uncle Harry." The heat had faded from Paul's face and left him pale. He avoided her eyes.

Remembering her reaction to the last letter Harry sent, the one Jackie forwarded from Calgary?

"I'm sending Garraway's cell number. If it's true that he's giving evidence to help put these scum away, he should tell Garraway where to find the money."

Paul licked his lips. "I hope someone else found it first. Got rid of it. These creeps don't deserve it. They shouldn't have it."

"Garraway said to give it to them."

"You think he'd use you as a decoy?"

"Who knows?" She scrubbed her cheeks with both hands. "I don't know what's going to happen."

Paul put his arms around her. "We'll be okay. We have each other, and we've got friends."

Carol hugged him, this boy-man who matched her height. She weighed more, in pounds and years, but here he was, offering to share the load. If only she could let him. Tears oozed between her closed lids. "I hope you're right."

She stepped away for a tissue.

"Mom?"

He stood with his hands braced on a chairback. The way he did when he was in for a lecture.

Crumpling the tissue in one hand, she waited. Hadn't she had enough for one night?

"Our speaker today was your friend Joey."

Her fist tightened on the tissue. "My former friend, since his drug use came out."

"He said he didn't know how to tell you. He can't change his past, but he genuinely seemed to care."

"And that should make me feel better how?"

"I'm just saying, if he's a real friend, you could use one now. Better than that Patrick guy."

"What's that supposed to mean?"

"He's plastic. Nobody living inside."

"That's a terrible thing to say." She'd seen signs of life—of pain—in his few unguarded moments. "He's reserved. And classier than we're used to."

"Whatever." Paul pushed the chair into the table. "I thought you should know about Joey. Will you come Sunday night?"

"Did he put you up to this?"

"He didn't even mention it. Just asked how you were." Paul's shoulder dropped as if he wore an electric guitar. A pose he must have picked up from his father. "You worry about my friends—I'm going to follow up on one of yours."

He made for the living room but stopped in the doorway. "You can meet Tara-Lynn."

Carol's groan was half admiration. Her son knew which buttons to push. "Okay. Maybe."

Before she'd known who he was talking about, she'd agreed with Paul about putting a bad past behind and moving on. Isn't that what they'd tried to do too?

But Joey and drugs? She'd go, all right, to be sure Joey didn't lead Paul down that road. But she wouldn't talk to him.

She piled the supper dishes in the sink and turned on the tap. Mindless work might settle her nerves after Garraway's call.

Reaching for the soap bottle, she paused. Pictures of her—of Paul—how did Garraway know Harry received them if there was no communication?

Maybe one of the wardens saw them and passed on the information. Too bad he hadn't seen a treasure map for Harry's hidden money.

What a day, and this call was the final straw.

The call, not what Paul said about Joey. Carol's ex-favourite deejay was out of her life, period. At least until Garraway cleared him.

She sighed. Or asked her to string him along.

Chapter 22

PAUL CAUGHT THE early bus Saturday morning, but an accident snarled traffic. He bolted into Morelli's with seconds to spare. He hung his jacket in the break room, then tapped on the office door, one arm hugging the padded envelope he'd smuggled out of the apartment.

His boss turned from an open cabinet drawer. "Ah, Paul. Is it still raining?"

"It's drizzling now. Mr. Morelli, would it be okay for me to put a package in the store safe? Just for a little while?"

Morelli's shrewd eyes studied him briefly. The store owner spread his palms. "Of course. As long as it's not your dream guitar from the front."

Paul grinned. He didn't realize he'd wished so loudly. He held out the manila envelope, standard magazine size but much thicker and sealed with packing tape. Not fancy, but all he could find.

"Thank you. Someone broke into our place last week, so I don't feel comfortable leaving this at home. It's only paper, but I wouldn't want to lose it." No lie there, although describing a thousand hundred-dollar bills that way was a stretch.

Morelli's thick brows drew together. "I'm sorry to hear that. Was anyone at home?"

"No. The police think they were watching for us to be gone."

"Vandals and thieves are too common these days. I will lock this up immediately, and you tell me when you're ready to reclaim it."

"Thanks a lot." Harry's letter hadn't said how to open the desk's hidden drawer, but a bit of poking and prodding solved that problem. Paul jerked his head toward the storefront. "I'd better get out there."

~~~

Carol put on her favourite dress and a pair of flat sandals to meet Patrick on Sunday. He'd phoned Thursday night to make sure things were okay and mentioned a new exhibit at a private gallery she hadn't visited before.

Art rested her spirit. After labouring yesterday over a letter to her convict brother, she needed it. And it would keep her from wondering about tonight and rehearsing verbal defences to throw at Joey. Not that she planned to speak to him.

She tapped on Paul's door. "If I'm not home by five thirty, eat without me. We need to leave by quarter after six. See you later."

His "Bye, Mom" sounded muffled, like he had a mouthful of cookies.

Eyeing the container on her way through the kitchen, she suspected he might.

The sticky note on the back of the door reminded, "glasses," and she instinctively touched the bridge of her nose. Camouflage in place.

Creepy Voice was bad enough. The last thing she needed was a news-hungry journalist recognizing her—and the Calgary letter-writer tracking her here.

She undid the safety chain and let herself out into the early afternoon sunshine.

Patrick's glossy black Porsche eased around the corner of the building five minutes later and stopped behind her tired-looking Toyota.

She rose from her seat on the Johnstones' wooden stairs, but he was already out of the car.

He opened her door. "Sorry to keep you waiting."

"I came out early for some fresh air." Cecilia's barrels of giant pansies edged the fence behind the parking area. Carol liked the way the sun turned them to velvet. It wouldn't be long before the cool autumn nights finished them. "I need to be home before six. Should we take both cars?"

"And hope to find two parking spaces? It's unfortunate you have another commitment. I'd thought we could share dinner."

Carol clipped her seat belt and settled her purse on her lap. "I'm sorry, Patrick. I promised Paul I'd go out with him this evening."

He slid the car into reverse. "I'll take a rain check."

Linden House Gallery and Antiquities stood a few blocks aloof from the trendier art establishments, its elegant grey stonework and ivy-green trim evoking classic rather than current fashion.

The parking lot was nearly full. Patrick found a spot under the spreading limbs of a maple whose leaves already showed orange edges.

Carol didn't want to think about winter. It wouldn't match the marrow-freezing months she'd endured in Calgary, but there'd be snow and that awful grey slush. And cold.

They followed a slate path to the gallery's entrance. Inside, water rippled down the sides of a black marble pedestal in the centre of the foyer. Groups of paintings hinted at what lay beyond the French doors that opened to each side and the rear. Nature. Impressionist work. Still life.

A small knot of people stood in front of the nature scenes, conversing in low tones.

Patrick angled his head in their direction. "That's the new exhibit. Shall we begin there?"

Calligraphy on a white card beside the door announced, *Waters, Michael Stratton.*

Carol stared around the exhibit area as they entered. "These are amazing."

"Indeed."

They circled the room slowly, rarely speaking.

Peace welled in her soul as she studied each painting. Water was the uniting theme. Running water, in streams, fountains, waterfalls, even a whale's spray.

Ordinarily she preferred the softly blurred Impressionist effects, Monet in particular. These paintings, with their sharp, almost photographic detail, gave a different meaning to "timeless." Not eternal but immediate. Moments in time, fresh, strong, eclipsing past and future.

The painter's chosen moments sparkled with vitality. Carol lingered before a long, narrow view framed in weathered grey wood. Droplets of water cascaded from the battered spout of a blue metal watering can onto yellow and orange marigolds blooming in a faded work boot. Diagonals of sunlight caught the drops, filling each one with life.

Patrick called her to the next painting, a summer lake scene in a forest green frame. The picture spoke of early morning stillness, with shreds of mist curling from the water. A stillness shattered by a pair of mallards landing near one edge. She could almost hear the splash.

Another, of the gentle eddy around a canoe paddle working through a mat of green lily pads, glistened as if inviting her to dip her fingers into the cool liquid.

When they reached the door, they strolled through the other exhibits as well. Patrick checked his watch. "Care to investigate the antiquities on the next level or take tea in the solarium?"

"Tea would be nice, thanks."

"Afterward, I want to visit the Waters room again. My company has a small budget to support Canadian artists, and I need a new painting for my office." He smiled. "If clients see new décor from time to time, it fosters the impression that business is thriving. Which it is."

Potted greenery among the solarium's tables lent an intimate atmosphere.

The waitress brought Carol's mint tea in a rose-covered pot with matching china cup and saucer. Patrick's espresso came in a demitasse patterned in geometric earth tones.

He raised it for an appreciative sniff. "Ahh."

Carol swirled her tea gently in the pot, then poured. Tendrils of steam drifted from her cup. "You were right. Since the break-in, the apartment breeds stress. I did need to get out. This is a perfect place to spend an afternoon."

A smile softened his lean cheeks. "See? Trustworthy and reliable."

The smile hadn't touched his eyes. Carol laid her fingertips on the nubby linen of his jacket. "You miss her a lot, don't you?"

The green eyes blinked twice in rapid succession. "Is it that obvious?"

"Maybe not to anyone who hasn't grieved." She withdrew her hand. "It's not something to hide. You miss her because you loved her. Isn't that better than never knowing her in the first place?"

"Not in the dark just before dawn. For the other twenty-three hours each day, I agree. But I didn't invite you out to weigh you down. Any progress with your intimidating caller?"

"You were right about Harry's hidden stash. This guy thought that was why I moved here." She sipped her tea. Garraway's warning not to talk about it probably didn't extend to a person with Patrick's reputation, but anyone could be listening on the other side of the broad-leafed plant.

Patrick tilted his head sideways, a slight furrow between his eyebrows. "What are you going to do?"

"Write my ex-brother and ask him about it. It's worth the contact to clear this up. I mailed the letter yesterday, but nothing moves over the weekend."

"Think of how good you'll feel when this is behind you."

Taking her teacup in both hands, she propped her elbows on the pale peach tablecloth and rested the cup's rim against her chin. The wafting mint scent brought calm.

Patrick finished his espresso and patted his lips with a snowy cotton napkin. "Where are you going tonight? Not that it's my business."

"Church."

His eyebrows twitched. "I didn't realize you were religious."

"It's Paul's idea. My—Joey, the one with the sketchy past?" Heat crept up her neck over their argument in the café. "On Friday, he spoke at Paul's school for drug awareness. He's going to talk tonight about the difference faith made in getting him out of the lifestyle. Paul wants to see if he's telling the truth, and he asked me to go along."

Patrick leaned back in his chair, a faint crease in his forehead. "The man has already deceived you once. Is it wise to open yourself up for more?"

Her fingers tightened around the teacup. "I want to see how he explains himself, but mostly it's for Paul, to make sure this isn't some cult thing."

"Could this Joey be using Paul to find another way into your life?"

A giggle cracked her tension. "I'm hardly worth that much effort."

"If he's after the money, he needs to stay close to you."

The warning lifted the tiny hairs along Carol's arms. She swallowed a last mouthful of tea and set the cup in its saucer.

"Why allow your son to attend?"

Spoken like someone who'd never wrangled a teenager. Carol breathed out slowly through her nose. "I appreciate your concern, but I really don't want to spoil the afternoon by arguing."

"I apologize. Of course, this fellow may not be what I fear. If he is, you're on guard. Adding church into the mix makes me question him more. Faith presumably helps spiritual issues, but it isn't much good against addictions. Or disease."

"Your wife?"

Patrick slid his espresso cup aside and spread out the white napkin. Starting at one edge, the first two fingers of each hand rolled it into a tight cylinder. "Rita had faith even at the end. I tried—"

He sucked a sharp breath, his gaze fixed on the table linen. "I'd have done more than that to save her. When the doctors couldn't help, we tried everything from alternative medicine to faith healers. Even this bizarre Mexican clinic where they filled her with vegetable juice."

He pushed the napkin roll into a U, then a circle, then pulled the ends to make a white bar. "Rita fought valiantly. Her final wish was to die at home in peace." A bitter laugh escaped him. "And never see another vegetable."

"That's so sad."

"The doctors, licensed and otherwise, did their best. The faith healers loaded it onto Rita and me. We weren't believing hard enough. The last one—a whale of a man, nearly hairless, with bright pink lips—he shook, and he ranted, and the spittle flew. Rita fainted from fright, but the cancer thrived."

Patrick unrolled the napkin and folded it into a neat square.

It reminded Carol of a shroud. She looked away.

He paid for their drinks, and they strolled back through the Waters exhibit.

The space wasn't crowded, but she spoke softly. "When Joey talked about faith, it sounded gentle, not pushy. Like it wasn't about rules but opportunity. Maybe there are different kinds of faith."

"Perhaps."

They stopped in front of a cascading waterfall. One supple branch, weighted with swollen buds, drooped over the torrent, coated in glistening beads of spray. It spoke to her heart. "I'd like to believe in a God who did miracles. But..."

She glanced at Patrick, standing stiff beside her. Sad story for sad story. Maybe it would take him out of his thoughts. "In Calgary, I worked with a woman who was a real holy roller. She'd been healed of a brain tumour. When I found out Keith was into drugs, she helped me pray for him."

The memory leaked acid into her stomach. "She said he'd break free. She prayed it and claimed it. I was so relieved. The next week, Keith was gone."

Patrick's hand found hers, surprisingly gentle. His eyes said he understood.

A bitterness she couldn't quell pushed out the final piece. "She blamed me. She'd had faith to be healed, so it wasn't her. My failure killed my son."

"A real God wouldn't make the innocent suffer because you or I couldn't manufacture sufficient faith to appease Him." Patrick stared at the painting, no doubt giving her space to collect herself.

She dabbed her eyes with a tissue as three stout ladies in flowered dresses approached. She'd seen a washroom beside the solarium. "Would you excuse me for a minute?"

When she returned, Patrick stood at the entrance to the Waters exhibit, talking with a brown-haired young man in khaki Dockers and a creamy yellow polo shirt. Patrick beckoned her to join them.

"Carol, meet Michael Stratton. This is his exhibit."

Friendly blue eyes met hers, and Carol liked the artist on sight. He couldn't be past his mid-twenties. Young, to achieve a showing like this one.

"Your paintings are beautiful."

Michael shook her hand. "Thank you. Water speaks to me, but it's tricky to capture on canvas."

Her attention strayed to a mid-size painting grouped with three smaller ones. A waterfall, with three vignettes of spray-drenched foliage. "You've done it, though. The drops sparkle, and the water looks alive."

"Thank you again."

Patrick took a business card from the half-moon table under the exhibit sign and studied it. "You're based in Nova Scotia?"

Michael rocked slowly from heels to toes and back. "I'm in the process of relocating. My website and email address won't change. The gallery owner will include the new information when she delivers your painting after the show."

Carol turned to Patrick. "Which one did you choose?"

"The lake with the ducks."

"Splashdown. I liked that one."

Michael acknowledged her comment with a gentle nod. "If you'll excuse me, I ought to mingle. It's been good to meet you both. Thank you, Mr. Stairs."

Carol smiled as she watched him introduce himself to an elderly couple admiring a nearby picture. "He'd rather be painting."

"Schmoozing is part of the job. He'll get used to it."

"Without losing the part of him that sees the magic in the water, I hope. Can we take a last look around before we go?"

"A brief one. Your son won't think much of me if I'm late bringing you home."

Gallery staff had already placed a "sold" card below the frame of Patrick's lake scene.

Carol's soul drank from each painting, a last bit of refreshment before plunging back into the fray that was her life.

Threatening callers. Writing to her convict brother. Joey... and church.

Chapter 23

CAROL DUG IN her purse for her keys as Patrick turned the car into her driveway. "I enjoyed our afternoon. Thank you."

"We'll have to book our dinner soon." Patrick's tone gave no hint of his mood.

"This isn't my idea of fun, but I'm a parent first." She didn't linger when the car stopped.

When she unlocked the apartment door and stepped into the kitchen, Paul was fixing a peanut butter and jam sandwich. "Hey. Have a good time?"

"I did. The paintings were beautiful." She hung her purse on the nearest chair. "Didn't you see the leftovers in the fridge?"

"I wasn't very hungry. This'll do."

Thoughts of church—Joey's church—had her stomach fluttering, but she'd better eat now or she'd binge later. "Make me one? About half as thick. That would stick my mouth shut for a week."

Paul's muffled snort earned him a cuff on the shoulder. She wished they could have more light-hearted moments like this.

They ate quickly. Carol washed the dishes while Paul fed Chance. The dog's lonely whine filtered through the door as she locked it behind them. "He's doing that more since the break-in. Do you think he's scared to stay alone?"

"Maybe. Or he thinks we're having fun without him."

She opened the driver's door and slid behind the wheel. "We should take him to the park next weekend. He probably gets bored with the same trip around the block every day."

Traffic was light, and with Paul reading directions they made good time.

A grey Volkswagen appeared in the rear-view mirror and stayed there as Carol wove through a network of suburban streets to reach the church.

She clutched the steering wheel. Coincidence. It had to be. Or intimidation. They knew she didn't have the money yet.

Paul checked over his shoulder. "That guy following us?"

"I don't know, but I'm more likely to lose us than him if I start making random turns."

"Come on, Mom, you know you want to play James Bond."

Tension crept up her spine. "If he wants to follow us to a church, maybe it'll do him good. If he passes us when I park, see if you can get his plate number, but he's probably a harmless citizen."

Grace Community Church was a sprawling flat-roofed structure with no steeple. A huge white cross adorned the side facing the street. When Carol signalled a turn, the Volkswagen zoomed past.

Paul shook his head. "No luck."

"At least he's gone." She found a place in the parking lot and they walked to the door.

A smiling Korean man welcomed them each with a warm handshake. Inside, people stood in buzzing groups while others found seats. No wooden pews here. Rows of green-upholstered chairs faced the front.

Paul tugged on her arm. "This way."

When he led her toward two girls standing at the end of a row, she scanned them with a mother's eye. Neat, pretty, with surprisingly modest clothes. One had a sweet smile, but the other's eyes held a sad wariness.

Carol relaxed slightly when he introduced them. Tara-Lynn, the special girl, wasn't the dangerous one. Amber must be the one they'd taken to the movies. *Keep your trouble to yourself.* Aloud, she said, "Nice to meet you. Were you waiting long?"

Tara-Lynn grinned at Paul, who seemed not to notice. "Not really, and the music's good."

They filed into the row, Amber at one end and Carol at the other.

She hadn't paid attention to the music earlier, amid the conversation noise, but now she caught bits of an up-tempo tune and singing.

This was nothing like the few churches she'd visited before. It didn't feel as reverent. Or as intimidating. Dark green carpeting matched the chair seats. Creamy walls and indirect lighting gave a sense of space. Overhead fans whirled lazily.

The stage—was that a word you used in a church?—spread across the front. She didn't see a pulpit. Instead, a set of drums crouched in one corner behind an electric keyboard.

Gradually, the chairs filled. A man and a teen boy stepped onto the stage carrying electric guitars, followed by five men and women. One man took a microphone and walked to the front of the stage.

"Welcome, everyone." He waited until the chatter subsided. "I'm Wade Caines, pastor of Grace Church. I'm glad to see so many of you here tonight."

Rev.—Pastor—Caines scanned the crowd. "Some of you are Christians, and some haven't given Christ much thought. Don't bother eyeing one another. It's neither visible nor contagious, whichever category you're in. We're going to get started with a few songs. If you want to sing along, please do. If you'd rather observe, that's fair too."

The pastor took his place behind the drum set. "I love this congregation. They let me preach and drum. But they don't let me sing." He held the microphone high and exaggerated the "off" motion before laying it down.

As the musicians began, song lyrics appeared on the screen behind them. Carol appreciated the pastor's permission not to fake knowing the songs.

On the other side of Paul, Tara-Lynn's voice rose clear and strong. Carol couldn't tell if Amber was singing. Paul's fingers tapped the beat on the armrest.

By the end of the fourth song, most of the audience joined in. They stood for what the leader promised was the final number.

When it ended, the pastor surfaced from behind the drums. As the others left the stage, he moved the leader's microphone stand to the centre.

He looked toward the front rows nearest the steps, where the musicians had resumed their seats. "Before Brother Joey comes to speak, I want to say a short prayer and we have a special musical guest."

Eyes closed, Pastor Caines raised his face to the light. "God, You are real and present with us here. Bless this time, and give us ears to hear and hearts to respond. In the name of Jesus, Amen."

A stocky man in an untucked plaid hunting shirt and faded blue jeans approached the microphone. Pastor Caines clapped his shoulder. "This is my good friend, Tristan Knox. Welcome, brother."

Scattered whistles punctuated the polite applause as the pastor left the stage. The lights dimmed, leaving a circle holding the newcomer who stood, head bowed. Music flowed from the speakers.

This was their singer? The sweet strings and piano didn't match the lumberjack effect.

The man in the spotlight lifted his head and began to sing, and all Carol could do was stare. His countenance glowed with a sweet joy that made her heart ache.

He sang about God, but it felt like a love song, personal instead of formal. No one in the audience made a sound.

When the song ended, wild applause broke the spell. He sang again, a faster song that brought the same expression to his face. Naked, innocent love, unashamed and consuming.

Carol's eyes prickled with tears. This time she was glad when the song ended.

The singer looked out at the audience. "Thank you. Thank God for loving us." Waving, he stepped out of the light.

The lights came up as Pastor Caines rolled a lectern toward the microphone. Joey walked beside him. They clasped hands with the singer as he passed. Pastor Caines smiled at the crowd. "What an amazing gift, amen?"

"Amen!" echoed around Carol. She'd always thought of the word as a special form of punctuation for ending prayers. Apparently, it was another way to say "yes."

Pastor Caines nodded. "I don't know how you're going to follow that, brother, but it's all yours. Friends, let me introduce Joey Hill. He's been a member of our church for seven months now. Joey moved here from Vancouver for a fresh start. He wanted to leave his past behind. After he'd worshipped with us for a few months, he came to me with his story."

The pastor drew Joey closer to the microphone. "This is a man of integrity, and the Lord will use his experience to help others."

Joey scrubbed a hand through his hair as the pastor walked away.

He hadn't dressed in Carol's idea of church clothes either, but he looked good in an open-necked, long-sleeved button shirt and grey pants. He laid some papers on the lectern. "To keep me from rambling too long."

Facing the crowd, he spread his feet, hooking his thumbs over his belt buckle. "Thank you for coming this evening. I'm no stranger to public speaking, and I've visited three high schools this week to talk to less willing audiences. But as Pastor Wade said, this is my spiritual home. This is also the most personal part of my story, so I hope you'll forgive me for being nervous."

He pulled a water bottle from inside the lectern, twisted off the cap, and took a sip.

Carol felt a twinge of sympathy. She could never do this. Then again, if Joey hadn't made such stupid choices, he wouldn't have to either.

Except he didn't have to. Why would he willingly expose his shame? Hers was mostly reflected from her brother, and she hid from it.

He capped the bottle and rolled it between his palms. "I was a well-known public figure in Vancouver, host of a daytime radio show. Young, popular, more money than brains. I didn't *not* believe in God. I simply didn't think He was relevant to my life.

"I got caught up in the tabloid version of the celebrity lifestyle. Parties, fancy car, living for the weekends. Cocaine to 'accelerate' the fun. What it actually did was give me enough rope to hang myself."

His shoulders rose and dropped. "In jail, I did try to hang myself. Literally. I couldn't even do that right, thank God."

Carol felt his shudder run through her too. The Joey she knew—or thought she'd known—was together, grounded. Secure. Not suicidal. He wouldn't make this up just to play on her sympathy. And he didn't know she was here.

As he narrated the collapse of his life, she felt a grudging admiration for his courage to be so open. His voice broke when he spoke of the prison ministry team, and he took another drink of water.

"Three ordinary guys who got more satisfaction on the right side of the law than I'd found chasing the devil. Two were labourers, one an accountant. They didn't preach, but they listened week after week and helped me discover I needed Jesus.

"I learned salvation is more than fire insurance. It's for now, so we don't have to stay trapped in the messes we make. So we can call God 'Father'—not the lousy kind some of you have but a good one who knows what's best and wants to help us."

Carol pushed aside the memory of her own father. Matt Silver had been as tortured as Joey, but it came out differently. How much of her fear of God came from her father's rages?

Clenching her hands together, she glared at Joey. She hadn't come here for a sermon. Prayer made things worse, not better—at least when she prayed. That proved she was better off out of God's line of sight.

Joey's voice regained the friendly assurance she knew from his radio show. "That's my story, folks. It's not pretty, but neither are parts of yours. I hope you can accept me as I am, a forgiven sinner who's still learning how to let God steer my life. Thanks for listening, and God bless you."

He headed off stage, and Pastor Caines stepped up to the microphone. "I hadn't heard the car story before. I'll think twice before offering you my keys."

At the crowd's laughter, the pastor pulled a jingling ring from his pocket and tossed it to Joey. "I trust you, brother."

Pastor Caines raised both hands, palms toward the audience. "Lord Jesus, You change lives. Thank You for what

You've done in Joey. Please touch each one here tonight in a very personal way. You know the cry of each heart. Help those hearts cry out to You and not settle for less. Because of Your Cross, Amen."

The music started again, and a buzz of conversation rose among the crowd. Most people headed for the exits, but Carol watched those who clustered around Joey near the base of the stage.

She couldn't refute what he said about how trusting God had changed him.

Unless he was one of those stage Christians who took forgiveness as freedom to indulge themselves. Or genuine, but blackmailed by his former suppliers. He'd said Creepy Voice contacted him. Maybe the man called again with another "assignment."

Hugging her arms tight to her ribs, she couldn't stop a shiver.

Beside her, Paul seemed thoughtful. Was it safe to let him go on the interview with Tara-Lynn? Could she stop him without a reason?

The seats around them were empty. She stood, hoping to get away before Joey spotted them.

Paul and his friends didn't move. Amber's head hung down, her hair fallen forward to hide her features. Tara-Lynn leaned close, one arm around her shoulders. Paul glanced from his friends to Carol.

She nodded. "No rush. I'll wait in the car."

"Don't you want to talk to Joey?"

"Not tonight."

"Okay. I'll be out soon."

Carol shouldered her purse and hurried up the aisle. She noticed a man near the back as he turned away. Patrick? Short black hair, a similar set to his shoulders.

She slid past two women talking in the aisle and saw him profiled in the doorway, caught in an usher's handshake. She darted forward, but he stepped out into the dusk.

"Excuse me." She waved off the usher and ran down the path to the parking lot. "Patrick?"

A few people moved among the vehicles. There—a lean figure stiffened, then turned toward her and waited.

She crunched over the gravel at a slower pace. What to say now that she'd caught up to him?

Patrick stood with one hand in his pocket. "I saw you with your son and didn't want to intrude."

"Why did you come?"

He tipped an eyebrow. "The sign said 'all welcome.'"

"Were you checking up on me?"

"A strong choice of words. Suffice to say I shared your concern about the validity of his story and wanted to hear it for myself."

"And?"

His lips thinned. "Your friends are none of my business, and my opinion may upset you, but I don't trust him. Anyone who dumps that much personal baggage in public may be trying to divert attention from another pile."

"He's not bragging about it. He's saying it was stupid and that people can change."

"Chemical dependence or spiritual, either way it's unhealthy. If it's legitimate. I'm glad you didn't stay to chat with him. I have to go. Early meeting tomorrow. Would Friday work for dinner?"

"I'm not the best company after I've been on my feet all week."

"I'll phone you midweek and we can make an arrangement for the weekend. In the meantime, take care. Your enemies sound like they mean business."

Patrick saluted with his keys and walked away.

Chapter 24

PAUL SCRABBLED HIS belongings together as math class ended Monday afternoon. A hasty glance showed Tara-Lynn wasn't in the first wave of students surging out the door. Turning, he saw her leaving her seat. He stood and set a pace to intercept her.

She smiled and headed his way.

With math at the end of the day like this, he hadn't had an excuse to find her at lunch. Instead, he'd hung out with the guys from the band and Nicole, who went wherever Barry did. Funny how the hour seemed to drag.

Falling into step beside her, he said, "Sorry I couldn't stay last night. Mom wanted to get out before Joey saw her."

She pulled some hair free from between her purse strap and shoulder. "He seems like such a nice guy. Do you think hearing his story helped?"

"I don't know if *she* knows. Did you and Amber talk to him?"

"Once she calmed down. She's so mixed up and hurt. I'm trying to be a friend, but I don't know what to do."

"You did okay last night."

Tara-Lynn opened her locker and loaded more books into her backpack. "Listening and crying I can do, but she needs more than that. Social workers can only do so much when

179

they're not allowed to mention God. I phoned my church, and Pastor Stu said he'll meet with us if she wants."

"You think religion makes that much difference?"

When she closed her locker, they threaded through chattering students toward his. "Religion only brings more rules. Didn't you listen to Joey last night? It's about relationship with Jesus, letting Him carry us when we can't do it alone."

"I heard him, I just don't know if I got it. So you think he's legit?"

"What would he gain by faking? A conversion story like that attracts more skeptics than if he said he changed on his own. But yeah, with Amber's and your mom's feelings on the line I prayed about it. God didn't raise any warnings. Joey's story clicked with me, and I believe him."

They reached Paul's locker, and Tara-Lynn leaned against the one beside it, watching him. "Joey said we could meet one evening this week since I'm busy after school, or on Saturday. Are you still okay to come with me?"

Paul crammed homework into his backpack and stuck his arms into his jacket sleeves. "Sure. Maybe Thursday? The other times I'll be working or rehearsing."

"Okay, I'll phone him."

The metal door to his locker clanged shut. He clicked the lock. "Walk you to your bus stop?"

"I have the car today. Can I drop you anywhere?"

They didn't have to walk so close as the halls cleared. He was glad to escape the irregular brush of her arm against his. It distracted him. "I'm okay, thanks. We're going to Barry's after the school band gets out for our own practice. How'd you get your mom's car again?"

Colour crept into her cheeks. "It's mine. Dad's way of showing affection."

"Sweet. I'll come outside with you. Might as well get some air while I wait for the guys."

"Your mom wouldn't let you join the school band?"

"No way. Too much like my dad."

The school doors shut behind them, and Tara-Lynn pulled out her keys. "It must be hard to keep the secret."

"I do what I have to do."

Once she drove away, Paul walked to a nearby Tim Hortons. If he'd taken a ride, she might have had time for a drink. But he needed to make this call before meeting his friends.

He and Barry had noticed a pay phone outside the coffee shop earlier and laughed. Who used them anymore? But if this call backfired, he sure didn't want it traced to his cell. He dug coins from his pocket and unfolded the paper he'd kept from Joey's church.

"Grace Community Church, good afternoon."

"Hi, um, if a person gives money and doesn't leave a name, is that okay?"

"We like to give tax receipts when we can, but anonymous gifts are accepted. God knows the giver."

God could know. The authorities, and Harry's enemies, were another matter. Paul watched a group of teens exit the shop carrying brown takeout cups. "Will it get used for what the note says?"

"Assuming it's nothing against our church policies." Question marks filled the woman's voice. "I should tell you, we don't accept funds that were illegally or immorally gained."

"This comes from a bad source—I didn't do it, someone else did—and I want to use it for good, to help drug users."

"Oh. I think that should be given to the police."

"Except it'd end up paying city salaries or something. Not helping people." Paul massaged his forehead. He should hang up, but he had to get rid of this money. "So, is it true God can forgive anyone? No matter what he's done?" Even Harry?

"Yes, if they ask Jesus into their heart."

"And that makes the person clean?"

"Yes." The woman sounded surer now as if she'd rather deal in souls than dollars.

Paul stabbed the pay phone with his finger. "But God can't clean dirty money?"

Two cars pulled into the drive-through while he waited for her to decide what to say. "I never thought of that. I'll have to ask Pastor Caines. If you could leave your number?"

"Never mind."

"I'm sorry. But I promise you, God can forgive—and change—anyone."

"The guy did a lot worse than earn this money. He can be clean, but the cash is a lost cause? I know you don't make the rules, miss, but that sure doesn't click for me."

He checked the remaining change in his pocket and joined the line of customers inside. After that, he deserved Tim's largest Iced Cappuccino for the walk back to school.

Dispose of the money, give it to a good cause. It sounded so simple. He had to do it fast, before Harry's enemies found it. And before he gave in and spent some of it on the Les Paul guitar at Morelli's.

~~~

Near the end of Carol's shift, Detective Garraway stopped at Sticky Fingers for coffee. She slid a giant cookie onto a plate for him too. "I mailed the letter on Saturday."

Garraway ripped open two packets of sugar and dumped them into the coffee, then added cream. "Good. We want this behind you so you can get on with your life."

"So long as he stays out of it." She'd been clear in the letter. No more contact.

The detective's spoon tinkled against the mug as he stirred. "Your friend checks out clean for now. His connections from Vancouver could easily have led to more here, but from what we can see he's made a fresh start. He seems sincere about the call he got from you-know-who. All I can say is to trust your instincts, but that goes for anyone you've met since you moved here. And keep the low profile."

As if she knew another way now. "Thank you, Detective. Enjoy your coffee."

She cleared the next table and carried the tray to the kitchen. *From what we can see.* Garraway's subtle hint about what they couldn't see? Or had Joey truly changed? She missed his friendship, but maybe life was safer without him.

That night she baked thank-you cookies for Garraway and his crew. They'd been so good about Chance. She turned on the first hour of Joey's show but decided not to call.

When the nightmare woke her at two, she listened again for nearly an hour before falling asleep. As she was drifting off, she heard Joey say "This one's for Carol. I hope you're okay. Hope you're sleeping, but just in case here's Billy Joel."

She almost called him the next night, but phoned Jackie instead. So many things she couldn't mention over the phone in case someone was listening, but they caught up on surface news. Whatever her enemies already knew, she could say. The problem was, they knew more than she did.

Jackie was angry about Chance. "Your thug was a coward. All that sweet pup would do is lick his hand."

"He's fine now and milking it for all it's worth. We've been taking him for extra walks, and your out-laws brought him a juicy bone yesterday."

"I'm glad they're there to keep an eye on you."

"Me too. Good night, Jackie."

Carol checked the locks and shut off the lights. She checked the street. A grey Volkswagen sat parked at the opposite curb. Should she phone the police? Not Garraway, not this late at night. Would the non-emergency response number send a car to check it out? Maybe trace the licence plate or follow it when it left?

As if the driver had read her thoughts, the vehicle sped away.

~~~

Paul arrived at Morelli's early for his shift on Wednesday and reclaimed the envelope from the safe. "Thanks for keeping this, sir. Worst case, I'll have to ask again, but I think I'm good."

The music store owner pressed a hand on Paul's shoulder and peered at him. "Is the situation secure at home?"

"Probably not, but Mom doesn't want this in the apartment anyway. I'm getting rid of it." Before she could give it to those scuzz-buckets to ruin more lives.

The grip on his shoulder tightened, then released. "You talk lightly, but a heavy load should be shared. If I can help, my support is yours."

"Thank you." Paul stuffed the envelope inside his shirt and headed for the storefront. His shift didn't start for twenty minutes, but there'd been customers browsing and Morelli encouraged staff to demonstrate the instruments.

He lifted the Les Paul down from the display, plugged it into a small amp, and ran through a series of tunes. Holding the guitar made the temptation worse.

Only Harry knew how much money filled the envelope. Paul could buy the guitar—buy half the store. Except Mr. Morelli knew he couldn't afford it, and Paul couldn't tell him where the money came from.

Barry might make the purchase and keep it at his place, but could Paul tell his friend about Harry?

Schemes grew and faded until his brain hurt, but he couldn't evade the key point. The money wasn't his, and it felt wrong to gain from drug trafficking even if it was second-hand. He knew what the lady at the church meant when he applied it to himself. But to use the money for unselfish good was different. He'd stick to his plan.

He caught Jubal when the older teen arrived for his lesson. "Stop for a minute before you leave? I need to ask a favour."

"Can we talk now instead? After my lesson I've got to run. My girlfriend wants to see a movie."

The lone customer browsed the sheet music. Paul jerked his head toward the counter.

Jubal followed. "What's up?"

"Remember I mentioned my uncle?"

"You still in touch with him?"

The envelope of money felt heavy inside his shirt. "Yeah. He hid money before he got caught. Drug money. It wasn't his idea—they forced him to transport."

Why did he need to defend Harry? The man had earned his conviction.

He checked his watch and talked faster. "The drug guys want it back. I want to do something good with it but the church I phoned said they wouldn't take dirty money."

The practice room door opened and the previous student came out. Jubal stood his guitar case on end. "What's next?"

"Will you stick it under the office door at your church? If they don't know where it came from, is that wrong?"

Jubal waggled his head. "I don't know, man. Gotta get to my lesson. I'll let you know when I come out."

Paul slipped the envelope from under his shirt and scrawled *To help drug addicts* across both sides. He tucked it behind the cleaning supplies.

The sheet music customer finally made his choice, and Paul rang in the sale. A couple more people drifted in and out. Paul kept checking his watch, afraid the customers were waiting to flock in when Jubal finished his lesson.

Tara-Lynn came in with five minutes to go.

He swallowed a groan and forced cheer into his voice. "Hey. What brings you in?"

"I wanted to tell you we're on tomorrow evening to see Joey. Want to get a pizza first? I can pick you up after I'm done with the kids."

"That'd be great." Anything to get her out of here. Now. Had he told Jubal he didn't want her to know about Harry?

Her smile flipped his stomach despite his tension. A girl like this, why waste her time on him? He straightened the brochure rack beside the cash. "Might be busy later. I'd better start cleanup now."

Before she could take the hint, Jubal hurried from the practice room. "Hi Tara-Lynn. Paul, he kept me late and I've gotta fly. I'll keep thinking about what you said. When are you in next?"

"Not till Saturday." His desperation must have shown in his voice, because they both stared at him.

Jubal raised a hand. "Easy, man. Phone me before school tomorrow, and we'll make a plan." He rattled off his number and dashed out the door.

Paul scribbled the number on a message pad and shoved the paper into his pocket.

"Paul?" Tara-Lynn wore a worried frown.

"It's nothing."

"If you say so." Her tone frosted. "I won't keep you from your work. Have a good evening."

How did girls pack so much hostility into something non-verbal like walking out of a store? Paul stuffed the envelope back inside his shirt. It looked like a long evening.

Chapter 25

THE THICK ENVELOPE mocked Paul all night, like a monster looming in the corner of his room. If Jubal didn't take the money—today—he'd buy the Les Paul. Lying to his boss about how he could afford the guitar felt almost as bad as using the money in the first place, but he couldn't hold out much longer.

Finally, near dawn, the answer hit him. He'd thought giving it to God would balance some of the evil Harry had done, but if a church wouldn't take it, what about a shelter or a soup kitchen?

He didn't know whether to laugh or kick himself. All that agonizing for nothing! He could hop a bus downtown after school and leave his burden in one of the spots on Yonge Street.

He'd finally settled into a decent sleep when his alarm went off. Too tired to risk lingering, he jumped out of bed. When he phoned Jubal, the older teen surprised him with a groggy promise to take the cash. They attended different schools, but Jubal had a car.

Now, it'd really been a waste of time stressing last night. The envelope held an incredible amount of money to carry around in public, but who'd know he had it? He could pass it off and catch a nap while Tara-Lynn was volunteering.

As he finished breakfast, his mother shuffled into the kitchen, blinking in the light.

"Hey, Mom. Rough night?"

"You look pretty ragged yourself. Are you okay?"

"I'm fine." He hugged her a bit tighter than usual. She was losing weight, and he didn't think it was a diet. The cops had better nail this drug ring soon.

Should he tell her about tonight? Why stir up fireworks? But she'd freak if she found out later. "After supper, I'm going with Tara-Lynn to meet Joey. She'll drive me home, so you don't have to worry."

Assuming the plan was still on after the way they parted yesterday. Maybe he should just tell Tara-Lynn about Harry and scare her away.

She wouldn't write the sort of tabloid stuff his mom feared. If she did though, he was dead. Either way he lost his math helper. If he hadn't already.

At lunchtime, he shared Mom's chewy oatmeal raisin cookies. Tara-Lynn's brittle ice cracked to let her take a second one.

After school, he handed off the envelope to Jubal and holed up in a corner of the library.

Tara-Lynn's words in his ear pulled him from a bottomless sleep. He straightened and peered blearily around, rubbing his cheek where the textbook pillow had left a crease.

She grinned. "I heard you snoring from the doorway."

He dragged his sleeve across a damp patch on the book, then shoved his work into his backpack. "I told you I'm no good with homework on my own."

At the pizza joint, she didn't eat much. She made up for it with nervous chatter.

He reached for another slice. "You'll do fine. You've got solid questions, and Joey likes to talk. Worst case, he gives you too much material and you get writer's cramp."

She giggled. "It's awfully kind of him to do this."

Paul frowned. Nerves were okay, but he hoped she hadn't developed a crush on Joey. "He's old enough to be your father."

"That's fine for an interview. I'm more interested in boys my own age." Her cheeks flamed, and she gulped her root beer.

He concentrated on finishing his pizza. "We need to get going."

They found the apartment without trouble. When Joey opened the door, strains of "The Long and Winding Road" drifted out to greet them. "Hey, guys. Paul, thanks for coming. Me alone with an underage female is just asking for rumours to start."

Tara-Lynn shrugged. "We could have met at Starbucks or somewhere."

"The background noise would have messed up your recording. Plus, what if I break down and cry?"

Her eyes went wide, and Paul snickered. She shot him a glare.

"Kidding." Joey showed them to a round wooden table. "I promise I'll behave. Drinks?"

"No thanks." Tara-Lynn pulled out a chair.

Paul followed her lead.

Joey brought in a pitcher of ice water and three glasses on a tray. "I get dry if I talk too long."

Tara-Lynn set her phone to record and laid it on the table. She positioned a sheet of questions beside her blank notepad. "Thanks for letting me interview you, Joey. I've picked up a lot of information from your talks, so today I wanted to explore a few areas in more depth."

She looked—and sounded—confident, professional. Like a good musician, she'd worked the nerves out of her system before hitting the spotlight.

"You said your life is better without the party scene, even if it's not what society calls exciting. Can you tell me more about that? What defines quality now?"

Joey considered. "Life was erratic before, like a manic scavenger hunt for something to make it vibrant. You know the U2 song, 'I Still Haven't Found What I'm Looking For?'"

Paul knew it, and Tara-Lynn nodded without interrupting the flow.

"With Jesus, I've found it. I can be who I am without always trying to live up to the hype. I'm not so hung up on myself, so I can give time to you, to the kids when I speak at schools, to anyone Jesus connects me with. He's the boss now so I don't have to be. It gives me a kind of purpose, like I'm on a mission. And when nothing's happening, it's okay to be quiet. I find that liberating after a lifestyle of perpetual motion."

Tara-Lynn scribbled rapidly, although her phone would catch it all. "Can you share examples of connecting with people?"

Joey tipped his head to the side. "At the schools, I've had chances to encourage students after my talks. If I can be one more nudge on the path to wholeness, I'm grateful. For me, wholeness includes a personal relationship with God. I can't say a lot about that in the public school venue. That's why I invited students to hear me at church that Sunday."

He poured a glass of water and set it on a coaster in front of him. "Even when I was keeping quiet about my past, there were good opportunities through work. So many people need someone to talk to. Maybe my past gives me more compassion, or maybe it's Jesus in me. Again, I can't preach on the job, but I can listen. Let them know someone cares. And I pray for them."

"So you'd say prayer makes a difference?"

"It invites God into the situation. I'm no theologian, but I can understand how free will means we choose whether to exclude or include Him."

Paul listened to the rhythm of questions and answers, intrigued by how comfortably Joey could talk about applying faith to life. A couple of times he barely caught himself before throwing his own question into the mix. Hard to remember this was an interview, despite Tara-Lynn's feverish writing.

Joey sounded content in his new life. It must be fulfilling to help others while doing a job he loved.

"That wraps up my questions." Tara-Lynn tapped her pen against the paper. "Paul, you looked like you had an idea earlier. Something we should ask?"

"I don't know for your interview, but the forgiveness bit..."

Joey took another sip of water and studied him over the rim of the glass. "How can I be so arrogant to claim God forgives me? Or how can I be sure it matters if we're forgiven?"

"Neither! I'm not going to argue about what you believe. It's just—do you think there are limits? Can God forgive anything? And how would you be sure?"

He caught Tara-Lynn's sudden glance. He hadn't meant to sound so intense. What was she thinking?

She turned to Joey. "Great questions. Probably not what I need for the interview though. Joey, could I use your washroom?"

"Of course. It's around that corner."

"Thanks. You two carry on." She dropped her pen on the pad and stopped the recording.

Joey set down his water glass and leaned his elbows on the table. "Are you thinking of yourself, or is this for a friend?"

"Does it matter?"

Joey's moustache twitched. "Not really. The answer's the same. The way I read the Bible, it says anyone who asks to be forgiven receives it. Assuming they mean it, of course. You get more than the forgiveness. It's about asking Jesus to move into your heart, to break your destructive habits whatever they are, and to clean you up and give you a new life. You can't have the forgiveness without Jesus."

"That's what he said, but I couldn't believe him."

"Who said?"

Paul's ears warmed. "I have a relative in prison. He says he's a Christian now and that God forgave him. But he's a dangerous offender."

Joey let out a low whistle. "Your uncle?"

"Mom told you about him?"

"The internet told me. I didn't know he'd accepted Christ."

"Do you think it could be real?"

Joey's eyes narrowed. "Could be. With a sentence like his, it's not like he's trying to get out early on good behaviour."

"I'm not talking about him faking it, I want to know if it's possible on God's end."

"What's too hard for the One who made the universe?"

The toilet flushed, and Paul jumped. "I don't want Tara-Lynn to know."

"I won't say a word. But I think you should. Trust me, keeping secrets can cost more than you want to pay." Joey lowered his voice. "Your mom told me about your brother. I'm sorry."

"I'm starting to understand him a little better now, but then I just thought he was a jerk."

"No matter what he was, he was her son. She'll remember how he was in the good years and how she hoped he'd turn out."

"Funny, she acts like she remembers the bad years and expects me to do the same thing." Paul stared helplessly at Joey. "Sex and drugs and rock-n-roll—playing in a band is the least dangerous of the three. It's all I need, but she's smothering me!"

Joey glanced over Paul's shoulder. "Tara-Lynn, did you know Paul's an aspiring musician?"

"He's good too, so I'm told." She sat beside him and poured herself a glass of water. "Not that he's ever let me hear him play."

Heat crept up Paul's neck. Who'd said he was good? Barry? Maybe Jubal? That'd be praise indeed. He held Tara-Lynn's gaze, challenging. "Saturday night at The Wall. It's alcohol free. We're all underage."

Her chin lifted. "I'll be there."

Chapter 26

FRIDAY AFTERNOON, CAROL stood in the kitchen at Sticky Fingers swirling cream cheese icing onto a trio of carrot cakes.

Lily poked her head in from the café. "There's a man asking to see you. Can you spare a minute?"

Carol's hand froze in mid-swirl. "Short? Tall? Scary voice?"

"Does it matter? This isn't *The Dating Game*."

Carol laid her spatula on a piece of waxed paper and followed her boss to the door. This guy wasn't a regular customer or Lily would know him. Joey? He had no business following her around. Her mystery caller, come to intimidate in the flesh? More time. She needed more time.

Detective Garraway waited at the counter. Good. Carol scanned the café. If Creepy Voice was here, Garraway could protect her.

Then her brain caught up. The detective was the one asking for her. This stress was making her paranoid.

"Hello, Ms. Daniels. I'm mixing business and pleasure. I wanted to touch base, and my wife asked me to pick up dessert." He tapped a white cardboard box on the counter. "Caramel pecan cheesecake."

He motioned her closer. "Your letter produced a phone call. Will you be home this evening?"

"After seven thirty."

"May I drop by around eight? I have interesting news."

"Please." *Help me find that money and get on with my life.*

Lily followed her into the kitchen. "Are you okay? You seem jumpy."

"I'm fine. It's just a follow-up to the break-in."

Carol finished the carrot cakes and carried them to the display case. Almost time for the supper crowd. Patrick wouldn't be in tonight. He'd phoned the apartment mid-week to invite her to dinner on Saturday. Joey hadn't returned. She told herself that was good.

She changed into her serving apron and tucked a fresh order pad in the pocket. Waiting tables over supper kept her in touch with the regulars. Tonight, the tables filled quickly. That suited her fine. Taking orders and chatting with customers kept her mind from chasing Garraway's news.

Too bad she ended her shift by going home to an empty apartment.

Chance barked a loving welcome at the door, then promptly ignored her once his food dish hit the floor.

She surveyed the dated kitchen. Sure, home wasn't exciting, and she'd been even more itchy to be out at Paul's age. Look what she'd done to escape.

She couldn't be as hard to live with as her aunt had been, but she didn't blame Paul for being out so much. At least she could always reach him on his cell. Still, it left her feeling... lonely.

The empty nest was coming, like it or not. She'd better get used to it.

She closed the door on that thought and pulled leftover chicken soup from the fridge. While it heated, she made a pot of tea.

Had Harry buried the money in one of the city parks? She imagined a midnight trip through a graveyard, or perhaps a coded treasure map. He couldn't have made it too hard to get at, but it must be in a spot where nobody would find it by accident.

Maybe she could convince Garraway to send an undercover agent. Creepy Voice would insist she make the drop-off herself, no doubt. The detective could coach her through that. Then she'd be free.

Free to start the new life she'd wanted for herself and Paul.

After cleaning up the kitchen, she stationed herself on the couch to watch for Garraway. Chance climbed up beside her and rested his muzzle in her lap.

The detective's car pulled into the driveway shortly after eight. He knocked on the rear door this time.

She hurried to let him in, Chance by her side.

Garraway crouched, extending a hand to the dog. "Hey, fella. It's good to see you walking around."

Chance sniffed his fingers, tail wagging.

The detective straightened. "I'm glad he's okay. Before I forget, my wife said to tell you the cheesecake was excellent. I agree."

"Thank you."

He squared his shoulders. "To business. You have a desk that belonged to your mother?"

"Yes, why?"

"Sent to you by Silver?"

Carol gasped. "I've had it so long, and the money just came up. I never thought of it."

She dashed for Paul's room, Garraway at her heels, Chance barking behind them. She flung open the door and flipped on the light.

"Excuse the mess." She pulled the chair away from the desk, then removed the drawer over the knee-hole and set it on Paul's rumpled bed. "Harry sent this when he was arrested the first time. It came empty. I assumed our old hiding place was empty too."

Garraway stood three paces into the room, arms folded, watching. The dog pushed past him.

Carol knelt and ran her fingers along one side of the drawer cavity. Slide that piece of wood—there—press the latch, slide the wood back into place. Click. The panel popped open.

She reached into the narrow cavity, a shallow ledge above the three drawers that opened from the desk front. Her fingertips slid over paper, but not bundles of money. She felt down the side.

Magazine spines. "I think my dear ex-brother lied. This must be a stash of his pornography."

As she pulled out the top magazine, her eyes flicked the cover. The air left her lungs.

Music magazines. She dove under the desk and seized the rest.

"Ms. Daniels, you don't need to look at those."

She crawled into the open and stood, glaring wildly around before drilling into Garraway.

Lines bracketed his mouth. "I don't know what Silver's playing at, but I'll find out."

"It's not him. These are Paul's."

Garraway's lips twitched. "They're more likely Silver's, as you said. If they're not..." He drew a slow breath. "Teen boys often sneak a magazine or two. It doesn't mean he'll turn out like his uncle."

"They're Paul's." She flung them on the bed, one by one. *Guitar Player. Rolling Stone. Guitar World.*

Garraway stared from the instrument-splashed covers to Carol's face. "So, we have a bigger problem."

"Not that I approve of pornography, Detective. A man looks at that, then he looks at me—I don't want his dirty little thoughts touching me. But I can't let Paul grow up like his father."

Garraway's expression had gone blank except for a slight narrowing of the eyes. His chin lifted. "Ms. Daniels, if your son wanted to use the desk as a hiding place, he had to empty it first."

Carol pressed a fist to her mouth, her jaws aching with all she wanted to call down on Harry. When she could trust herself, she whispered, "If anything happens to Paul..."

"Will he be home soon?"

"It's Friday night. He doesn't have to be in until eleven."

"Can you track him down?"

Leaving the magazines and desk drawer as they lay, Carol marched to the kitchen. She picked up the phone and punched the numbers for Paul's cell. When his voice mail picked up, she wanted to scream. Instead, she left a curt message to phone home.

She turned to the detective. "I thought the whole point of having a phone was to answer it. I'll try again in a few minutes. Would you like a brownie or a cookie?"

He patted his stomach. "No thanks. I'm still digesting cheesecake."

Carol's nerves screamed for chocolate, but eating in front of the detective would be rude. Instead, she led him into the living room and flung herself into a chair. Chance settled at her feet.

She huffed a sigh. "I can't believe Harry sent me that desk full of money! I'd have had a heart attack if I'd found it before now."

Garraway sat opposite her. "He said he sent it with other pieces of furniture and hoped you wouldn't think to check the drawer. Apparently, he was keeping it as a form of insurance."

"Silly me, thinking he cared about heirlooms."

At the detective's curious glance, Carol said, "It was furniture my grandfather built for my mom." She was telling him about her mother when the phone rang.

Chance barked. Carol dodged him and sprinted for the phone. "Hello?"

"Mom, what's wrong?"

"I need you to come home. Now. Detective Garraway's here."

"Are you okay? Did they come back?"

"They didn't, but where are you? I'll pick you up"

"One of the guys will bring me."

"Okay, but hurry."

Carol stalked to the living room. "He's on his way. I think I scared him."

"He needs to be scared of this crowd. They're not playing."

"Detective, you know that and I know that, but he's a typical teenager. He thinks he's invincible." She checked her watch. "He usually hangs out at one of his friends' houses. I don't know how far away it is."

Finally, the back door opened and slammed. Chance ran to investigate.

Paul dashed into the living room with the dog on his heels. "What's up?" He stared from Carol to Garraway.

Garraway placed his palms on his knees. "The money, Paul. Silver told us where to look."

Paul sighed. He dropped his backpack beside the couch and shed his leather jacket on top of it. "Don't worry about it. It's gone."

"Gone!" Carol jumped to her feet. "What do you mean, gone?"

He faced her, a weary determination in that guitar-player stance she hated. "Tell them it's gone. Someone else found it first."

He looked at Garraway. "If they got it, they'd buy more drugs to sell. This way it'll help users, not make more."

Garraway held his gaze. Neither faltered. "Paul, these people mean business. I applaud your sentiment, but one person can't take them on and come out on top."

"I did what I had to do. It's gone. So, they can leave us alone."

"Or take some form of revenge." The chill in Garraway's voice made Carol shiver.

Paul blinked. "They wouldn't."

"Your uncle knows they would. He warned you when he told you about the money."

"Wait a minute." Carol sprang to her feet and lunged toward Paul, fingernails biting her palms. "You've been talking to him?"

Paul spread his feet and hooked his thumbs into his belt loops. "We've been writing." He scowled at Garraway. "Thanks for keeping my secret."

"Your mother would have busted you before breakfast. Who else could have told you about the hiding place?"

"Whatever." Paul shrugged. "For what it's worth, Mom, he sounds like he cares. Maybe he did change. Joey says it's possible."

"You told Joey?"

"Not about the money, about Uncle Harry and forgiveness. Joey's had his own turnaround. I thought he'd know if Harry had a chance."

Groaning, Carol palmed her forehead.

Paul straightened. "Uncle Harry knew they were turning up the heat about the money. You wouldn't let him reach you, and he didn't want to tell them in case they broke in and trashed everything to get it—maybe including us."

Garraway leaned forward in his seat. "Silver couldn't risk approaching a warden. These guys have eyes everywhere. He did ask his contact—Paul—to either tell you or the authorities. Which brings us to the original question. Where is the money?"

Paul shook his head. "Gone. I gave it away."

"To whom?"

"To help addicts. Anonymously. Through a third party."

Carol dropped into her seat. "Joey."

"I told you, I didn't talk to him about it. A friend you've never met."

On the couch, Garraway rubbed the bridge of his nose. "Why doesn't anyone just let the nice detective do his job? Sit down, please, Paul. Tell me where the money went."

Paul sat at the opposite end of the couch, arms folded across his chest. "No."

"Do I have to take you to the station until you've had time to think?"

"I won't—"

Carol cut across the detective's words. "We've had enough threats. My son stays here. The money's gone, and if it could save even one life it'd be worth it. How do we convince these creeps it's really gone?"

"You can't."

Chapter 27

CAROL STARED ACROSS the living room at Detective Garraway. It was his job to protect them. To save her son. But Paul had given away their bargaining tool. "Can't you use fake money? Or borrow more? It's just for the transfer so you can catch them, right? Not like you want them to keep it."

"That's a lot of money. It'd have to be real. Some of it might filter into circulation before we tie this up." His gaze flicked to Paul. "This would have been using Silver's money for a good cause too."

Paul flushed. "I didn't think of that. But I can't get it back. How could I prove it came from me?"

"I can look after that, but it'll take more time. Ms. Daniels, if they call this weekend, tell them you know where it is but can't get at it until Monday." Garraway turned to Paul. "Assuming you tell me how to find it."

Shoulders slumped, Paul retrieved his backpack. After a bit of digging, he pulled out a paper. "Should I call him now?"

"Use my phone." Garraway held it out. "In case your line's tapped. This one we don't want them hearing."

They waited as Paul phoned. "Jubal? It's Paul. Did you have a chance to drop off my package?"

Garraway pulled out a notepad and pen and slid them across the couch seat.

Paul picked up the pen. "What's the name of your church? The police want to get it back."

He wrote on the pad. "Okay. Thanks, man. Sorry I dragged you into this." He slumped back against the couch, eyes shut. "No, I'm okay, just feeling stupid. See you later."

Garraway took the phone and checked the name on the pad. "I should be able to get a number for their minister tomorrow. This may be easier than I thought. Paul, I appreciate this. For what it's worth, I applaud your desire to help drug users. Shelters and counselling centres are always under-funded."

"Jubal's church works with them too. Spiritual help might make it easier to break the addiction."

Carol glanced at her son. How much attention had he paid to Joey on Sunday?

Garraway stood. "For now, I'll get out of your hair."

After locking the door behind the detective, Carol turned to see Paul standing feet apart, shoulder dropped into his father's guitar-player pose. The magazines in his room rushed to her mind.

His lips twitched. "So you found them."

"Yes."

"I meant to take them to school today. They're only magazines—"

"That I forbade you to buy."

"Why can't you be glad I'm into music and not drugs?" Paul's eyes flashed. "I know you loved him, but Keith made lousy choices. I'm not like that. All I want—*need*—is to play guitar. How's that going to hurt me?"

Carol gripped a chair for support. "It'll hurt everyone around you. I want you to have a good life with a decent salary and happy family. Not live off your wife and take your kids' inheritance to buy a better guitar."

She stared at the chipped tabletop, holding her breath as if that might erase her words.

Paul spoke from far away. "What inheritance?"

"Your grandfather Silver's life insurance. I didn't mean to tell you."

"Mom, he was a talented musician and he'll always be my dad, but I can see the truth. Music mattered more than we did."

Her head came up. "What makes you say that?"

"Some of what I read about him online. And last month, I met a guy who used to play with him." Paul's fingers twitched like he was playing air guitar, then stilled. "He left the band after a few years, said Dad was too high maintenance."

"What was his name?"

"Donnie Leyland."

Carol's fingers tightened on the chairback. She tried to make her question come out casually. "What else did he say?"

"Not to tell you I'd talked to him. But it's true. Isn't it?"

She inhaled. "Yes."

"That won't happen with me. If I have a family, they'll come first."

"It won't happen at all if you quit dreaming about guitars and pick a stable career."

Paul's mouth tightened. He rocked on his feet, watching her.

Carol knew that look. She'd given it to Skip each time he came up with a crazy plan she'd have to work around. She circled the kitchen. "Where did you meet Donnie? Don't tell me he came to your school too."

"There's a music store where I go and—dream. The owner introduced us."

A new thought made Carol flinch. "That money. Did you keep some to buy a guitar?"

His smile held regret. "No."

"Paul, I'm begging you, even if it feels like cutting off your arm, stay away from the music. Listening's one thing, but I saw what playing did to your father. You're too much like him."

"What if it's tearing out my soul?" His chin jutted. "Maybe I am like him. Donnie said I've got Dad's gift, only better."

"His gift was a curse. Donnie saw what it cost us. I'll kill him."

"Find him first. He was only in town for the weekend. Mom, I'm sixteen. I can make my own choices. I'm sorry, but I'm not going to hide it anymore. Donnie said to serve the gift and he's right. I have to play."

The pleading in his eyes hardened into resolve, and his lips formed a grim line. He held Carol's gaze for a long beat before he spun and walked out. Seconds later, his bedroom door banged shut.

Carol dragged out a chair and slumped at the table, head in her hands. How long had her son been going behind her back, buying guitar magazines and scheming?

At least he had no money for a guitar. Talent or not, he couldn't join a band without one.

Thank God Skip was out of their lives. Bad enough to give their son his gift for music. He'd have had Paul on stage. And chasing women and drinking, no matter if Paul was underage. Like father, like son, that would be Skip's line.

Skip had been twenty-one when they met, playing at Carol's high school dance. A real rocker, talented, sexy, a little wild. Carol couldn't keep her eyes off him. She was sixteen, living with a repressive single-parent aunt. She'd had to sneak out to the dance. Skip unlocked her dreams. It took getting pregnant to force permission for the wedding, but baby Paul was a sweet price for freedom.

Baby Paul, baby Keith, both named after musicians Skip loved. A miscarried baby girl.

Now, she was alone. Helpless to stop her surviving child from messing up his life. She clamped trembling lips together and brushed away her tears. When you're the only one left, you can't fall apart.

She paced the kitchen, listening to the radio, until her eyes stayed dry and the hiccupy half-sobs vanished. It was barely ten o'clock, which meant eight in Calgary. Not likely she'd catch Jackie home on a Friday night, but she needed human contact.

Jackie's machine picked up on the third ring, but Carol didn't leave a message. A friendly, perhaps inebriated, voice waking her later wouldn't help. She opened the container of brownies, snapped it shut, and wedged it into the cupboard. Regaining the weight she'd lost wouldn't help either.

A fresh batch of brownies would make a thank you for all Detective Garraway's help, and with a designated recipient she wouldn't eat them. Rock music filtered from Paul's room. The mixer wouldn't bother him.

While the brownies baked, she washed the dishes.

The radio ended a four-song set, and Joey came back on the air. "I was just talking with my young friend Amber, and if any of you are praying people, please remember her tonight. She's in a hard place. Amber, this one's for you. 'We Are the Champions,' by Queen."

Carol dropped her soapy mixing bowl into the sink and grabbed the phone. Busy. Her call rang through on the fourth try.

"Welcome to—"

"Did you talk about me on-air—and ask people to pray?"

"Carol? It's good to hear from you. I've been worried."

"Did you?"

"Of course not. I've never done it for anyone. People's needs are private. Plus, management doesn't like God talk. But she's still a kid. I met her at Paul's school, actually. She's facing some major stuff. My prayers need backup tonight."

The song ended, and an up-tempo, driving guitar lick opened the next one.

Carol stretched the phone cord to the sink and dipped her hands in the water. "I met her." No need to tell him she'd been at his church at the time. "Paul and a friend are trying to help."

"Tara-Lynn. She's a neat girl. I think she has an eye for your son."

"Yeah. I don't know how I feel about that." Carol rinsed the mixing bowl and put it in the drying rack, anxiety flashing in her stomach. Joey's plea for Amber had made her forget the crisis with Paul.

"From the look of it, he's not sure either. But you two have a lot on your minds right now. Did you find the mystery money?"

"No, but I found the guitar magazines he's been hiding."

"Ouch."

"I've tried to keep him from turning out like his father, and now he tells me he's going to play no matter what." She set a spatula in the draining rack and pulled the sink plug. "I just want him to have a good life with a family. Is that so bad?"

"Fame's a trap, but there are musicians, even stars, who keep it together and stay married."

Her shrug nearly dislodged the phone from between her ear and shoulder. "Skip and I stayed married. For all the good it did."

"I never met your husband, but Paul's got his head on straight. We talked after Tara-Lynn interviewed me. He's sensitive, caring, responsible even. He's not out to be a rebel. He loves music. I think he needs it."

"He's only sixteen."

"Would it matter if he were twenty-five? Carol, Paul's a good kid. If you can't change him, why not try trusting him?"

She put the bowl she'd been drying into the cupboard and hung up the tea towel. "Music's too dangerous."

"Some days it's all that keeps my sanity. I think you're the same."

"Playing is different. It owned my husband's life. Most of his friends weren't much better."

"It doesn't have to be that way. You can be brilliant in one area, but if you keep your balance with the rest of your world you add to it instead of taking away."

"People mess up."

"All the time. What you can do for Paul is encourage him. Let him see music and relationships aren't an either-or deal. Prayer would really help."

The scent of baking brownies teased her. She checked them through the glass. "I don't want to go there."

Joey's chuckle sounded sad. "Another day. In the meantime, I'm praying for you both but not on the air. I need to get back to work. Keep in touch?"

"I don't know."

She hung up and filled the kettle for tea.

On the radio, Joey said "This next one's for Carol. Billy Joel's 'The Longest Time.'"

The opening notes tugged her lips into a smile. Had she told him this song always lifted her mood?

Joey could be so sweet, and she needed a friend. But could she trust him? His past. Paul's music. What other secrets was he keeping?

The phone rang and she dove for the receiver, her fragile peace shattered. Almost eleven—please be a wrong number!

Another unknown caller. How much more of this could she take?

She pulled in a deep breath through her nose and set her shoulders. This man would not break her. Not with her son's future at stake.

"Hello?"

"Ah, Ms. Daniels. Working late in the kitchen tonight?"

She checked the window. Black—he could be anywhere out there. She turned away and leaned against the counter, cupboards behind her head.

The chilling voice continued. "I thought of asking my minion to put on a mask and stick his face up to your window, but we wouldn't want to frighten you, now, would we? Do you have my money yet?"

"No. I mean, not yet. I can get it next week. Monday." Garraway had said Monday, hadn't he?

"I'll hold you to that." Click.

Chapter 28

CAROL LOVED THE way city sidewalks took on a different feel after dark. As she and Patrick walked the block from the restaurant to his car, she caught snatches of happy chatter from the people around them.

Patrick took her arm to guide her around a knot of laughing girls dressed for a Saturday night on the town.

She remembered going out with Skip, those times they hired a sitter and prowled Calgary's party district. Most nights he'd been playing, and that was fun too. Listening and dancing, pretending she was as free as the others her age instead of a mother of two.

Music invited from the bars they passed, but she knew better than to suggest it to Patrick. She grinned at the thought of him wild-haired and tie-less on the dance floor.

He'd been a perfect dinner partner though. As they reached his car, she thanked him again.

"My pleasure." He opened the Porsche's door for her and leaned an elbow on it as she slipped in. "Care to stop at my place for an after-dinner drink, or are you on a curfew?"

The look she gave him must have been sharper than she'd meant, because he stepped back. "That wasn't intended as a come-on. I occasionally find the evenings long."

She pictured him wandering the big house with a hostile cat for company. "I can relate, with Paul being out so much. A drink would be fine."

When they stepped through his front door, she couldn't repress a quick look around.

Patrick chuckled. "Isis never comes to greet me. If you don't sit in the rocker, she should ignore us both, but I'll shut her away."

They spent a companionable hour or so on the couch, sipping wine and listening to orchestral music by the dancing flames of the gas fire. Sometimes they talked, but Patrick seemed to have relaxed enough from his role as host to allow stretches of silence.

That suited Carol. The luxurious room and the wine had a mellowing effect.

A phone chirped.

She jolted upright. How could she have drifted to sleep against Patrick's shoulder?

He stood and pulled his cell from his pocket, walking away from the couch. "Hello?"

A male voice reached her, muffled and indistinct.

Patrick paced a slow half-circle. "Give me fifteen minutes." He snapped the phone shut and dropped it into his pocket.

"Carol, I'm sorry. I need to follow up on this. I'll get you a cab."

"Is everything all right?"

The lines deepened around his mouth. "When the right person speaks, even investment consultants are on call. I'll survive."

As they walked into the entryway, he asked, "Have you heard from your brother?"

Her pleasure in the evening fled. "I have the information. It'll take a couple days to get the money."

"Can I help you?"

"I appreciate your concern, but I'll be fine. What I can't figure out is why Harry revealed his hiding place. He never cared what happened to me."

But Harry had phoned Garraway—and sent the pictures before that. He'd asked her to be warned in the first place. Why?

She stepped into her shoes and let Patrick help her into her jacket. His chivalry could grow on a person.

Headlights swept along the street, and the taxi slid into the drive behind Patrick's Porsche.

She turned to him. "Thank you for a lovely evening."

He clasped her hand briefly. "Thank you for sharing it with me."

He opened the door but stopped her as she stepped through. "Would you join me for the symphony on Wednesday?"

White around the lips now, he didn't give her time to respond. "I realize it's in the middle of your work week, but it's a refreshing evening out. Beautiful music, comfortable seats. You can forget the outside world for a few hours. Will you come?"

"I'd be delighted."

"Thank you. We'll discuss details later. My phone will ring any minute."

It hadn't been nerves over inviting her out. He still looked like he expected to meet a ghost.

They walked to the car, and Patrick paid the driver in advance. "Good night, Carol."

"Good night, and thank you again."

He hurried toward the house without a backward glance.

The taxi driver kept up a light chatter about the weather and the Maple Leafs' hockey chances, but the ride home seemed longer than usual.

Carol's thoughts kept returning to Patrick. She'd never seen him tense before, only smooth and collected. And why did she say she'd go to the symphony?

She arrived home a little after eleven.

As she cracked open the door, Chance's eager whine reassured her the intruders hadn't returned. "Hey, fella." She ruffled his fur and locked everything except the security chain.

"Paul's not in yet, is he?"

The dog's tail wagged at the name. He followed her as she put away her jacket and purse.

Carol changed into her pyjamas and robe and headed to the kitchen to make tea. She listened to the radio until the tea was ready, then settled on the couch to flip their few television channels.

Midnight passed, and her restlessness grew. Paul had asked to stay out later tonight to catch a show with his friends, but he should have been in by now.

She climbed off the couch, careful not to step on the sleeping dog, and peered out the window. No traffic on the street.

No sign of the grey Volkswagen either. It wasn't here often. What if they'd gone after Paul?

After pacing the living room as long as she could stand it, she went into the kitchen and picked up the phone. Paul would be annoyed with her for checking up on him, but she had to know he was safe.

On the third ring, an unfamiliar voice asked, "Paul?"

"This is Paul's mother. Who are you, and why do you have his phone?"

"Um... Hi, Ms. Daniels. This is Barry. Paul and Tara-Lynn left before I did, and he forgot his jacket with his phone in it. They were going to drive a friend home. He should have been in by now though. Do you want Tara-Lynn's number?"

"Yes, please." Fighting panic, she scribbled down the digits, thanked him, and disconnected.

Tara-Lynn's voice mail picked up after the second ring. The girl's cheery message, innocent and normal, made Carol's fear worse.

Paul was never late. If something came up, why hadn't he phoned?

Trembling, she moved around the kitchen straightening chairs at the table, realigning the already-orderly canisters on the counter.

Batteries. Maybe Tara-Lynn's phone died. Or maybe she'd forgotten it at home.

That didn't explain Paul being late.

She stood in the middle of the room, fist pressed against quivering lips. Crying wouldn't help, nor screaming.

The city loomed huge and shadowed around her, a maze where evil lurked. Where people disappeared.

Her son could be anywhere, hurt or in danger.

Carol's nightmares crashed into the present. She fled for her room. Dug through her wallet for Garraway's card.

Chance glanced up with a sleepy whine as she ran past the living room to the kitchen.

One ring, two... please not another voice mail!

"Garraway here."

Relief melted her. She leaned on the counter for support. "Detective, it's Carol Daniels. This may be nothing, but Paul should have been home by midnight." She swallowed a sob.

"Try to keep it together, Ms. Daniels. You can help us find him. Worst case, if your enemies have him they'll call you. I got through to the church late this afternoon, but their new admin assistant deposited the money right away so it wouldn't get stolen. We can't follow up with the bank until Monday. If you get a call, tell him the truth. In case they're listening now, I'll repeat that we will not mark those bills. I'll use undercover operatives, informants, and the like, but I will not endanger a civilian like yourself."

"Thank you." Her words pushed through trembling lips. Had she made things worse by calling? Why hadn't she picked up a cheap cell for herself as well as for Paul?

Garraway continued. "Best case, Paul and his friend lost track of time and they'll be embarrassed. Now, tell me everything you know about what he did this evening."

"I don't even know where they went. A concert somewhere. He's so secretive about his plans. I relied on being able to call if I needed him. But he left his phone behind." She gave him Paul's number, and Tara-Lynn's, and repeated what Barry had said.

"I'll follow up with these. Do you have a friend who can stay with you?"

"I'll find someone."

"Good. And keep your phone line clear."

A friend to stay with her? She glanced at the ceiling and shook her head. Not Cecelia. The landlady's smothering comfort would drive her crazy. Patrick's cool reserve would be the other extreme, probably with the same result.

It didn't matter that she hadn't forgiven Joey's deception. She raced to her bedroom, grabbed her purse, and dumped the contents onto her bed. Did she still have his phone number? Receipt, receipt, shopping list... at last she found it.

She hurried to the kitchen. Almost one o'clock. He'd be sleeping. She held her breath while his phone rang.

"Hello?" Groggy voice. She'd woken him.

"Joey, it's Carol. I—Paul's missing. Can you come?"

He made a soft grunt as if already getting out of bed. "Tell me how to find you."

She gave him directions, plus her number in case he got lost. "I'll be watching for you."

"I'm on my way."

215

Chapter 29

CAROL PACED THE living room, Chance at her heels. She'd traded her nightclothes for leggings and a baggy sweatshirt and started a pot of coffee for Joey. How much longer?

A motor broke the night's silence, and her heart rate spiked. She hurried to the window. Joey? Or Paul? *Come home. Please come home.*

An unfamiliar car pulled up to the curb, and Joey sprinted across the lawn.

She ran to fling open the front door.

Chance followed, rumbling a low growl, and pressed against her leg.

"Hush, fella. He's a friend."

Breathing hard, Joey stopped in the doorway. "What happened?"

"He was supposed to be in by midnight. He's with Tara-Lynn, and she's not answering her phone, and please don't make any innuendos. Harry's money—I don't have it yet. They broke into the apartment before. What if they've taken Paul?"

She found herself in his arms, holding on for dear life.

His fingertips circled slowly on her shoulder blades.

Little by little, she gathered strength to stand on her own. Fighting tears, she led him into the living room.

He tossed his jacket on the coffee table and sat beside her on the couch, the dog watching each move. "Have you phoned the police?"

"Paul forgot his phone with another friend. The detective said he'd call and try to find where they might have gone. He told me not to wait alone. I'm sorry I dragged you out of bed."

"Don't be. I want to help." Joey squeezed her hand. "I'm not the most eloquent, but would you like me to pray with you?"

"Thanks, but no. I don't have a very good track record with faith."

"Want to talk about it?"

She shook her head. "If you're happy with it, I don't want to discourage you."

"Hey, faith is like life. It's messy and confusing at times, but I've experienced God's work in my heart. I know He's real." Joey hiked a shoulder. "I still have questions, and I doubt I'd be able to answer yours, but you won't scare me off."

Carol hadn't thought in terms of questions, but she sensed them now, lurking beneath the hurt. "I prayed for my mom, and she died. When Keith got into drugs, a friend prayed with me. Prayer healed her from a brain tumour. Keith died, and she said my faith was too weak."

She slumped forward, hoping Joey wouldn't see her tears. "I can't pray for Paul. I might kill him."

Chance left his post beside Joey and pressed himself against her leg.

Joey yanked tissues from the box on the coffee table and pressed them into her palm. He rested his hand between her shoulders. "It doesn't work like that. Someone who's studied could try to explain how our faith and God's power interact, but look at it this way. Did you mean what you asked? Did you think God could do it?"

She nodded, not trusting herself to speak.

"So, you did your part. Keith had a part to play too, and maybe he couldn't because of the drugs. But your toxic friend blaming you... if your prayers had the power of life and death, wouldn't that make you stronger than God?"

"I couldn't be."

His thumb wiped a fresh tear from her cheek. "Precisely. You're a strong woman but not that strong."

Another tear slipped down her cheek. Her entire body vibrated, the muscles so tight it felt like they'd rip free.

Joey drew her into the curve of his arm. "We don't know anything's happened. Paul may be fine—at least until you get your hands on him."

"If they've killed him, I swear I will burn their money and give them the ashes." She pulled free of his embrace. "I can't take this, Joey, I think I'm going to explode."

She read compassion in his eyes, in the wry twist of his lips.

"Then we'll pick up the pieces together. Listen, when my world crashed it wasn't this bad, but it was still messy. Pieces everywhere." Gentle hands clasped hers. "The same God who picked me up off the floor can help you now. He didn't do too bad a job on me, did He?"

"What if there's nothing left to put together?"

"There will be."

An Eagles ringtone sounded. Joey dove for his jacket pocket. "Hello?"

He straightened at once and thrust the phone toward her. "Paul."

Carol clutched it to her ear. "Paul! Are you okay?"

"Mom?"

She heard wariness and embarrassment in his voice but no danger. Relief clogged her throat. Shaking her head, she passed the phone to Joey.

He thumbed a button and held the phone between them. "Where are you?"

"Why's Mom at your place?"

Chance sat up and stared at the phone, ears perked.

"I'm at *your* place. Waiting for you. Why'd you phone me instead of your mom?"

"I hoped she'd be asleep. Listen, we need help. Amber's in a bad way, and if her parents see her like this again they'll kick her out. I know it's asking a lot, but could we crash at your place for the night?"

"Come home." Joey hiked a questioning brow.

Carol nodded.

"I can't bring Amber like this. She's tripped out on something, and it'll make Mom think of Keith. We hoped you'd understand."

"Just get home. Your mother's been frantic."

"I can take care of myself."

"Like your dog when those thugs broke in. How far away are you?"

After a muffled conversation, Paul said, "Maybe half an hour."

"We'll be waiting. And I'm glad you're okay."

"Yeah. Bye."

Joey dropped the phone on the coffee table. "No danger, only an idiot teenager. Make that three. I could pound him for putting you through this."

Carol wilted against the couch. Anger would come, but right now she felt damply giddy with relief. "Thank you for coming."

"Thank you for trusting me enough to call."

"I need to let the detective know, and Paul's friend." She pushed to her feet, stepped past Chance, and headed for the kitchen to make the calls.

Garraway first. The detective kept his tone matter-of-fact, but his words came out clipped. He had to be angry about a midnight false alarm. "Ms. Daniels, I'm glad this turned out well. Paul needs to understand the danger until the money is transferred. Abduction was a very real possibility tonight."

"After this, he may be grounded for life. I'm sorry to ruin your night's sleep."

"Don't mention it, ma'am. It's why they pay me the big bucks. Good night."

When she reached Barry, the boy sounded like he hadn't been worried. He must not know about the drug ring.

She poked her head into the living room. "Would you like a coffee and some cookies?"

Joey left the couch and came to her side. "I'm good, thanks, unless you need to keep busy."

"I think I'll make hot chocolate for the kids. If they've been driving around all this time, not knowing what to do..."

"In that case, I'd better eat my cookies before they arrive."

It felt good to laugh again.

Leaving a carafe of hot chocolate on the counter, they took their cups and a plate of cookies into the living room where they'd be able to hear Tara-Lynn's car.

Carol's teacup trembled in her hand, and she braced it against her leg. She'd been so scared, but she didn't want to explode in front of Paul's friends. And Amber... "I don't like Paul being around a drug addict."

"She doesn't want to stay that way. And she needs good friends right now."

"It's just, after Keith—"

Joey took another cookie from the plate. "These are terrific. Have you talked to Paul about Keith? He saw more than enough. He sounds like nothing's going to tempt him down that road."

"Will Amber make it? Keith tried."

"I made it. We have to hope."

A car pulled into the driveway. Carol ran to the front door, Joey at her heels.

He stepped into his shoes. "They might need help with Amber."

A minute later Joey and Paul appeared, half carrying the crying girl. Tara-Lynn followed.

Carol spread towels over the couch and directed them to lay Amber down. "Is she vomiting?"

Paul looked up, a tight cast to his pale lips. "Not now."

As soon as he straightened, Carol seized him in a fierce hug.

He gave her an awkward pat on the shoulder. "I'm sorry."

Joey asked Tara-Lynn into the kitchen.

When she could trust herself to speak, Carol held her son at arm's length. The blistering rant faded unspoken at the exhaustion in his face. "You look terrible."

"You don't look so good yourself." He touched her hair. "Mom, I never meant to scare you like this. We didn't know what to do."

A sniffly, singsong giggle came from the couch. "Do you know the muffin man..."

~~~

Carol tucked a soft blanket around Amber and drew Paul into the kitchen.

Tara-Lynn sat at the table with Joey, her features as strained as Paul's. She broke off what she'd been saying and looked up at Carol.

"Ms. Daniels, I'm so sorry. Amber can't go home like this, and we've been driving for hours trying to find a place for her. My mom's having a party, Pastor Stu must be out on another emergency, and we didn't know what to do."

Tears sparkled on her lashes. "I was so afraid the police would stop us. I don't have my full licence yet, so I'm only allowed one passenger under twenty after midnight."

Carol rested a gentle hand on the girl's shoulder. "It's okay now. It's over."

Joey gave his seat to Carol. "Paul, you sit too. I'll get the drinks your mom made."

"In a minute." Paul hurried out and returned carrying his wooden desk chair, singing, "One of These Things is Not Like the Others." He broke off the Sesame Street classic. "Amber's got me going now."

Joey set steaming mugs of hot chocolate in front of the teens and refilled the cookie plate. He poured hot chocolate into his mug. "I haven't had this stuff in years. Can I make you more tea, Carol?"

"Yes please." She'd reassert her independence soon. Right now, it felt good to be looked after.

While the water boiled, Joey came to stand near the table. He fixed one teen, then the other, with a stern gaze. "Promise me you'll never pull a stunt like this again."

Tara-Lynn's chin quivered, and Paul shot back, "It was my fault. I'll take the blame. Tara-Lynn didn't know we'd had a break-in or about those creeps and their money. If it was anything but drugs, we'd have come here right away."

His tone warmed. "Mom always made home a safe place, even if we got in trouble. But drugs are too much."

Carol focused on Tara-Lynn. "Should you phone home?"

The girl's mouth trembled. "I told Mom I was staying with a friend. I just... haven't found where yet."

Joey brought Carol's tea and sank onto the remaining chair. "Sorry, gang, but no underage females—or males—spend the night at my place unless I'm somewhere else with witnesses to prove it."

"They can stay here." Another time Carol would have laughed at her son's incredulous expression. Protective determination hardened her voice. "Amber needs help. If her parents won't give it, I will."

Her lips firmed. Kick the girl out, indeed. Life on the street would make her situation worse. "The girls can have my bed. I'll sleep on the couch."

Joey yawned. "My bed's sounding good right about now. You've got this zoo under control, so I think I'll head out." He blinked at his watch. "Wonder if I'll make it to church this morning."

After he left, they moved Amber into Carol's room and tucked her into bed fully clothed. Carol found an extra sleep shirt for Tara-Lynn. "She's quieter now. I hope she doesn't keep you awake."

Tara-Lynn shrugged. "I think I could zonk out standing up. I don't want her to wake alone and disoriented in a strange place."

Carol slept fitfully and woke mid-morning, her mind full of dream fragments in which Keith, Amber, or both, ran mazes and fought monsters. She dragged herself through the shower and changed into the clothes she'd taken from her room before bed.

None of the teens stirred until she was taking banana muffins from the oven.

Amber walked into the kitchen, rumpled and wearing a puzzled frown. She squinted at Carol. "Hi."

Carol set the muffin tray on a potholder and took off the oven mitts. "Hi. I'm Paul's mom, Carol. Do you remember them bringing you here for the night?"

Amber twisted a lock of hair around her finger and didn't meet Carol's eyes. "I'm not sure. Thank you for letting me stay. I'm sorry to be a problem."

Carol longed to gather the girl in a comforting hug, but that would probably embarrass her more. Instead, she set a plate of steaming muffins on the table and invited her to sit. "Help yourself when they cool. There's coffee on. I thought we'd all need it."

Amber's lower lip trembled. "No thanks."

Carol sat beside her. "Amber, I don't know what happened last night, but you can beat this. If you lose hope, nobody can help you."

Keith's face rose in her memory, and her voice broke. "I think that's what happened to Paul's brother. But you have friends who care enough about you to drive around the city half the night instead of leaving you on a street corner or sending you home to face your parents. They believe in you."

Amber's eyes swam with tears.

Carol went for the tissue box and set it on the table. "Can you try a muffin or a drink? Your body's probably empty."

"Maybe a coffee, please? Double-double."

"Coming right up. I'll make a solid brunch once the other two appear."

"Thank you, Ms. Daniels. Paul's a lucky guy."

Carol chose a pretty floral mug from the cupboard and reached for the coffee pot.

Behind her, Amber continued, "He told me about his brother. I'm really sorry. But you must be proud of Paul. He's responsible and keeps out of trouble, and what a musician."

Hot coffee sloshed onto the counter. Carol set down the pot and grabbed the dishcloth to wipe up the spill. "What?"

"I went last night to hear his band. They're a bit novice, but he blew the audience away on a couple solos. Then stupid me bumped into some of my old friends, and I couldn't walk away."

Ice slid around Carol's heart. Fear, or anger?

A detached part of her mind noticed Amber sounded more disgusted with herself than hopeless now. Good. Maybe the girl could make a clean start.

But a band? All the time Paul spent with his friends—it was band practice. Where did he get a guitar?

When he'd admitted he needed the music, was he trying to prepare her?

Her hands shook as she finished filling Amber's mug. She stirred in a double shot of milk and two sugars, the spoon clinking. *Please don't let him turn out like Skip.*

Desperate wishes to the universe couldn't help Paul. And no matter what Joey said, she was afraid to try praying.

Paul had told her, and Joey reinforced it, that seeing Keith's addiction made him avoid drugs. Could what he learned about Skip keep music from ruining his chances for a happy family?

Skip's drug of choice had been alcohol, and he'd been happiest in the middle of a party. She'd seen none of that from Paul, but even the small fame of a raw high school band would bring temptation.

Despite her turmoil, she carried Amber's coffee to the table without spilling. The girl nibbled at a muffin. Good, she'd need something healthy in her stomach.

Paul walked into the kitchen, yawning and scratching his head, as the phone rang.

Carol tensed. She couldn't handle another threatening call right now.

Chapter 30

JOEY'S NAME SHOWED up on the call display and Carol's lungs unlocked. "Hello?"

"Did you get any sleep?" Beneath his concern, exhaustion roughened his voice.

"A bit. How about you?"

"Short but sweet. I'm on my way home from church. Do you need me to pick anything up at the store to feed the crew?"

She'd already pulled extra meat from the freezer. "We're okay. Why don't you join us? I'm about to start brunch."

"You don't have to ask me twice. If you're sure you want to add to the crowd."

"Are you kidding? I need reinforcements."

He laughed. "See you in about forty-five minutes."

As she hung up, Paul asked, "Did I hear brunch?"

Did I hear band? She couldn't let that out now, not in front of Amber. "Brunch. Yes. Joey's coming too."

Amber pushed limp hair from her cheeks. "Would it be okay if I had a shower?"

"Tara-Lynn's in there now, but she said she'd be quick." Paul grabbed a muffin and joined her at the table.

Carol eyed the girl's slight frame. "If we can find something to fit you, I'll throw your stuff in the washer."

"I've been too much trouble already." Amber brushed at the wrinkles in her shirt.

By the time Joey arrived with a fruit tray and a bottle of orange juice, Carol had bacon and sausages keeping warm in the oven. Amber and Tara-Lynn, each in borrowed sweats, set the table while Paul took his turn in the shower. He wouldn't be long. There couldn't be much hot water left.

Joey set his offerings on the counter and hugged each occupant of the kitchen. "Ladies, thanks for taking pity on a starving bachelor."

Carol opened the juice. "I'll bet you're a fine cook."

"Try me sometime. Microwave dinners, my specialty."

Amber stirred the hash browns. "I think these are ready."

Eggs sizzled in the frying pan while Tara-Lynn buttered toast. Before long, they all sat in the living room with plates of food and glasses of juice, laughing at Joey's and Paul's bad jokes.

After the food disappeared, Joey spoke into Carol's ear. "How about a walk?"

"You got up for church this morning. Don't you want to nap?"

"I'll sleep later. Right now, I want to make sure you're okay."

Behind him, Paul said, "Go on, Mom. We'll clean up and finish the laundry. We owe you one."

The girls nodded.

"Okay, thanks." She'd probably have to clean the kitchen again after them, but if it made them feel better, a walk with Joey sounded fine.

On the way out the door, she snatched her glasses off the counter.

Joey gave her a sideways look. "Your brother's enemies already found you."

"So I don't need paparazzi too."

He shrugged. "It's old news."

"The prison escape and his recapture were this year. There are probably still trial proceedings. I try not to keep up." And Garraway said Harry's drug information would come out eventually.

She opened the door. "Murphy's law—when I decide it's safe to stop hiding, his enemies will eliminate him in prison and the whole media circus will blow up in my face."

Chance bounded across the kitchen, toenails skittering on the floor.

Joey laughed. "Here's another kind of circus."

"There's a park a couple of blocks away. Or did you want to drive somewhere?"

"Your guard dog wants to come too. Let's walk."

In the park, Carol lengthened the retractable leash. She and Joey wandered paths while the dog orbited, poking his nose into the vegetation. He ignored the joggers, but she pulled in the leash whenever they met another dog.

Crisp autumn smells and the painter's palette of leaves filled her senses. "I needed this."

"Me too."

Eventually, they settled on a bench, Chance content for the moment to lie at their feet.

Carol tipped her face to the sun and closed her eyes. "I wouldn't have made it without you last night."

Joey laced his fingers through hers. "That's what friends are for. I'm glad everything worked out okay. It was scary though."

"I heard what you said about God, but I'm not ready. If I can't trust people, how can I risk trusting Him?"

His fingers moved on the back of her hand. "I know you've had bad experiences, but if you can trust someone's heart... Paul's, maybe mine, especially God's... it's okay to let them choose how to act even if it's not what you want."

"God let my mother, my unborn daughter, and my son die." She twitched Chance's leash to get him up. "Let's walk."

Joey kept hold of her hand as they stepped onto the path.

The silence between them weighted her spirit like a sack full of wet laundry. She picked up a stick and tossed it out of the way. Chance retrieved it, and she sighed. "I shouldn't have said that. You don't need all my baggage."

Joey stopped, his eyes haunted. "Carol, if it's tearing me up to think of all the pain in your life, imagine what God feels. He didn't cause it, and He loves you more than you can imagine."

"He's got a funny way of showing it." She tugged the stick away from Chance and threw it out of reach. "Come on, you crazy mutt."

The dog raced after the stick until the leash brought him up short. He looked from his quarry to Carol and back again. When she didn't give him more line, he tossed a defiant bark at the stick and trotted to her side.

Joey laughed. "Well, there's one guy who'll always do what you want."

They kept walking, the sun warm on their backs. Joey picked up a fallen maple leaf and twirled it by its stem. "Whatever you think of God and me, your son has his head screwed on right. He's a fine young man. You could take time to get to know him. Find out who he really is."

"You mean let him go his own way. Even if it's not what I want for him."

"He's growing up. Last night was a blip, but his heart was in the right place. He'll choose differently than you would. He's a different person. He'll be okay."

"I wish I could believe you."

Joey's moustache twitched. "So do I."

~~~

"Amber told me about the band."

Carol intercepted her son when he arrived home Sunday night, the first chance she'd had to get him alone. The girls had stayed all day, and then the trio went to Tara-Lynn's church for the evening service to let Amber meet the pastor.

Paul gazed slowly skyward and let out a slow breath. He locked the door and hung up his leather jacket. "It was our first gig. I wanted to wait until we'd been playing awhile, so you'd see it hadn't changed me."

He braced himself against the wall. "I'm sorry I kept it a secret. But when I play, I'm alive, energized. Happy. Don't ask me to give it up, because I can't."

The longing in his face and voice made Carol think of a little boy begging to keep a stray puppy. Except this puppy could grow up to savage the hand that nurtured it. "Music took over your father's life, and we paid for it."

"Don't you think Dad had responsibility for that? Donnie Leyland said to serve the gift, and he's right. That doesn't mean to obsess over it or let it replace common sense."

Thoughts of Donnie brought a half smile. Carol tugged it into a frown. "Where did you get a guitar? Or learn to play well enough to perform?"

"A friend in Calgary showed me. His teacher gave me some contacts here. Mr. Morelli's a musical genius. He gave me a job to pay for lessons. I use one of Barry's guitars in the band."

"So hanging out at Barry's has been cover for band practice?"

"We hang out while we practise. His parents have this huge house, and he's the only kid." Paul rolled his eyes. "His mom's in this losing battle to turn him posh. His name's really Thaddeus Barrington, but don't tell him I spilled it. His mom calls him TB. Says it makes him sound important."

Now, Paul's grin turned into a snort. "His girlfriend says TB is for Teddy Bear. Poor guy."

Carol rubbed her neck. Did she feel a migraine coming on? Too many emotions churned in her heart. "Don't try to change the subject. Music is an unstable career, and it demands your whole life. Skip wasn't the only musician to neglect his family."

"I'll pay what it costs before I start a family. And if I can't make it, there's always flipping burgers."

Carol opened her mouth, but Paul shook his head. "I'm kidding. But I need to pay my dues while I'm young. Get myself started. If I don't have what it takes, I'll find out in time to choose a different path."

"Amber said you're good."

"Thanks. Donnie said I have potential."

Surprised pride jostled with a surge of anxiety in Carol's heart. "He'd know what he was talking about. He was there last night?"

"No, he came into the store that one night and we played for a bit. Is he ever something."

"The band wasn't the same without him." She avoided her son's eyes.

"Donnie said Dad wanted the lifestyle more than the music. You know that's not me. I like my space. When it's time, I think coming home to a family will be the best balance to life on stage."

He flashed her a grin. "Now that I don't have to hide what I'm doing, coming home here will be better too."

"What if I forbid you to play? You're still under my authority, and I don't want you ruining your life." Carol's whole body ached. It felt like trying to stop a flood with her bare hands—Paul's dreams, his life, pushing through her fingers.

His shoulder dropped into his defensive, guitar-player stance. "I'm old enough to choose for myself. If that includes leaving home, I will. We've had this conversation."

Her heart broke at the determined edge to his words. Now, she knew why he'd been so adamant not to move again. He'd do it—choose the music over his own mother. The desperation in his eyes said loving her wouldn't stop him. She touched his shoulder. "Stay."

Paul pulled her into a rib-cracking hug. "I promise I'll keep my head."

Letting go, he said, "Music will be first when I'm playing, but I won't forget the people I love. Tara-Lynn puts God first, and it doesn't mean the people around her get left out. I think it helps her see them better. Look how she's been with Amber."

"You've both been wonderful to Amber. True friends."

"Then let me prove I can play music and not neglect my friends."

Carol swallowed her tears. "You haven't left me much choice."

~~~

The school corridors rang with laughter, raised voices, and banging locker doors. Monday mornings might start in irritable silence, but by day's end the thought of escape lightened the mood. Paul and Barry forged through the throng.

A hand slapped Paul on the back. "Hey, buddy, hear you got some action Saturday night. Way to go."

Scowling, Paul hunched his shoulders and kept walking. Losing his temper again would gain nothing.

He glared at a boy who looked up from a nearby locker, jerked his own open, and thrust his stuff into his backpack.

As the other boy walked away, Barry leaned toward him. "Lighten up, dude. They're just trying to welcome you into their world."

Paul straightened. "I don't want to be in their sick little world. And nothing happened. Tara-Lynn hugged me after we came off-stage, and somebody saw me helping Amber to the car later. Suddenly I'm the star of a threesome."

Barry shrugged. "Wish they'd want to welcome me."

"Amber doesn't need this crap, and Tara-Lynn's a Christian, for Pete's sake. She wouldn't be doing stuff like that. How's it going to make her feel?"

Paul rammed his arms into the sleeves of his leather jacket and pulled it on. "Tara-Lynn wouldn't even look at me in math class. Maybe she'll never talk to me again."

"And that matters why, Mr. I-don't-have-time-for-a-girlfriend?"

Heat washed Paul's face. "You heard?"

"Half the school heard you rip into those guys. Maybe that's why she's mad."

Something in Paul went quiet. "What do you mean?"

Barry hiked a shoulder. "A lot of guys look at Tara-Lynn, but she only looks at you."

Paul blew out a long sigh. "I can't deny the music, so I've gotta stay single. She deserves better than time-sharing anyway."

He zipped his jacket and hefted his backpack. "At least helping her with Amber let us be together. Until those jerks had to ruin it."

He slammed his locker door, sending a chain of vibration all along the hall.

Chapter 31

CAROL USUALLY LOVED Mondays at the café. Not this Monday. Before the supper crowd started, she'd ruined a batch of cookies and nearly added a second measure of sugar to a bowl of cake batter.

Paul had no idea what he was getting into with a band. She'd seen the dangers. Lived their effects.

Since her talk with Joey in the park, she felt more alone than ever. Alone and unable to keep her son off his father's path.

After her shift, she hurried to her car, berating herself for mixing up the Termolis' orders. The older couple's warm concern had only made it worse.

A hand caught her shoulder. "Keep walking to the car. Don't turn around."

Carol stumbled.

The hand shifted to support her elbow, the grip closing tight to keep her from running.

A thousand visions of terror flooded her mind.

Before she could scream, the man spoke again. "Act normal. I have a message for you, and then I'm gone."

Would he keep his word? No way would she get in the car with him.

"My boss wants an update on the money."

"I haven't heard—I'm waiting for a call—it was supposed to be today. I don't know what went wrong, but I need to wait for that call. Please—I need more time."

"Boss is getting impatient. You don't want that."

She swallowed hard. "I'm doing my best."

They reached her car. "Get inside. Put your head down and count to a hundred. If you can ID me, he won't think you're worth much alive once he has the money."

Her key shook so badly that she couldn't fit it in the lock.

Her assailant grumbled a curse. He kept one hand locked on her elbow while his other one grasped her fingers and rammed the key home. The movement pulled her close against his body.

Don't scream. Don't draw attention. He was just a messenger. He'd said he would leave.

The man twisted the key in the lock. He pulled the door open, shoved Carol through, and slammed it behind her.

Heart pounding, she hit the lock before leaning her forehead on the steering wheel. She twisted for a peek in the side mirror but couldn't pick him out among the pedestrians.

A vehicle zoomed past. She looked up to see a grey Volkswagen turn the corner.

It took another five minutes for the shakes to subside so she could start the engine.

She checked the rear-view mirror as she drove. Not that anyone from the gang needed to follow her. They knew where she lived.

A gentle rain began to fall, and she switched on the wipers. She hit a string of red lights, but as she turned a corner the next two lights changed to green. She sped up.

Blurred motion to the right made her jump on the brake. She clung to the wheel and swerved to miss the black SUV that came out of nowhere.

Her front bumper caught its rear. Both vehicles spun.

Her car's right rear tire whomped the curb, and the car jolted to a stop.

Three figures bolted from the SUV, leaving the doors wide open.

Carol stared after them. A tap at her passenger-side window made her jump.

A young couple peered in. The man mouthed, "Are you okay?"

Nodding, she unfastened her seat belt and leaned to roll the window down a crack to communicate.

The man spoke through the gap. "We were right behind you. Do you need us to call the police?"

"Yes, please." It took three tries to grasp the key and shut off the engine. She should get out, assess the damage, but weakness pinned her to the seat.

While his companion spoke into a cellphone, the man studied her through the glass. "You're white as a sheet. I'll get you a coffee."

Tears prickled her eyes. She found her purse and fumbled coins from her wallet. "Thank you so much. Could I have a peppermint tea instead, please? Just tea, nothing added."

"No sweat. I'll be right back." He jogged away.

The young woman tucked the phone in her pocket. "They're coming. With that SUV in the middle of the intersection, they might even hurry."

Carol unlocked the passenger door. "Would you like to sit in the car?"

"Sure. I could wait in our Jeep, but you could probably use the company. My name's Mia."

"Carol." She pulled a shuddery breath as Mia climbed into the car. "I didn't see that guy until he was on top of me. My light was green from the last corner."

"Crazy joy riders, probably. Or impaired. They took off in a hurry."

Traffic crawled around the wrecked cars with surprisingly few angry horns. Mia's boyfriend, Kit, emerged from the drizzle carrying a takeout tray of brown paper cups and a yellow cardboard box.

He slid into the back seat and passed a cup to Carol. "I got you a large." He passed a cup to Mia and offered around the open box.

Mia giggled. "No calories tonight. Stress evaporates them."

Carol set the hot cup in a holder and reached into the box of donut holes. She picked a glazed chocolate one and another one rolled in white coconut.

The young couple kept up a light chatter that distracted her from glancing too often at the clock.

Finally, a siren swelled, then cut off. A black-and-white pulled up across the street. A second unit followed.

Two officers flanked the stranded SUV to direct traffic. A third strode toward Carol's car.

The combination of stress and sugar gave her the energy to step out to meet him, but she held onto the door in case her trembling legs gave way.

The officer wore a friendly smile on broad features of First Nations heritage. His name tag read *T. Berens*. After making sure Carol wasn't hurt, he listened to her story and took statements from Mia and Kit.

When the couple was free to go, Carol hugged them both. "Thank you so much. I don't know what I'd have done without you."

She sat in her car while Officer Berens sketched the vehicles' layout and measured the skid marks.

Alone.

She used to handle everything alone. It was easier. But since moving to Toronto, getting to know Joey over the phone, she'd leaned on him with her nightmares—even more on Saturday with the panic over Paul.

Imagine, waking a friend, especially one she'd tried to cut off, in the middle of the night. Patrick's face rose in her mind. Reputable, serious Patrick should have been the logical choice for support instead of the guy with the sketchy past.

Support, perhaps. Comfort? Sometimes the heart had to overrule the head.

She'd made the right call. Joey's response proved his friendship. Tears welled again and she blinked them away, concentrating on Berens' movements as he measured the vehicles' distance from the traffic lines and each other.

In all truth, she'd relied more on Jackie than she realized before the move. And her praying friend before that, the one Joey called toxic, until they lost Keith.

What happened to the strong woman who kept her family together despite her husband, who fought for a chance for her kids? Maybe she'd died with Keith.

I don't want to be alone anymore.

Her lips twisted. If her subconscious wanted to use Billy Joel titles to sum up her emotional state, "Close to the Borderline" fit better than "I Don't Want to Be Alone." Besides, she *was* alone, like it or not.

She clenched her fists and breathed deeply through her nose. A hint of fighting spirit stiffened her spine. She stepped out of the car and approached Officer Berens.

He glanced up from his clipboard. "We'll have you on the road shortly."

"I need to contact Detective Garraway."

The officer's eyes narrowed. "This is a straightforward traffic accident."

"Not about this. It's something that happened when I left work. Please. I know it's after hours, but he said to call if I needed him. I don't have a cellphone. It'll be even later when I get home."

"Garraway gave you his direct number?"

"I'm the pawn in the middle of one of his cases." She fished the detective's bent card from her wallet. "See? Cell number on the back."

Berens' smile made his brown eyes twinkle. "Okay, you're legit. I didn't really need to see the card. I'll try him in a minute." He raised a palm to the persistent drizzle. "Why don't you wait in your car?"

Shivering, she went back to the battered vehicle and turned the radio on low. The music helped keep her thoughts out of the dark corners.

Officer Berens had gone to the squad car, and now he walked over to her. "I'm waiting for a call-back from Detective Garraway. The SUV's stolen, by the way. Lady didn't know it was gone until we called. There's a tow truck on the way. Do you need one too?"

"I'm not sure."

"Let's move you off the road while we wait for the call. That way we'll know if you're mobile."

The engine sounded rougher, but maybe that was her imagination. She steered carefully out of the intersection and pulled into the coffee shop lot on the corner.

Officer Berens sat in his car. As she approached, he beckoned her to join him. "Detective Garraway's in the middle of a situation right now. Let me take your information, and he'll get it from me later. Sounds like he could be awhile."

Carol bit her lip to stop it quivering. She didn't need a personal dependence on Garraway, just a citizen's reliance on the police force as a whole. But what if Berens was a dirty cop?

Her skin chilled. What if Garraway was?

Angry at her own crazy head games and the fear behind them, she tried to keep her voice steady. "Did he have any message for me?"

"He said to tell you the bank wasn't cooperating and he couldn't get the money today. A policy about giving notice for large withdrawals. He'll explain when he talks to you."

Fresh fear pierced her anger. "That could take days!"

"Not many. He's using the department's influence." Berens turned to a fresh sheet of paper on the clipboard. "That's all I have. I'll make sure he gets what you tell me."

Flashing yellow lights meant the tow truck had arrived. Carol watched it collect the SUV. "The money's connected to people he's investigating, and it was deposited by mistake. Could you tell him one of them intercepted me after work and threatened me?" Her voice wobbled as she gave the details.

Berens frowned. "Have they made personal contact before?"

"No, it's been phone calls."

"They're increasing the pressure. I'll talk to Garraway as soon as I can." He laid the clipboard on the seat between them. "If there's nothing else, you can go home and unwind from all this."

Carol shook his hand. "I don't know how you do it. I'm seeing a tiny picture of what you deal with every day, and I'm a wreck."

Officer Berens smiled. "Positive contacts, people like you, help us keep perspective that not everyone's out to take down the city. Try not to worry, Ms. Daniels. Detective Garraway's the best."

Carol walked to her dented Toyota. Would Garraway's skill be enough? More immediately, would the car make it home? And what kind of run-around would the insurance people give her?

Paul was gone when she arrived. Naturally. Her heart twisted at the knowledge he was either practising with the band or working at the music store.

She locked the door, dropped the mail on the counter, and collapsed at the kitchen table. So alone. If Harry's enemies killed her, Paul would have no one.

Those joy riders almost did the job for them.

Tears soaked the sleeves that pillowed her face.

"What do I do? God, I don't know if I can trust You, but what do I do?"

Chapter 32

HALF AN HOUR later, Carol hung up from the insurance company. She carried a steaming cup of peppermint tea and the unopened mail into the living room. What would the appraisal show? An old car like hers... if they wrote it off, they wouldn't give her enough to replace it.

A sip of tea did nothing to settle her nerves. She turned the radio on and plopped onto the couch to distract herself with the mail. Advertisements, a bill, and a small hand-lettered envelope that held a black-edged, typed card.

Dear Mrs. Daniels, as my son's wedding will not take place, I have cancelled the travel reservations he made.

Regretfully, Honore Renaud.

Not take place? Gilles had seemed like such a sweetheart. Maybe he had a dark side and Amy found out in time. Or maybe his mother had squelched the relationship. She sounded like the forceful type, from this note. Carol frowned. More probably, Isobel's damaging influence made Amy the cause.

"Maybe you're better off, Amy. I hope it works out. For both of you." Carol snorted. She wondered about her cousin, yet here she was talking to the air.

She picked up her cup and filled her lungs with peppermint scent. The radio was playing Gordon Lightfoot's "Early Morning Rain." A lonely song, but his music always loosened her tension.

Chance lay on the floor, as close to her as he could get. Did he sense her need of comfort? She rested one foot against the steady rise and fall of his ribs.

At the sound of the back door opening, the dog broke off in mid-snore.

Paul bolted in from the kitchen. "Mom, are you okay? What happened to the car?"

"Kids in a stolen SUV ran a red light. It could have been a lot worse." *Don't think about could-have-been, focus on the fact that you're okay.*

Her son fended off Chance's welcome-home licks and dropped down on the couch to give her a one-armed hug. "You should have called."

"I'm okay."

"You don't look it. Maybe you need to get to bed early."

"Yes, son." She mustered a grin. "I wanted to see you first. How was your day?"

"Better than yours, I guess. Practice was good. The guys were pumped after playing on the weekend." He yawned. "I finished most of my homework after school, so I won't be up late."

"I don't know if I'll be able to sleep, but I'll try. Joey's show starts soon. It'll take my mind off the accident." She shut off the radio and carried her empty mug to the kitchen.

Paul followed her and picked up his backpack from beside the door. "Joey's a decent guy. He's been great with Amber. He came to check out Saturday's gig too."

A pang stabbed Carol's heart. "He did?"

"Too bad he didn't stay till the end. Things might have ended better for Amber. I'm glad I can talk about the band now. I hated sneaking around, but I figured you'd go ballistic." Paul grinned. "You took it pretty well. I'm proud."

He slung his backpack over one shoulder and headed down the hall.

Carol stared after him. She'd told Joey a bit about Skip and how hard she worked to keep Paul off that path. So he found out about this band and instead of telling her, he aided the deception?

She locked the doors and changed into pyjamas. Instead of climbing into bed, she returned to the kitchen and turned on the radio.

Joey was chatting about a busy weekend and how good it felt to come back to work and rest up.

When the next song started, she picked up the phone. Busy. While she waited to get through, she rehearsed what she wanted to say.

"Welcome to All-Request Oldies. What would you like to hear tonight?"

His voice stirred memories of his hand holding hers as they walked yesterday. Of his comfort Saturday night when she thought she'd break.

"How could you know Paul was in a band and not tell me?" Tears vibrated in her voice. That made her angrier. She didn't want to be vulnerable.

"I'm glad that's out in the open. He asked me to respect his privacy, but you needed to know."

"You should have told me Saturday night that you'd seen him. What if he *had* been abducted?"

"You said the detective was calling Paul's friends. They'd have given him the details. Paul said this was a venue for the under-age crowd. Since he wouldn't tell you, I went along to make sure the manager actually enforced the alcohol- and drug-free rules. I should've stayed til the end, but everything seemed fine. Paul said he'd be home by midnight. By the time you phoned me, if he'd been abducted they could have been anywhere. Hang on, commercial's ending."

Joey introduced the next line-up of songs on air, then came back to the phone. "They're still working out the kinks, but they've got a good sound. You should hear them, Carol. Your son is really something. He's a deep thinker for a teen. I can't see him turning out like his father."

"You don't see a problem, so my parenting rules go out the window?"

He let out a slow breath. "Someday, we'll have a normal conversation. 'Hi, Joey, could you play me a song?' and 'Sure thing, Carol. Want to catch a show on the weekend?'"

Her fingers tightened on the phone. "Here's a request— instead of taking it upon yourself to decide what's best for my son and me, how about playing 'My Life'? From me to you."

She hung up before he could hear her cry.

Her control didn't break until she reached her bedroom. Curled in bed in the dark, she clutched a pillow to the hollow ache in her chest. Tears poured from the deepest reservoir of her heart.

The radio played on. She'd shut it off once she found out if he actually played her request.

The song ended. She waited through ads for pizza and real estate services until Joey started speaking.

His voice made the tears flow hotter. "We'll open this next set with two in a row from the same artist. The first is a request, and the second is for Carol in Toronto. It's one of the few Billy Joel songs you've never asked for. I thought it might be time."

She glared at the radio. What had he picked as a parting shot?

Her mind echoed every defiant word as "My Life" played, and she whispered the closing plea to be left alone, despite the pain in her heart.

Then a light, rapid beat caught her by surprise. Joey was right. She'd never asked for this one, perhaps because she didn't think the subject existed. "An Innocent Man."

Joey was defending himself. Trying to justify what he did.

But she knew that wasn't the song's message. The lyrics offered unselfish motives and support, and as she listened she longed for the fairy tale to be true.

By that definition, there weren't any innocent men—or women. Even Amy's Prince Charming didn't last.

Yet it was what she thought she'd seen in Joey. Since their first conversation, he'd seemed friendly, truly concerned. Like he was on her side.

Maybe he treated everyone that way, and she'd read too much into it. That hurt even more, because he acted like he genuinely cared. Even in the pain and anger over the secret of his drug use, she'd counted on him caring.

She remembered how he held her Saturday night, and his anger telling Paul to come home. His anguish on their picnic when he tried to tell her about his past. Her heart whispered that she mattered to him.

Carol silenced the radio and rolled onto her back. A sliver of streetlight angled across the wall from where she hadn't fully overlapped the curtains.

It made no difference how Joey felt about her. No matter how pure his motives, she couldn't trust him to stay within the framework she'd erected for her and Paul's lives.

Not that Paul respected the boundary either. She couldn't blame Joey for her son's defection.

As she lay on her back, tears leaked from the outside corners of her eyes and down both sides of her head to her pillow. One trickled into her ear. She dried it with her sleeve and curled onto her side.

The silence oppressed, but music wouldn't help now, nor chocolate. The memory of Paul's eyes haunted her, pleading for understanding.

He needed to play.

She couldn't fight a longing that strong without crippling her son. Or losing him.

Who knew what kind of red tape Garraway had to cut through to reclaim Harry's money? If the drug lord grew impatient, would Paul lose *her*?

Dread slithered into bed with her.

Trembling, Carol drew her knees to her chest. She'd always coped with life by controlling it. Now, everything was spinning out of her grasp.

God, I don't know what to do. I can't keep my son safe, or myself. I'm scared to trust You. Help me.

Had she just *prayed*?

She curled even tighter into a ball. As if God might have heard and be looking in her direction.

Logic said it wasn't her prayers that failed Keith. God wasn't blaming her for her son's death. Or her mother's. Or Skip's, or their unborn baby girl.

Joey had pleaded with her to trust God's heart—said that God had the best plan anyway. Instead of trusting Him, she'd managed her own life. Done it her way without even asking for His input.

And God didn't push like she did with Paul.

Her throat tightened until each breath was fire. Doing life her way brought them here—to an obstacle course she could never navigate alone. Speeding out of control with no brakes.

Tonight's accident replayed in her mind. The helplessness, the certainty of impact. She'd heard a song on the radio once, "Jesus, Take the Wheel." Heard it and made a cynical joke.

Could it be that simple?

Her mother had clung to faith, claiming it helped her endure their abusive home. Joey had claimed God could pick up the pieces if Carol broke.

A different type of fear threw her heart into overdrive. What if she got it wrong—or it wasn't enough?

Forcing trembling lips to shape the words, she whispered, "God, I'm sorry for trying to run my life. Help me trust You like Joey does, like Mom did. Even if things get worse. I don't care what You do with me, but please protect Paul and grow him into a good man. An innocent man like in Joey's song. And bless Joey for being such a good friend. I'm sorry I lost him."

Chapter 33

SHOULD SHE CALL Joey?

Driving home after work the next day, Carol still didn't know. The question had tugged at her thoughts all through her shift, and she'd had trouble focusing on her duties.

Last night, she'd killed their friendship. She didn't want him to remember her rudeness as their final contact, though. And he'd be happy to learn she was on track with God.

She waited for a pedestrian in the crosswalk, then turned onto her street. If she did call, would he hear apology or appeasement? What if he thought it was just a new step in their strange dance?

Her prayer had come from a longing for control in her world—if not hers, then God's. She hadn't done it to please Joey, but she couldn't deny wishing for another chance with him.

Those thoughts aside, she had a bigger problem. Letting go of the control she'd never had meant releasing Paul to make his own decisions.

She pulled into her driveway and shut off the engine.

Paul had been doing his own thing anyway. Would God keep him on track? Or simply pick up the pieces afterwards?

Resting her forehead against the steering wheel, she tried to exhale some of her tension. *All I want is a guarantee my son won't end up like his father!*

Before she reached the apartment door, her landlady bustled down the stairs. "What did the insurance people say?"

"I have an appraisal tomorrow before work." Good thing the car was driveable in the meantime.

Cecilia and Basil had both come down that morning to inspect the damage and get the story. "Crazy drivers! You could have been killed."

The older woman didn't know about the drug dealers. It could still happen.

That thought solved Carol's dithering. Peace with God meant accepting that she and Paul were in His care whether she lived or died. She wanted peace with Joey too. Just in case.

She escaped her landlady's mothering and unlocked the apartment.

Chance squeezed past her to greet Cecilia.

By the time Carol called him inside, the dog's dish held a mound of food. A plate of leftover macaroni casserole spun in the microwave. Hunger made a good excuse not to resume the conversation with her landlady.

Halfway through her meal, she paused for a hasty prayer of thanks. "Sorry, God, I'll get this."

Her mother had found strength in her faith and from Christian friends. She'd needed it.

Carol speared some pasta with her fork. She'd liked the informality of Joey's church, but her presence might make him uncomfortable. Maybe she'd ask Paul about Tara-Lynn's.

Joey. Should she call him at home or wait until he got to the station? Home felt more personal, and they could talk longer if he wanted.

As she washed the dishes, her landline rang.

Garraway's cell. "Ms. Daniels, I'd like to drop by if you're free. Say in fifteen minutes?"

Hope seared her veins. Had the bank released the deposit? "I'll be waiting."

He arrived bearing a thick brown envelope.

Manic butterflies filled Carol's stomach. The money! She'd waited for this, wanted it to be over, but now she had to get through the exchange.

"I can have my life back!" She couldn't stop the tremor in her voice.

"That's our hope. No more contact since yesterday?"

"No." Arms crossed, she stared at the bulky envelope he laid on the table.

So much money—from drugs. From Harry. "I don't think I'll be able to rest until this is done. What if some random burglar breaks in and thinks he's hit the jackpot? Or if there's a fire?"

Garraway shrugged. "Worst-case scenarios rarely happen. I'd stick it back in that hidden desk drawer if I were you, to minimize the risk."

"When they contact me, what do I do?"

"Exactly what they say." He pulled a phone from his pocket. "My cell is programmed into this. So is dispatch. Keep it on your person."

"What—"

"Ms. Daniels, the minute you receive instructions about the drop, use this phone to contact us. We'll track your movements through its GPS. Our officers will be present even though you won't see them. Their job is to observe and gather evidence, but they will break cover to protect you if necessary."

"Thank you."

Chance padded into the kitchen. He circled Garraway once on the way to his food bowl.

"I guess he knows you're one of the good guys. Detective, why are you giving Creepy Voice the money?" Her words whispered like dry leaves in the wind.

"Rope to hang themselves. Our evidence is almost complete, and with luck we'll recover a portion of the cash. Not that I'll see a new office chair or anything."

"Was it the truth when you said you wouldn't mark it? Or what about a tracking device in the envelope?"

"Too risky. This is a sophisticated group. Any sign of interference and they'll disappear before we get them. We recorded the serial numbers so we can identify what remains in their possession when we bust them."

The detective tapped the screen on the new phone. "Let me show you how to access speed dial."

When he'd gone, Carol stared at the device. Would she remember what to do?

Remember—she'd been about to contact Joey when Garraway called.

She grabbed the kitchen phone and pressed Joey's number. Three rings took her to his voice mail. She hung up. Leaving a recorded apology felt like the coward's way.

Paul was working tonight, and she'd offered to pick him up. About quarter to nine, she grabbed her purse and keys and headed out. She might not like her son's choice of employment, but knowing was better than the wall of secrecy.

He wanted her to meet his boss, but Mr. Morelli wouldn't be there tonight. Maybe she'd get in on Saturday.

She found the store without trouble and collected Paul.

Now that her son didn't have to keep his music secret, his love of playing, of parts of his job, flowed out. She listened, letting him rebuild the bridge her guitar hostility had severed.

He sounded balanced, grounded. Completely different from Skip's all-about-me take on music. And he talked all the way home.

She kept her concern for his future to herself.

After Paul took a cup of hot chocolate to his room to finish studying, she realized she hadn't told him about her faith decision.

Her lips tightened. He didn't seem to have a problem with Tara-Lynn's Christianity, but his mother might get a different reaction.

For now, she needed to apologize to Joey. It took the first half hour of his show to work up her nerve.

Five tries to get through tonight. Tuesdays weren't usually this bad.

When Joey answered, his friendly greeting caught the words in her throat.

"It's Carol. Don't hang up, I called to say I'm sorry about last night." She twisted the phone cord around her index finger. "Do you have a song that says 'I was stupid, you were right, and please forgive me?'"

His soft laugh let her relax. "One or two. I'm sorry too. You're under a lot of stress, and I shouldn't have lost my patience. I didn't think you'd answer if I phoned, so I came by this evening to apologize in person. I saw another car parked behind yours and figured you had company."

A wistful undercurrent in his tone made Carol rush to explain. "It was the detective dropping off Harry's money. As soon as I get instructions, I can get rid of it and be free."

"That's fantastic."

"And I've found someone else to lean on, so I won't have to unload on you so much."

"I didn't mean it that way."

"You were right, we should be able to have a normal chat. So, could you play me a song? Your choice."

"How about the show?"

Good, he'd picked up her reference to last night's conversation. "If you let me cook dinner for you first."

"Now, you're talking."

"I'll take that as a yes." She licked her lips, nerves singing again. "I want to tell you something."

"Carol, is Saturday a date or goodbye?" The intensity in his voice shook her.

"What?"

"Are you letting me into your life, or is it a way to say thanks and so long?"

"Saturday is... whatever we make it." A warm glow lit her heart.

"Okay, allow me to introduce myself. My name is Joey, and I'm an idiot. Good thing you can't see me blushing. I guess saying you found someone else sounds like goodbye, even for friends. What did you want to tell me?"

"Um... someone else... What you said about God. I'm going to learn to let Him be in charge."

Joey gave a low whistle. "Now, that I can live with."

Chapter 34

"HEY." PAUL KEPT his voice gentle as he slid into the empty seat beside Tara-Lynn in the library.

She glanced up from her textbook. Her smile looked fake. "Hey, yourself."

"Are you doing okay?"

Her eyes could have drilled steel. "You couldn't ask me Monday, when they were throwing all that garbage?"

"I—"

"You were too busy defending yourself to care how Amber or I felt."

"That's not—" Paul remembered where they were and lowered his voice. "That's what made me so mad. I don't care what they say about me. I was steamed for your sake."

"Thanks for the support." Her focus never left her book.

"Tara-Lynn, please. Okay, I was embarrassed and angry, and maybe I was afraid talking to you would fuel the rumours. You seemed like you were handling it okay."

"You couldn't even call us after school to be sure?"

"I..." Sure, he'd been busy, but he could have phoned. "The best I can do is ask now. And tell you I'm sorry."

Tara-Lynn turned a page in her book, and he waited while she read. Or pretended to read. Finally, she looked up, tears on her lashes.

"Amber's blaming herself. If she'd stayed away Saturday night, this wouldn't have happened."

"It's not her fault these losers have mouths. She still wants to get off drugs though, right? Sunday, I thought the embarrassment would make her fight harder to get free."

"That's what she says. You could join us. Show the gossip crowd they can't intimidate us. I—we miss you."

"I've missed you too. Math homework isn't the same."

"Homework! If that's all that matters to you, forget it!" She slapped the book shut and grabbed her belongings before he realized what was happening.

Her chin quivered, and the tears in her eyes made something die inside him.

He reached out a hand, but she ignored it.

"You want to be a lone wolf musician? Enjoy being alone." She stalked out of the library.

Paul gaped after her. "It was supposed to be a joke."

Lone wolf musician... enjoy being alone. Barry was right, she'd heard about his no-girlfriend rant. And the tears said it hurt.

He could go after her, but then what? He needed music like he needed air. If that meant staying single, so be it.

If only he could convince his heart.

~~~

Patrick held the door to Roy Thomson Hall for Carol, then stepped through behind her. For once, traffic had cooperated. He detested being late, but with her not leaving work until seven it had seemed inevitable.

A respectable number of patrons milled about the lobby, although most would already be seated. Patrick guided his guest through the crowd and handed their tickets to a smiling attendant.

Steeped in elegant music, the auditorium pulled him into its comforting embrace. He led Carol to their aisle. As they settled into their seats, he watched her admire the surroundings.

She leaned closer. "Pretty full house. I'm amazed you got such good seats."

"Season tickets. Rita loved the symphony."

Carol's lips worked as if to find words, or perhaps to hold them back.

He offered a tight smile. "I'm in her seat. Forgive me, but it's one of the few points of contact I have."

Her nod said she understood. And pitied him.

Rita had been the love of his life, his raison d'être. He'd walked empty since the cancer defeated them.

The orchestra took position on the stage.

Patrick sat straighter. Had he made a mistake inviting Carol? Impulsive actions ran contrary to his nature, yet once the words were out he'd been unable to retract them.

She makes a pleasant companion, Rita. Are you angry?

The music began with a swell that unleashed a chill of pleasure through his senses. He glanced at Carol to see if she felt it too.

She gazed at the stage, lips parted in a smile.

He relaxed into his seat, closed his eyes, and let the music carry him.

Tonight, the program offered mostly show tunes. Not his favourite, but pleasant and well executed. As always, he was startled by how quickly the intermission arrived. When the house lights came up, he turned to his companion. "What do you think?"

"I love it. Thank you for inviting me."

He felt no unease from Rita. "Can I buy you a drink?"

In the lobby, chilled water bottles in hand, they strolled among the other patrons. Patrick recognized many as long-time concert-goers. He knew few by name. Networking came with his job, but not here. This was his haven.

He hoped his companion didn't notice the speculative glances that came their way. He was about to suggest they return to their seats when a hand clapped his shoulder from behind.

"Patrick Stairs, you old dog. Decided to rejoin the human race and bring a lady friend, did you?"

He turned to meet the bleary eyes of one of his clients. The older man leaned nearer, wine-warmed breath enveloping Patrick like an invisible fog.

Composing his features into a smile, Patrick resisted the urge to step away. "Ellis Richards, meet Carol Daniels. Ms. Daniels is a lady, and she is my friend, but we should leave it at that."

Richards dropped one eyelid in a slow wink. "Mustn't be premature. You understand rumours, in your business." He gave Carol a careful once-over, which she seemed to ignore. "Pleased to meet you, my dear. If this whippersnapper gives you any trouble, come see me."

Patrick took Carol's elbow. "We need to return to our seats. Enjoy the rest of the concert."

He spoke low in her ear as they walked. "The man is a client. I couldn't risk losing him. I apologize for his words."

She looked up at him. At this distance, her eyes were startlingly liquid. "He was less subtle than the rest, but people love to play matchmaker. We came as friends, and I won't read more into it than that. I know you're in love with your wife."

Something was wrong with Patrick's breathing. He wrenched his gaze from hers, catching the soft concern before he anchored his focus on the door ahead. "You're exceptionally understanding."

He ushered her into the auditorium and they found their seats, but his breathing didn't settle until the music resumed.

The symphony's performance earned a standing ovation.

Carol had tears in her eyes. "Thank you for bringing me. That last part felt like a prayer."

He hadn't thought her a religious person, although many people had a spiritual side. Had she been influenced by the story Hill spun at his church that night? As if a person could walk away from being in that deep and get close to God.

Closer to God meant farther from Patrick. The crowd was thick tonight. He took her hand so they wouldn't get separated.

In the car, he played an orchestral CD to sustain the evening's effect.

Carol leaned against the headrest and closed her eyes. "That was amazing, but I'm bushed. I didn't sleep much last night."

Patrick spared a glance from the road. "Silver's money?"

"I finally got it, and now I have to wait for them to call again. I want my life back."

His fingers tightened on the wheel. *Don't we all?* "Would you like me to hold it for you? My home has a wall safe and a high-end security system."

"And an attack cat." Carol hesitated. "I appreciate it, Patrick, but I need to have the money ready when they call. You haven't heard this man. He's frightening."

"All the more reason to allow me to be your go-between. My offer stands. At least consider it when he calls."

"Maybe. Thanks."

Maybe meant "no."

Patrick needed an antacid. She couldn't suspect him. Nevertheless, her stubborn independence would prevent him scoring points with Lear and keep him tied to the drug lord.

At the very least, he could be the one to alert Lear to the money's availability. Once the cash was out of her hands, she should be free from danger.

When they reached her apartment, a light burned in one of the front rooms and another in the kitchen. Patrick parked and escorted her to the door.

She held her coat tightly and shivered in the night air.

He rested a hand on her shoulder. "Thank you for coming out this evening. I hope we can do this again."

"Thanks for inviting me." She smiled, then unlocked the door and ducked inside.

One thought pierced the numbness in Patrick's mind. In that moment when their eyes met, he'd been going to kiss her.

He practically ran to his car. It took all his control not to squeal the tires as he drove away.

Later, in the quiet of his home, he poured a glass of red wine and carried it to the rocking chair. *Rita, I know you told me to move on, but I don't know if I'm ready. Help me, please.*

It was after midnight when he went to bed. As he drifted into sleep, he realized this was the first symphony night he hadn't needed to phone the agency. A few of their employees resembled his wife, as long as he removed his contact lenses and dimmed the lights. They didn't mind starting out in one of Rita's negligees, and they were always gone before his alarm sounded in the morning.

Perhaps he was moving on. A tear slid onto his pillow.

Chapter 35

CAROL SLID A pan of brownies from the apartment oven Thursday morning and inhaled the rich chocolate steam. Eleven to seven wasn't the greatest shift in the world, but at least when she came home the chores were done. Tonight, supper would be waiting too. Meatball stew, and brownies with ice cream.

Another half hour before she had to leave for work. She changed into her café uniform and settled on the couch with a recipe magazine.

The phone rang. Adrenaline pumped, like always. It was probably a telemarketer. But surely the drug dealer would call soon. *Please, God, I want this over. With Paul and me safe.* Did she need to spell it out like that? Better safe than sorry.

She dashed into the kitchen and checked the caller ID. Another unidentified local number. This could be it. What did the guy do, steal cellphones in bulk?

"Hello?" Could he hear the tremble in her voice?

"Ms. Daniels. You have a package for me."

"Yes." The word came out as a squeak. She cleared her throat and tried again. "Yes."

"Answer your front door in one minute, and hand out the package. Don't try to ID my messenger." Click.

One minute, and here she stood, staring at the phone.

She slammed it into its cradle and bolted for Paul's room. Her fingers fumbled with the catch for the hidden drawer. At last, she yanked it open and grabbed the envelope.

The doorbell rang.

She cracked her head on the desk. Shaking off the pain, she bolted for the front door, clutching the envelope.

The silhouette through the frosted glass loomed like a giant. His raised his arm. Pounded a series of thundering knocks.

Her heartbeat hammered in her ears. She forced herself to unlock the deadbolt and turn the knob. This had to end. Now.

Security chain in place, she cracked the door open and stuck the envelope through the gap.

Rough hands snatched it from her fingers.

Throwing her weight against the door, she clicked the deadbolt home, then sprinted for the front window. Was he leaving?

A hairy pink gorilla opened the driver's door of a grey Volkswagen, squeezed in, and sped away.

Carol sagged against the wall. A giddy mix of tears and laughter bubbled over.

When she caught her breath, she rooted Garraway's loaner phone from her purse and selected his cell number from the menu.

"Garraway."

"Detective, it's over. Sorry, this is Carol Daniels. They picked up the money. I only had a minute's notice so I couldn't call you. But it's gone. I'm free!" More giggles erupted. She pressed her lips together.

"Did you get a look at them?"

"It was a guy in a gorilla suit. Pink. With a 'Granny's Singing Telegrams' sign on his back." She couldn't keep the lilt of laughter from her voice. "He drove the same grey Volkswagen I told you about. Did your patrols ever get a plate number from it?"

"We've got that angle nailed, and we'll check out the telegram company. Sign's likely a fake. Best you can't identify the guy anyway, from your point of view. Too bad. I'd have liked another witness. Well, Ms. Daniels, keep vigilant, but you should be clear now. I'll be in touch to collect the phone. Have a good day at work."

"Thanks, Detective. You too."

Work! Carol gasped and checked her watch. Two minutes later, she pulled the insurance company's rental car out of her driveway and joined the traffic flow. With luck, she'd make it on time.

~~~

Carol woke in the middle of the night, sweating and tangled in the bed sheet. Her breath rasped in the darkness. The only other sound came from Chance snoring on the floor. A fine comforter he was tonight.

"I can't take this. What do I have to do for a decent night's rest?" She swung her feet to the floor and turned on the bedside lamp. The nightmare faded, but so had sleep.

The dog's feet twitched, and another snore shook his ribs.

In slippers and her robe, she wandered into the kitchen. She turned on the radio, remembering the loud rap station and the horror of a violated home. And Chance's brush with death.

Waiting for the water to boil, she cut a big piece of brownie and heated it in the microwave. Warm chocolate with ice cream could at least reduce the nightmare's effects.

Joey's show made good background music, and she enjoyed his casual chatter between sets. Snack finished, she rinsed her plate and left it in the sink before shutting off the radio. At least tonight she hadn't needed to load him with another high-maintenance call.

Chance didn't stir when she entered the bedroom.

Tired as she was, his snores didn't keep her awake.

She'd been asleep less than an hour when the second nightmare hit. She woke in a panic, heart pounding, eyes wide and filled with the afterimage of flames devouring her son.

Sobbing, she rolled to bury her face in her pillow. "God, can't You stop this?"

She fumbled for her robe and made a beeline for the kitchen phone. For once, her call went through first try. "Joey, it's me, Carol."

"Hey there. I'd given up on hearing from you tonight. Hope your being awake doesn't mean another nightmare."

Pain constricted her throat. "Why doesn't trusting God take them away?"

"I don't know. They've been going on awhile, like a habit for you or a pattern. Maybe it's something your mind has to unlearn."

"I can't go on like this."

"Let me introduce you to my pastor. He'll connect you with one of the women at church who'll know how to help."

The ridges of the phone cord dug into her fist. "What do I do now? Tonight."

Joey's exhale chased along the phone line. "I wish I had an easy answer. Faith isn't just about God getting us out of trouble. It's about knowing His presence with us in the middle of it. Even if your worst nightmare comes true, He'll be with you to bring you out the other side."

Goosebumps washed Carol's arms. "Don't talk about them coming true!"

"They won't, they won't. What I mean is, no matter what, God is there. Nothing can scare Him away. I need to set up the next songs. Can you wait for me?"

She leaned her head against the kitchen cabinet, remembering his arms around her the night Paul was missing. The echo left her feeling more alone than ever.

When the next song started, Joey came back on the phone. "Okay. Fear was never one of my issues, but the same principles apply. I'm sorry I don't know more, and I'm sorry we have to do this over the phone."

"Do what?"

"We're going to pray, and it might sound kind of weird. Can you trust me?"

"Yes." The realization both thrilled and scared her.

"That means a lot. You can trust God too. As I pray, you agree in your mind." He paused. "Here goes. Father, You are holy and all-powerful, and You love us more than we can know. Thank You for drawing Carol—and me—to trust You."

His voice broke. Steadied. "Because of Jesus, we are free. Carol is free. Free to be Your daughter and learn to love You."

Carol stood with her eyes closed and head bowed, phone pressed to her ear. The love for God in Joey's tone warmed her, but how could this help?

"In the name of Jesus, by His authority because of the Cross, we declare that Carol's mind belongs to God. Evil influences and thought patterns, we banish you in Jesus' name."

Her eyes flew open. Evil? But it sure wasn't God.

"Now, will you say this part after me?"

"Um... okay." She wet her lips with her tongue. *Don't let Paul walk out into the middle of this.* Good thing he was a sound sleeper.

"Good. God, I surrender my heart, mind, soul, and body to You."

She repeated the sentence in a whisper.

"I invite You to take full control."

The words stumbled, but she pushed them out.

"I'm sorry for allowing fear to take hold in my mind."

"I didn't do it on purpose!"

"I know you didn't, but it happened. Let's get rid of it."

Pacing the length of the phone cord, she continued. "God, I'm sorry I let fear get hold of my mind."

"In the name of Jesus, I ask You to remove the fear and replace it with trust in You."

She had no trouble saying that. Her heart ached for the prayer to come true.

"Amen. You did great. Here's the tricky part. Since fear is a behaviour pattern for you, your mind will go back to it. Like a path worn in the grass. It takes time for the grass to re-grow while you wear a new path."

A heaviness settled in her stomach. "So I'll have more nightmares?"

"Whenever you catch the fear response starting, or if you have another nightmare, remember you don't have to surrender. Say it out loud. Things like, 'Jesus is my shepherd. I don't have to be afraid.' Believe it's true even if you don't feel it, and change will come. It worked for me."

"You said fear wasn't your issue."

"Mine was depression. It was a long fight, and I still have to be on guard. You can do this. God is on your side. And so am I."

Tears blurred her sight. "Thank you."

"I need to get back to work. Father, please guard Carol's dreams tonight and give her rest. Good night, my friend. I'll play you a song in a bit."

Chapter 36

PAUL SPREAD PEANUT butter on two pieces of toast while his mother finished making his lunch. Most of his buddies bagged their own lunches, except Barry, who always bought his.

There were definite pluses to having a parent who said "I love you" by what she did for him.

His mom put his lunch bag beside his backpack at the kitchen door and carried her tea to the table. When she sat facing him, the circles under her eyes made him frown.

"Mom, are you feeling okay?"

"I'm okay. I had a rough night, that's all."

Worrying about him? He chewed a bite of toast to keep from scowling. This was why he hadn't wanted to tell her about the band. Her fears wouldn't keep him from playing, but they could add a load of guilt.

A pale smile lifted her lips. "I want to tell you—I made a decision earlier this week."

He braced for it.

"You think I worry too much. Try too hard to control things. I'm taking Joey's advice and letting God lead."

Paul blinked. This couldn't be the next round in their music battle, unless she thought God agreed with her.

Her breath came out in a nervous laugh. "It's a little scary, and it's going to take some getting used to, but I think it'll help."

No lecture? No warnings about flirting with danger? He tried to wrap his brain around what she'd said. "Hey, that's great. I've been thinking about this faith stuff too. And if God really is in control, that should make it easier for you not to... worry." He'd almost repeated *control*.

"Joey said people at his church can help. And maybe I can go with you and Tara-Lynn someday."

"Maybe." Tara-Lynn wouldn't invite him to church—or anywhere—after the way she'd stormed out on him at the library. His heart twisted. He'd deserved it.

Mom's brows pinched. "Trouble?"

"Just life. It'll work out. Joey's a good guy. Are you two an item now?"

A hint of colour came into her cheeks. "We're friends."

"If it grows, I'm cool with that. Just saying. Gotta go."

He crammed the remaining toast into his mouth, gave her a one-armed hug, and headed for the door.

"Slick diversion."

"Mmfh?" Chewing, he put on his running shoes.

"Tara-Lynn."

Paul turned to stare as he shrugged into his jacket.

Mom came to stand by the door. "You were right. Your father didn't choose music over family, he chose himself. Maybe you can make music and still commit to a relationship. If you want them both."

"I don't—"

"Besides, high school sweethearts are a long way from married with kids."

He shook his head, grinning, then planted a kiss on her cheek before picking up his backpack. When she talked about

Dad, which wasn't often, she didn't dwell on the negatives. What she'd said now about a selfish choice matched Donnie Leyland's words at the store.

As he ran for the bus, his thoughts kept pace.

He saw Tara-Lynn in the hallway before class, chatting with her friends. She wouldn't look his way. If she wanted it like that, fine.

Walking away, it felt like part of him stayed behind.

What if he could have it both ways? He reached his locker, stowed his jacket and backpack, and gathered his books for English. If he couldn't keep up with a girlfriend, he'd know not to hope for a family.

The thought tied a knot in his stomach. What if he ended up single for life?

For now, he missed Tara-Lynn. Better take a shot. At least find out how she felt about him. He dodged through the knots of students, but she'd gone.

She wasn't in math class, and he couldn't find her at lunch. The longer he prowled the corridors, the fainter his nerve grew.

He spotted Amber walking out of a washroom and ducked into a side corridor. "This is crazy." It took all his willpower to step into the open and catch up to her.

"Hi, Amber."

She skewered him with a don't-waste-my-time look, but she didn't turn away.

"I messed up on Monday. I was too angry to think straight. I'm sorry."

Her eyes narrowed.

Heat crept up his neck. "Things have quieted down. Are you okay?"

A bit more silent treatment, then she shrugged. "I'll be fine. So will Tara-Lynn, no thanks to you."

"Hey, I didn't start the rumours."

Amber let out an explosive sigh that ruffled her bangs. "Forget the rumours. Think about announcing to the whole school how little we meant to you. Fine way to be a friend, Paul."

"I said I'm sorry. I was angry, and all I could think was how upset you two were, and would you think I was the sort of jerk to actually spread stuff like that..."

"Never been a gossip tidbit before, huh?"

Duh. His uncle's arrest, his brother's death. Yeah, he'd kept the gossips in business for months. Then this one broadsided him, and he forgot all he'd learned about keeping his mouth shut.

He offered a sheepish smile. "Guess I knew better. I just blew it. You were starting to get off drugs, and Tara-Lynn..."

"Paul, she's a good girl. She doesn't deserve to be hurt by you or any other self-absorbed idiot. She thought you were different. I did too."

A few students wandered in the hallway, but none paid them any attention. He stepped closer. "I tried to talk to her, and she walked out. I haven't seen her since this morning."

Amber studied him. "She said she had a doctor's appointment today. Come to the pizza and bowling party at her church tonight and try again. If you do care, do something about it."

"I have band practice, and—"

Her glare gutted his excuse. "She's better off without you."

She whirled away.

Paul ran to catch up. "Look, this is new to me. I've never asked a girl out before."

When she slowed to let him walk beside her, he said, "Honestly, I do have practice. And she might not want to talk to me, especially in a group. Maybe I can phone her, or send her flowers, or something."

Amber held his gaze for a long moment. "You were really good to me Saturday night, and that means a lot. But if you mess her around, I know people who can hurt you."

Chapter 37

THE BUZZ SOUNDED three times before Patrick realized what it was. He clawed out of a dream of giant mosquitoes and swatted at his night table.

A fresh vibration slid the cellphone even nearer the edge. He grabbed it and thumbed the button. "Yes?"

"Bring her in."

"What?" He sat up in bed. "Carol? You have the money."

"It's time to send a message to Silver. If he talks, things will get hot."

Patrick's sleep-gummed eyes discerned faint grey around the bedroom curtains. Dread coalesced in his chest. "You planned this from the start."

"I always knew you were smart."

So how did I fall for this one? "What do you want with her?"

"There's her and the kid. I can make a point with one and still have the other for leverage."

Patrick's teeth ached with restraining the words boiling in his heart. "She says they're not in touch. That he doesn't care what happens to her."

"Then he wouldn't have told her about the money. Unless she already knew and played you for a fool."

Fisting his bedsheets, he fought to keep his voice steady. "Proper damage control would be to eliminate him."

"There's the small matter of his being in segregated custody. Don't worry, I'm working on it."

"Then leave her alone and send him another threat. You know he's unstable. If you hurt her or her son, he might risk the other one to take revenge."

"It's unprofessional to get emotionally involved, bright boy. Forget I called. But remember, if he talks, you go down too." Lear clicked off.

~~~

Paul hung his jacket in the break room at the store before pouring himself a paper cone of water from the cooler.

Mr. Morelli poked his head in the door. "Good morning, Paul. I've been meaning to ask, are you successfully rid of what I kept for you?"

"Actually, yeah. That's all settled. Thanks again."

"I'm glad to hear it. See you out front shortly."

Paul drained the cup and sailed it into the bin. With the money gone and the drug dealers off their case, and not having to keep the band or his job secret, he was on easy street. Mom even drove him to work this morning on her way for groceries, so he'd been able to sleep in an extra half hour.

The pressure wasn't off, though. Just different. He had to talk to Tara-Lynn. Phoning her was risky, but waiting until Monday to see her at school would be worse. He'd call after work.

If she agreed, they could go for pizza. And talk. Joey was coming for dinner. Mom said it wasn't a date, but Paul figured she wouldn't mind if he skipped out.

He stepped into the storefront as Mr. Morelli unlocked the door and flipped the window sign to "open."

Light rain kept the customer traffic down, but students streamed through for their lessons.

Paul returned from his afternoon break to see Tara-Lynn giving a book to his coworker at the cash register.

Eric smirked at the cover before he stuck the book under the counter. He winked at Paul. "This is for Jubal when he comes in."

Tara-Lynn avoided Paul's eyes. "He asked me to bring it for his girlfriend. I don't think he reads romance, Eric. Thanks." She turned to go.

Paul dashed to intercept her. "Can we talk?"

She kept walking. "I thought this was your Saturday off."

"I traded. Please, I was going to phone, but I need to say this in person. I'm sorry I've been such a selfish jerk."

"Have you?" Tara-Lynn stepped toward the exit.

They were alone in this part of the store, but Paul lowered his voice. "I abandoned you and Amber after the gossip started."

"You said you thought it would protect us from more rumours."

His cheeks warmed. "Tara-Lynn, I really like being with you. Monday, I was yelling at everyone because I realized we could have been more than friends—not what they said, but you know—"

He glanced wildly around at the instruments. "I couldn't face being pulled in two directions. I can't lose the music, but maybe I've lost it anyway. It feels hollow now."

The phone rang. Eric answered, but he'd been waiting on a customer.

Paul gulped air. "I'm making a mess of this, and I need to help Eric. Will you answer your phone if I call later?"

She shrugged. "Maybe. It's still all about you, Paul. What you want, what you don't want. I have feelings too." She flounced out the door.

~~~

Humming along with a Burton Cummings tune on the radio, Carol slid the last cookies off the baking sheet to a cooling rack. A big pot of hamburger stroganoff simmered on the stove. If Joey showed up early, she'd rather be hostess than cook.

One minute she wanted to dance, the next she worried about burning supper. Tonight meant something to Joey. She'd heard it in his voice. But what did he hope for? What did she?

She washed the baking sheet and drained the sink. As she finished tidying the kitchen, the phone rang.

How long until she stopped jumping at every call? The drug ring had their money. They wouldn't bother her now— unless they found out Harry talked. She could reclaim her life.

Should she pray for Harry? If so, how? Maybe she'd ask Joey.

Caller ID showed an unfamiliar number. It couldn't be. But her heart pounded in her throat as she answered. "Hello?"

"It's Patrick."

His voice sent a river of relief through her. "Your number used to show your name. I almost didn't answer."

"My cell was stolen. This is a loaner. Can you come see me?"

"How about tomorrow afternoon?"

"Tomorrow will be too late. I need to see you in person. It won't take long. Please."

She glanced at the clock. Three fifteen. Joey was coming at six. "Okay, but I can't stay. I have company coming for supper."

"I'll send a taxi." Patrick hung up before she could insist on driving herself.

She stirred the stroganoff and shut off the burner. Good thing she'd prepared it early.

After hanging up her apron, she hurried to the bathroom to check for flour smudges and apply some lipstick. Who knew how much time she'd have when she came home?

A taxi could be half an hour, but Patrick must tip well. They seemed to come faster for him. Carol jotted a note to tell Paul where she'd gone, in case he came in before she did.

Gravel crunched in the driveway, and a horn honked. She pulled her jacket from the pegs by the door, put on her glasses, and grabbed her purse.

She'd barely fastened her seat belt when the taxi reversed onto the street. Patrick must have told him to hurry. What could be so urgent?

Someone took his cell. In a public place? Or a home invasion, and he'd been injured? But he had an alarm system. And a homicidal cat.

I hope he hasn't had bad health news, not after his wife. But he'd said tomorrow was too late. Nobody got that short a warning. Maybe he'd been called away on business or something.

She'd been too occupied with her thoughts to pay attention to where they were going. A glance out the window showed warehouses on both sides of the street. She leaned ahead to tap on the glass. "This isn't the right way." So much for hurrying.

The driver didn't spare her a look. "Detour."

At the next warehouse, he cut a hard left and drove inside the building.

She spun to see hangar-style doors clatter shut to cut off the light.

"What's going on?" She fumbled with her seat belt and clutched her purse. Before she could bolt, both rear car doors opened. The dome light revealed shadowy figures blocking her escape.

God, help me! Patrick knew she was coming. How long before he phoned the cab company to check on her?

The man at the nearest door beckoned. "Move it. He doesn't like to be kept waiting."

A chill walked down Carol's spine. This was no random abduction.

The drug dealer.

She couldn't move. Couldn't breathe.

A gloved hand pulled her from the car. The man's face brought a scream to her lips, but then her brain kicked in. Blurred features meant a stocking mask. His partner, dimly visible on the other side of the car, must be similarly disguised. The cabbie's long hair and ball cap would keep him from being identified.

Precautions like this suggested they weren't going to kill her. That still left a lot of leeway. She faced the nearer man. "But he has the money."

He jerked his head toward the far wall and started walking.

Carol followed.

The other man fell into step beside her.

She licked paper-dry lips. Her gaze darted in all directions, but where could she run?

A line of light appeared ahead and widened into a doorway. Stocking Mask One stood aside to let Carol and his partner go through, then entered and closed the door behind them.

The cavernous space outside made this one seem small. Bright lights cast sharp shadows from the sole furnishings— two wooden chairs side by side in the middle of the floor. Stacks of boxes lined one wall. Another windowless door must lead deeper into the building's heart.

Stocking Mask One pulled Carol toward the chairs. "Have a seat." His grip felt like barely-sheathed claws.

She perched on the edge of the nearer seat.

Rough hands jerked her shoulders against the chairback, slung a rope across her ribs, and pulled it tight.

She ground her teeth to keep from screaming. Or crying.

The guards positioned each arm, palm up, on the wooden armrests, and tied her wrists and ankles.

Her hands curled into fists, and she strained at the ropes until her breath came in gasps.

Footsteps rapped the concrete floor. A heavyset man strode toward Carol from the other doorway.

The combination of stocking mask and well-cut business suit made her want to giggle. She bit the inside of her lip.

He stopped in front of her, feet apart and arms folded. Watching.

She pressed her lips together. Let him intimidate all he wanted. He had to speak first. What if she said the wrong thing and made this worse?

The man paced a slow circle around her, then resumed his scrutiny. Finally, he spoke. "A pleasure to meet you, Ms. Daniels. Thank you for dropping in. You'll excuse the masks, but they're for your protection. You may address me as Lear."

He motioned to one of the guards, who hurried into the hangar where they'd left the car. "I must apologize for my ex-employee in Calgary."

Carol stared at him.

"Ah, perhaps you didn't know he was mine. The unpleasant letter threatening your son?"

You and your son are easy targets. Especially the boy. As if she could forget. "I thought—" She shut her mouth. This man didn't care what she thought.

Lear's shoulders lifted. "You can imagine my fury. I had surveillance in place, and an overzealous cretin ruined it by scaring you away. You have no idea the trouble I went through to track you down after that." He spread his arms. "Then I find you on my doorstep, so to speak. How convenient."

He circled her again, then stood staring down at her. "Ms. Daniels, you may have guessed this meeting has do with your brother."

Shivers chased over Carol's skin. "You have the money. All of it. If something's missing, ask your gorilla—um—the guy who picked it up."

"Oh, I assure you, it's all present and counted. I've asked you and your son—he should be here any moment—here today to dispel a rather unsettling rumour that your brother may not have been as circumspect as he should have about our business affairs."

Son?

Fighting through the fear, she tried to process the man's full meaning. They thought Harry had let something slip. They didn't know he'd deliberately given evidence. *Don't let them hear it from me, God. Let them get what's coming.*

She stared at the masked face. "My son isn't involved. I'm not involved. You had to threaten me to make me even talk to him about the money. I don't know what else he's doing."

Lear shrugged. "A pity you were pulled into this. But we need to send Silver a clear message."

"What makes you think he'll listen to us?"

"He cared enough about you to work for me in the first place."

"What does that mean?"

"He discovered we were using his race car to transport our product, but chose to cooperate once he understood the potential repercussions to you and your sons."

Carol shivered. When Garraway first told her about the drugs, he said the dealers had threatened Harry's family before. She had seized the drugs as one more reason to hate her brother. She hadn't believed he'd cared about any danger to her or the boys.

She focused where the man's eyes would be behind the mask. "My brother and I lost contact years ago. I didn't know about his other crimes until I saw the news coverage. And I didn't know about any drug connection until you came after his money. Whatever else he's involved in, believe me, I don't know about it."

"You don't need to be close to your brother, merely deliver a message."

"A message. Fine. But leave Paul out of it. Please."

"Impossible. He'll be here any minute."

Carol's fists clenched, her forearm muscles straining against the bonds. "I was on my way to see a friend. When I don't show up, he'll phone the taxi company—and the police."

Lear raised one hand to the side of his head, thumb and little finger extended like a telephone receiver. "My cell was stolen. This is a loaner. Can you come see me?"

The voice turned her blood to slush. She'd thought Patrick had a slight cold or was upset. He didn't even know. Nobody knew. *God... You know. Help us!*

Lear resumed the deadly tone she knew so well from his phone calls. "No, Ms. Daniels, I think our meeting will proceed uninterrupted. As soon as your son arrives."

Chapter 38

THE DAY HAD never dragged so slowly at Morelli's. Paul bagged guitar strings for a customer and checked the clock again. Another two hours before his shift ended. Plenty of time to think about what a mess he'd made with Tara-Lynn and to imagine what she'd say when he called. If she answered.

Eric was on break, and the flurry of customers had ended. Paul picked up the polishing cloth and headed for the guitars. A couple of kids from school had been in earlier, and they'd left fingerprints on his Les Paul.

As he polished the ebony finish, the shop bell jingled. He turned to the door. At the sight of Tara-Lynn his smile froze.

Cheeks pink, she headed straight for him. She hadn't left so angry that she'd come back and slap him, had she?

He stepped away from the guitar just in case. "Hi."

"I'm sorry, Paul. I shouldn't have snapped at you like that—or jumped to conclusions."

Some of his anxiety disappeared. Some. "Don't apologize. You were right. I messed up again. I'm sorry."

"I went over to Starbucks for a pumpkin spice latte and an oatcake. And to talk to God. Not that I had to go to Starbucks to find Him, but I needed a pick-me-up, and I'm babbling again. I'm sorry."

Paul blinked. *God, if You're not still in the coffee shop, would You help me not blow it again?*

He fought to hold eye contact. "My dad was a musician, and he neglected Mom and us kids. You're the most special girl I've ever met. I've been afraid to ask you out in case I let you down."

He twisted the cloth in his hands. "If you're even interested."

Tara-Lynn's face had grown redder as he spoke. "That's not a choice you can make for me. Why don't you ask and see?"

"I—" The phone rang again. Paul rolled his eyes in apology, then hurried to the counter. "Morelli's, how may I help you?"

Tara-Lynn followed him and stood looking at the display while he talked. When he hung up, she stepped closer.

He leaned his elbows on the counter. "Come for pizza with me after work? So we can talk uninterrupted?"

She smiled. "Okay."

Eric came out of the back room. "Hey there, did you miss me?"

Paul wanted to growl at him.

The bell rang over the door, and he glanced up to greet the customer.

A burly man in a blue coat gave the store a once-over and strode to the counter. He fixed Paul with a hard stare. "Your mother's in trouble. Come with me."

One hand stayed in the stranger's pocket. Was that bulge a gun?

No way would Mom send a goon like this. She'd phone. Did the drug ring have her?

Sweat pricked Paul's neck. This guy could take him by force. And his eyes said he wouldn't care who else got hurt.

He locked the stranger's gaze and hurried from behind the cash register to stand between the man and Tara-Lynn.

"Okay. Thanks, mister. Let's go." He thrust his wallet at Eric. "Phone her boyfriend and let him know? His card's in there. Name's Garraway."

Heart thumping, he started for the door.

He looked around to see the man glare from him to Eric and back to him again before following. Away from Tara-Lynn. Good.

Paul kept moving.

He heard a thud from behind and spun to see Vincenzo Morelli holding a baseball bat.

The intruder was already pushing up from the floor.

Sirens wailed.

The burly man lurched to his feet and fled.

Morelli locked the door behind him and turned, brushing his palms together. "Not bad for an old fellow. Now, we wait."

Paul gaped at his boss. "I don't—"

"Eric triggered the silent alarm."

"Thanks, man." Eric could be a pain but right now, Paul loved him. "How did you know?"

"He walks in, makes a beeline for you, and tells you come. You call him 'mister' like you've never met, so how'd he know which of us was you?" Eric tapped his head. "I'm not just another beautiful bod, you know."

Tara-Lynn's giggle sounded a hair away from tears. She threw her arms around Paul.

When his boss merely smiled, Paul hugged her. Warmth blossomed inside amid the jangling panic, enough to unfreeze his mind.

Mom!

Paul squeezed Tara-Lynn and released her. "I've gotta call home."

Eric slid the phone across the counter.

As Paul counted the rings, a squad car pulled up outside.

Mr. Morelli unlocked the door and introduced himself to the responding officers.

Tara-Lynn stepped nearer to Paul's side. "Maybe she took Chance for a walk."

"Maybe." But his gut didn't agree. He hung up and opened his wallet to find Garraway's card.

She frowned at the card. "Does Joey know she has a boyfriend?"

"What? Oh, he isn't. He's a cop. I couldn't say it in front of that goon." He started the call before the officers with his boss could interrupt.

"Garraway."

Paul sucked air. He couldn't fall apart now. "It's Paul Daniels, sir. I'm at work and a man just tried to, I don't know, abduct me maybe. He said Mom was in trouble and I had to come. My boss chased him off. But she's not answering the phone. She should be home."

"I'll send a car. Has your boss called this in?"

"Yes, and the officers are here. But you're the one who knows what we're up against."

"You did the right thing, son. Let me speak to one of the officers on-site, please."

Covering the mouthpiece, he said, "Officers, Detective Garraway's on the phone, could one of you talk to him?"

They exchanged a glance. The taller, female officer strode to take the phone.

Paul turned to Tara-Lynn. "I thought this was behind us. I've got to stay away from you, I'm not safe."

Across the counter, Eric crooned, "I'm safe, sugar."

Tara-Lynn's mouth firmed. "Don't overprotect me. I can make my own choices."

The officer with Mr. Morelli finished taking notes, and both men approached Paul and Tara-Lynn. The woman who'd been on the phone hung up and beckoned her partner aside.

Paul seized his chance before he lost his nerve. "Mr. Morelli, I honestly thought this was over. I won't come back. I don't want to bring any more trouble."

The old man shook his head. "Trouble finds its own way. I want you to stay. The customers, they love you." He waggled a crooked finger under Paul's nose. "You may be my star pupil, but you have much to learn. I can't let you go unfinished."

Another time, the praise would have Paul flying, but all he could think about was his mother in danger.

He smiled his thanks, then stepped toward the two officers. "I need to go home. I think they got my mother."

Professional concern didn't quite mask their thoughts of what a teenager could do to help. The shorter officer, whose badge read *Watts*, flipped to a clean sheet in his notebook.

"A car's on its way to check your apartment. Detective Garraway brought us up to date. You and your coworker are quick thinkers." He eyed Mr. Morelli. "Although I don't advise the baseball bat approach. For now, I need you to tell me what happened here."

Paul gave his statement as quickly as he could, adding, "Please, I need to get home."

"I can take you." Tara-Lynn gave Officer Watts a sheet of paper. "I wrote out my contact information and what I saw."

He scanned the paper. "Very concise. Any relation to the Keirans who's running for mayor?"

Her cheeks pinked again. "She's my mother. I'd be happier if she didn't hear about this. She has a lot on her plate right now."

Paul hadn't put the names together, but he was only vaguely aware of the candidates anyway. The musician and the politician's daughter. Did he stand a chance?

He took her hand. Living on the fringes of media attention was something he understood, thanks to Uncle Harry.

Tara-Lynn was genuine, soft-hearted. Not glossy and image-conscious. He wondered if that caused problems at home.

When she smiled at him, he vowed with his eyes to be a safe place for her, where she could be herself with no pressure. He liked her true self. Wanted to know her better. For now though...

He turned to Officer Watts. "May we go?"

The man frowned. "The suspect may be planning to try again when you leave. We'll take you home when we finish here. It won't be long."

"So I'm a hostage?" He balled his fists. Would they stop him if he made a break for the door?

Tara-Lynn nudged his foot with hers. "Officer, what if I pulled my car up out front? You could be sure nobody grabbed him..."

Watts shook his head. "Our suspect could tail you in another car and take you both as soon as you hit a side street." He pinned Paul with a stare. "Promise to stay put, and I'll go light a fire under my partner."

Paul hesitated, then agreed. Becoming a fugitive himself wouldn't help Mom.

Watts headed for his partner, who stood at the counter interviewing Eric.

Mr. Morelli moved nearer to Paul and clasped his shoulders. "This city is not what it once was. Let me know when your mother is found safely. If I can be of any help, I will. And no more talk of quitting."

"Yes, sir. Thank you." He saw the two police officers approaching. "And thanks again for the baseball bat. That was a solid swing."

His employer's eyes crinkled in a smile.

The taller officer shook the older man's hand. "All done here, Mr. Morelli. We'll see Paul safely home and link up with the efforts to locate his mother. We'll be in touch."

Tara-Lynn jingled her car keys. "May I drive him? I'd feel safer than driving alone, and the sight of a squad car should keep the abductor away."

At the woman's nod, Tara-Lynn beckoned to Paul. "I'm parked in the lot down the street."

Chapter 39

AS SOON AS he stepped into the rain, Paul realized he'd left his jacket in the store.

Between the dash for the police cruiser and the transfer to Tara-Lynn's car in the nearby parking lot, he was soaked.

Tara-Lynn cranked the heater before leading the police car out onto the street. "It warms up fast."

"Don't worry about me. Just drive." He clamped his chattering teeth together.

She cut him a sidelong glance and hit the gas.

He kept quiet to let her concentrate on the road. That left the anxiety free to breed undistracted in his stomach. Before they reached his street, he'd imagined a thousand scenarios—all bad.

Another police car blocked the driveway. Tara-Lynn stopped across the street.

The officers who'd been riding shotgun continued on their way. Would Garraway know where to send them from there?

Paul leaped from the car before Tara-Lynn opened her seat belt.

She caught up and slipped a cold hand into his.

A muscular Black officer stepped from the cruiser.

Paul stopped in front of him. "I'm Paul Daniels."

"Constable Franklin. There's no response at the door, and nobody home upstairs. Do you recognize the car parked at the rear?"

The insurance company's rental. "That's ours. If she's in the apartment—"

Paul sprinted to the rear door, Tara-Lynn at his side and the officer right behind. He stuck his key in the lock and pushed into the kitchen.

"Mom?"

Chance bounded to lick his hand.

Paul followed a rich smell to the stove and lifted the pot lid. Stroganoff, still steaming although the burner was off. He scanned the room. "Her coat's gone."

Constable Franklin picked up a piece of paper from the counter. "Is this her writing?"

He snatched the outstretched sheet.

If you get home before I do, I've gone to Patrick's. Back soon.

Love, Mom.

Relief washed him. The next moment, he couldn't meet the officer's eyes. He felt hot and prickly all over. "Sorry for the false alarm."

"It's better to overreact than take chances. I'll update Detective Garraway, and he'll be in touch. The perp was definitely after you. You need to stay here and wait for Garraway's call. One question. Is this Patrick within walking distance?"

"He either picks her up or sends a taxi."

"Then that's the last loose end. I'll be on my way. Lock the door behind me."

Once the officer left, Paul crumpled the note and threw it in the trash. "Way to act like a complete idiot. I should have checked first."

Tara-Lynn shook her head. "What if she'd been hurt? You did the right thing."

"That cop didn't think so."

"He said he did."

"You heard the way he said it."

"Paul, you did the right thing. Don't beat yourself up over it. Let's just be glad she's okay. Are you going to phone her about that guy at the store?"

"She's expecting Joey for supper, so she won't be gone long. I wish I didn't have to tell her at all. She'll flip out." Paul shivered.

"You're soaked. Can I start water for hot chocolate while you change?"

"That'd be great. Thanks."

He pulled on dry jeans and a brushed flannel shirt, hung his wet clothes over the shower rod, and strolled into the kitchen. While the water heated, he scooped hot chocolate powder into mugs.

Trying to keep his voice casual, he asked, "You still want to hang out later, or will you be smart and find someone safer?"

"I'll be smart and stick with you. Will your mom let you out tonight after this?"

"I could be under house arrest forever." He'd fight that battle when it came. For now, it might be a good way to keep Tara-Lynn at a safe distance without hurting her again.

He opened his mouth to admit defeat and instead heard himself say, "That's a huge pot of stroganoff. Instead of pizza, you could stay for supper."

"Would your mom mind with Joey coming?"

"They were expecting me to eat with them anyway. It wasn't going to be romantic. I'll call her." He scrolled through the caller ID list and took a chance on the "P. Stairs" entry.

Patrick answered on the third ring. "Hello?"

"Hi, it's Paul Daniels. May I speak to my mother, please?"

"I'm afraid she's not here."

"Oh. When did she leave?"

"You misunderstand. She hasn't been here at all today."

"But she left a note—"

"Perhaps she came by while I was out, but I assure you, she is not here now. If you'll excuse me, I have urgent business." Click.

Panic boiled in Paul's stomach. "He says he hasn't seen her."

Tara-Lynn gasped. "But the note..."

"Yeah. And I'd swear it's her writing."

"Do you think someone forced her?"

"Maybe. But why leave a contact? I'd have just said gone out."

The kettle shut off. They both ignored it.

Tara-Lynn wrapped her arms around her ribs. "You need to phone the police again."

Officer Franklin's condescending tone echoed in Paul's mind, but what choice did he have? He pulled out his wallet. "Detective Garraway will listen to me."

At a sudden knock on the back door, their gazes locked. Paul hurried to answer.

Behind him, she whispered, "Be careful."

As if he needed reminding. He set the security chain and braced one foot behind the door before easing the door open a crack. "Who is it?"

"Joey. What's up?"

Paul's breath whooshed from his lungs. He fumbled to unhook the chain and flung the door wide. "Am I glad to see you!"

Frowning, Joey stepped inside and closed the door against the rain. "What's wrong? Where's your mom?"

"She's—" Paul's voice cracked. "A guy tried to abduct me from work. Said she was in trouble. When we got here, we found a note that she'd gone to visit a friend. But I called, and he said she's not there."

Joey didn't seem to notice Tara-Lynn take the roses from his hand and lay them on the counter. "Patrick."

"Yeah. Does it matter?"

"I never liked the sound of him."

Paul snorted. "I never liked the feel of him. But he said he hasn't seen her. I've gotta call the cops."

The phone rang, and all three of them jumped. Paul snatched it. "Hello?"

"This is Patrick Stairs. The drug ring has your mother. You need to call the police, but I see only one chance to rescue her. Will you trust me?"

Tara-Lynn and Joey were both staring. Paul mouthed "Patrick" and asked, "Do I have a choice?"

"At the risk of sounding melodramatic, not if you want to see her alive again. Do you have transportation?"

"Yes."

"Meet me at the old paint factory on Harkins Drive. We'll go together from there. Tell the police no sirens." Patrick clicked off.

Paul hung up and stared helplessly at Joey and Tara-Lynn. "He says Mom's in danger, but if I meet him he might be able to help. Joey, will you drive me? Tara-Lynn, I need you to go home. And pray."

As one, they shook their heads. Even their frowns matched.

Tara-Lynn stepped toward him. "I told you, I'm not leaving. I want to help."

"If you get hurt, it makes things worse!"

Her scowl said it didn't matter.

Joey shook his head. "Tell me where, and I'll go. You phone the police and stay here."

Paul stepped nose-to-nose with him. "She's my mother. I have more right than you."

"Granted. But if she loses you, it'll kill her."

Tara-Lynn came to stand by Paul. "I'll take you. Let's go."

Sighing, Paul shoved his feet into his wet running shoes. "I hope I live to regret this."

Joey growled, "Me too. Come on, I'll drive. You can phone the police on the way."

Chapter 40

JOEY FORCED HIMSELF not to speed—much. The GPS on his phone led him to the rendezvous point.

Paul and Tara-Lynn sat in the back, quiet and pale.

Not a good idea. Dare they trust Patrick?

He flicked the turn indicator and pulled into the parking lot. A gleaming Porsche sheltered beside the metal building.

He cut through a puddle and pulled up to the car from the opposite direction.

The Porsche's window powered down.

Joey opened his and matched the driver's glare with his own. Accusations clogged his throat.

Patrick checked the rear seat. His frown eased. "Did you phone the police?"

Paul had made the call while Joey drove. Now, he spoke through his own lowered window. "They'll follow from here. No sirens."

The boy was scared, but he sounded determined.

"Good." Patrick's jaw firmed. "I swear I didn't know this would happen. Lear will be furious that his goon bungled picking you up. If I take you in as a captive, we can get close enough to attempt a rescue."

Joey clenched the steering wheel. "Or delivering Paul is part of the plan and you get a reward."

"He'll have to trust me." Patrick's stare burned into Joey. "What are your intentions toward Carol?"

"Excuse me?"

"Answer the question."

He felt Paul and Tara-Lynn listening from the back seat. "I want to be her friend. More, if she'll let me."

"Treat her well." Patrick's eyes narrowed. "You had the guts to walk away from drug ties. I couldn't. But I will kill Lear before I let him hurt Carol. Tell her I'm sorry. And that I cared."

A rustle in behind him made Joey glance in the rear-view mirror.

Paul gave Tara-Lynn a quick kiss and opened his door. "I believe him. You two, pray. I've gotta go."

He ran around the vehicles and jumped into Patrick's car. The Porsche shot away.

Joey wheeled around to follow as two unmarked cars eased away from the curb. He tried not to hear Tara-Lynn's sniffles.

~~~

Lear strode across the warehouse room to meet his henchman. Carol couldn't hear the conversation, but the man's hunched posture spoke worry. The drug lord seemed to swell.

A brief conversation sent the other man scurrying toward the windowless door she assumed led deeper into the building.

Lear shoved his hands into his pockets and walked toward her across the cavernous space. "It seems your son declined the invitation."

His tight voice belied his casual stance. So did the fist shapes in his trouser pockets. "Which means he will be the messenger, and you the message. Hopefully not a significant reduction in my bargaining power."

Carol blinked at her captor, but she didn't really care what he meant. Paul was safe.

Lear peeled the stocking mask from his head. He pulled a black comb from his pocket and tidied his hair, then flashed a chilling smile. "With no witness, I might as well have an unobstructed view."

His henchman approached, carrying a briefcase. Lear dragged the other chair to the side, and the man set down the case. Lear twiddled the combination dials and opened it.

The array of syringes and vials made Carol's mouth go dry. She strained against her bonds.

The man stepped nearer and pushed up her sleeve. He ran a finger across the corded muscle in her elbow crease, then snapped a rubber tube around her bicep and pulled it tight.

She tore her gaze away and met Lear's over the man's shoulder. The satisfaction in his smile froze the plea on her lips.

He inhaled deeply and moved to study the vials. "Now, what would be best? And how much for her weight? No point wasting any."

It sounded more like musings than actual questions. The other man didn't answer.

Carol prayed for help with her eyes open.

Nobody even knew she was in danger, tied up here in some God-forsaken warehouse. What did she expect, a lightning bolt to fry these two? An angel with a sword?

She bit her tongue to stop a scream. Lear seemed the type to want her awake to experience his torment, but if she went hysterical she had no doubt he'd clout her. No matter how bad it was, she had to see it coming.

Carol shook her head. She was still controlling what little she could. *God, help me be brave. I'm not in control, but I choose to believe You are. Take care of Paul. I trust you with my son.*

Tears trickled down her cheeks, but suddenly Lear's meaning came clear. He'd wanted to do this to Paul. With her watching.

A wave of cold swept her. Thank God her son was free.

Lear's "message" must be death or he wouldn't have unmasked.

It wouldn't be Paul.

This would be brutal for him. But he'd have Tara-Lynn, maybe Joey. He wouldn't be alone.

Lear gave a vial to his helper. "This one, I think. She's on the heavy side, so be sure to use enough."

The man selected a syringe from the case and fitted a needle to the tip. He sneered at Carol, then loaded the syringe from the vial and held it to the light.

Behind them, the door to the cavernous loading garage banged open.

Lear whipped the mask over his head again.

"What do you mean, bypassing me on this?" Patrick's voice. Behind her—not from Lear.

She'd never heard him so angry.

Lear waved a casual hand. "You sounded a touch reluctant, Pat. By all means, join us. And introduce your friend."

Patrick strode into view. With Paul.

Carol couldn't stop a moan.

Paul gave her a sick smile, but Patrick focused on Lear. "I wasn't backing out, just asking for more time. I thought I'd been given it."

Her mouth opened, but she found no words. Nausea choked her.

Patrick pushed Paul aside and advanced on Lear. "It's a good thing you left me out, so I could clean up after the B team botched their pickup. Lucky for you the boy called me. He thought this was a rescue mission."

Swift as a hunter, Patrick stepped behind Lear and threw his arm around the drug lord's throat. Lear's body arced backward. From the crook of Patrick's other arm, Carol assumed he held a weapon.

Patrick still wouldn't look at her. He glared at Lear's henchman. "Sit on the floor. Away from the case. Paul, get your mother out of here."

Lear swore. "You're dead."

Patrick's features could have been carved from marble. "They leave first."

Paul's touch on her arm made her jump. His other hand gripped a knife. "It's okay, Mom. Hold still. I'll cut you loose."

The cool blade slid between her skin and the rope. She couldn't stop staring at Patrick. "Why?"

Patrick continued to focus on the man on the floor.

Lear spoke, his voice constricted by the arm across his throat. "Pat's one of my errand boys. I should have realized he was too squeamish for more than deliveries."

"Pat-*rick*." His elbow jerked Lear's chin higher. "Carol, I'm truly sorry. I lost the fight to save the first woman I loved. It won't happen again. I hope you can forgive me."

His looked her way at last.

A blur in her peripheral vision resolved into Lear's henchman launching at Patrick.

A gun roared. Lear crumpled.

Patrick turned the gun on his attacker. The two men shot simultaneously.

Both fell.

Paul cut the last rope and pulled Carol to her feet.

She clutched him blindly, then staggered toward Patrick.

"Mom, come on."

But she dropped to her knees at Patrick's side.

Blood pumped from a hole in his chest. His gaze sought hers, bright and aware.

She pressed both hands over the wound. Blood slid under her palms. "Patrick, your phone—which pocket? We'll call 9-1-1."

"Too... late." The gurgle in his voice stopped her breath. "For... give?"

She held his gaze, willing him to stay conscious. "I don't understand what you did, but I forgive you. Thank you for rescuing me. Rita would be proud."

"And... you?"

"I'm proud of you too. You saved my life."

Patrick's cold lips barely responded to her kiss, then stilled. The light left his eyes.

Paul tugged her shoulder. "We've gotta go. Garraway said get out fast."

Blindly, Carol stood and let her son pull her from the room. They fled through the loading garage and out into the rain.

A swarm of police officers surged for the building, but only two figures stood out to her—Joey and Tara-Lynn, running toward them.

She fell into Joey's arms, sobbing.

Chapter 41

THE PHONE RANG in the kitchen. Carol stayed flat on the couch.

Paul's bedroom door opened. He skidded into the kitchen and caught the phone on the fourth ring.

Carol rolled onto her side and drew her knees up. She pulled the faded red blanket tighter around her shoulders and stared at the darkened television. Beside her on the floor, Chance snuffled in his sleep.

Paul spoke from the kitchen. "Phone's for you. It's Joey."

"I don't want to talk."

"He's worried about you. So am I. If you don't take the call, I'll tell him to come over."

Her sigh came out like a moan. She pushed up from the couch and shuffled into the kitchen, trailing the blanket.

The telephone receiver felt cold in her hand, hollow. "Hi, Joey. Did you get some sleep last night?"

"Complete with terrible dreams. How about you?"

"Not much."

"Mmm. That's why I waited until after church to call. Do you want to take Chance to the park?"

She stared out the window. The rain had stopped in the night, and a weak autumn sun tried to warm sodden tree branches. "Paul can take him out later."

"Yesterday was a lot. I thought you might be baking."

Another sigh vibrated the emptiness inside her. "Coping mechanisms only go so far. I've tried to pray, but it feels like God's in shock too."

"I'll be there as soon as I can."

"No. I mean, I'm in my sleep stuff, and I haven't even showered. Today isn't a good day."

"I'll drive slowly. Paul can let me in if you're still in the shower."

"Joey—"

"No buts. Take your time, and I'll see you soon."

When he hung up, she stared at the phone before dropping it into the cradle. Joey, so warm and caring. Patrick, dead. She couldn't close her eyes without seeing his corpse.

On the way to her bedroom for clean clothes, she paused by Paul's door. "He's coming anyway."

Showering eased the numbness a bit, and at the last minute she couldn't meet Joey in stretched-out leggings and an oversized sweatshirt. She left her comfort clothes in a heap on the bed and put on her favourite dress.

As she stepped into flat shoes, it hit her. She'd worn this dress the day she went to the gallery with Patrick.

Fresh tears started. Okay, she'd let this be a kind of memorial to him.

She shrugged into a cardigan and went to tidy the living room before Joey arrived.

His car pulled up as she was folding the blanket. She picked up the morning's empty tea mug and carried it into the kitchen on her way to let him in.

Chance raced her. She nudged him aside with her knee and opened the door.

Joey's gaze flickered from her face to her dress and back again. "You sure clean up nice."

He stretched a thumb to swipe away the newest tear, then drew her into his arms. "You're safe now. The danger's gone."

"So is Patrick."

Releasing her, he offered a sad smile. "He loved you."

The numb mass that was Carol's heart couldn't respond. She reached past him to close the door. "So he said."

"How did you feel about him?" Joey's voice had gone quiet. "Not that I have a right to ask."

"I was sorry for him, living in that big house with only his dead wife's cat for company."

She stepped aside and picked up the kettle. "Paul made me tea earlier, but I need another cup. Can I get you something?"

"Not now, thanks. I had coffee with lunch. There's that fine line between keeping awake and getting caffeine jitters." He settled in a chair.

She reached for a teabag and a clean mug, then came to sit opposite him. "I can't get my head around what Patrick did. But in the end, he gave his life to save me."

Joey's hand covered hers.

The warmth steadied her. When the water boiled, she jumped up to make her tea. "I'm glad you came. I still feel lost in the gloom, but at least you got me off the couch."

"And into the kitchen, but there's no baking happening. Paul and I will waste away." He rubbed his stomach.

His forlorn tone made her laugh.

The next second, her tears flowed.

"Oh, Carol, I'm sorry. That one bombed big-time." He reached to hug her, but she dodged and grabbed a handful of tissues from the box on the counter.

Mopping tears, she turned toward him. "It's okay. Thanks for trying. Hey, I never said thank you for the flowers. Paul put them in water when we got home from the police station. They're in the living room."

His moustache twitched. "You're welcome. We dropped them and ran when Patrick called."

"At least the stroganoff got put in the fridge. I know this isn't how we planned it, but would you stay for supper tonight?"

"You sure?"

"Do I look like I want to eat leftovers all week?" She almost produced a smile.

"Then yes, please. But you're not off the hook for our dinner and movie when you feel up to it."

Light flickered in her gloom, small but steady. "Okay." She picked up her tea. "Let's go see your roses. Maybe Paul will come out of his room."

Following her, Joey asked softly, "How's he doing?"

"I think he's just glad it's over. He's shocked, but he doesn't have any grief to live with. Thank God. He's had more than his share already."

She tapped on Paul's door before they settled on the couch.

Eventually, he wandered out to join them. When he heard Joey was staying for supper, he said, "Don't take this the wrong way, but would you guys mind if I skipped out? Tara-Lynn and I were going to get a pizza last night."

He avoided Carol's stare and looked at Joey. "There's some stuff we need to talk about, but I didn't want to leave Mom alone."

Carol sat a little straighter. "I'll be okay."

"Mom—"

Joey nodded. "I'll stay as long as your mom wants me to."

Paul poised for a second on the edge of his seat, then walked into the kitchen to the phone.

Carol raised an eyebrow at Joey. "If we haven't scared that girl away yet, she's a keeper."

"For sure." He smothered a yawn.

"Coffee now?"

"No thanks, but could I pour myself a glass of water? After Paul finishes arranging his date."

"Of course. And I made your favourite cookies yesterday morning."

He stared toward the kitchen. "How long do you think he'll be on the phone?"

After Tara-Lynn collected Paul, Carol heated their supper. She set the roses on the table and turned on the kitchen radio, but she spent more time pushing stroganoff and linguine strands around her plate than eating. "You didn't have to bring flowers last night."

"I wanted to celebrate your step of faith... and our friendship."

Remembered terror spiked her pulse. "I'd have gone out of my mind without God yesterday. Nobody knew I was in danger, but somehow He was there. As scared as I was, I knew if I died, He'd look after Paul."

"He helped us find you." Joey's hand shook as he reached for his water glass. "Patrick's desperate plan. Tara-Lynn and I prayed up a storm in the car. It was awful not knowing what was going on."

"Patrick bringing Paul in... that was the worst." She pressed her lips tight, but the trembling spread and she started crying again.

"Hey, c'mere." His chair scraped.

The care in his voice made her cry harder. She pushed out from the table and went into his arms.

Joey's warmth, his steady heartbeat, Bob Seger's "Against the Wind" on the radio...

Gradually, her tears slowed. She leaned into the embrace, and their steps fell into rhythm with the song.

The music worked into her muscles. By the time the song ended, they were genuinely dancing.

A tiny bubble of laughter escaped her as they stepped apart.

Moustache twitching, Joey bowed. "Thank you, milady."

She dropped a mock curtsy. The next song's opening notes froze her feet en route to her chair. "Honesty." It didn't get more appropriate than that. She glanced at Joey.

He held out his arms.

She settled her palms on his shoulders, and they moved together to the beat. In flat shoes, she wasn't that much taller than him.

Their gazes locked. Joey's kindled, and his arms tightened around her. Their steps slowed.

Carol moistened her lips, anticipation tingling in her veins. She leaned nearer and closed her eyes for his kiss.

Joey pressed a finger against her mouth.

He released her and stepped away, his gaze still heated. "Yesterday shook us both, and people do crazy things for comfort. But I can't kiss you under false pretenses."

Carol worked to slow her breathing, to quell the sweet sensation that set her heart racing. She drilled him with a stare. "If you're married—or gay—I do *not* want to hear it tonight."

"Innocent on both counts. A friend could kiss you and forget it, but... I love you."

He spread his palms. "You didn't need to hear that tonight either. No pressure, no expectations. I know you don't need a man in your life. But I hoped if we kept spending time together, you'd begin to feel something for me."

Carol gave her head a slow shake, trying to sort through her tangled reactions. This man who'd knocked her self-reliance for a loop, who listened and supported and never demanded... loved her.

She could see it now in his eyes, and it warmed her deep inside.

It took willpower to put a bite in her voice. "I feel something right now, mister."

He seemed to wilt, and she couldn't keep from smiling. "Relief. I thought I was going to lose you." She threw her arms around him and buried her head against his shoulder.

Joey's arms circled her and held tight.

When she lifted her head, his hold loosened, but she didn't step back. "I'll take you up on that invitation. Let's see what happens."

Eyes closed, she brought her lips to meet his. This time, he didn't pull away.

Epilogue

CAROL HAD FORGOTTEN the delirious sound of a live band in a confined space. Standing against the rear wall with Joey, she drank it all in.

Driving bass line, passionate drums, hoarse vocals, lead guitar cranked into the sweet spot without slipping into a jangling buzz. Paul on stage, grey leather jacket hanging open and hair sweat-spiked, lost in Beatles chords.

The music, the excited high school crowd, swept her back to her own teens and the magic of those early years with Skip. Paul delivered a screaming guitar solo, and her pulse thrilled.

She put her lips to Joey's ear. "He *is* good."

Smiling, he tightened his arm around her waist. "Told you so."

They could have sat with Tara-Lynn and Amber, but Carol hadn't been sure she could stay. Now, she couldn't leave.

She caught Vincenzo Morelli's eye farther along the wall. Pride radiated from him in nearly visible waves, and no wonder. The music teacher nodded, and she smiled.

The Les Paul sounded as good as Paul said it would.

It was the guitar that made Carol accept the surprise inheritance from Patrick. Half his estate went to cancer research and half to her. At least he hadn't left her the evil cat.

The lawyer assured her it was legitimate even though Patrick had made the changes the morning of his death. She wouldn't see the bulk of the cash until all the paperwork was settled, but the lawyer had advanced funds to cover Paul's dream guitar.

She couldn't think of Patrick without sadness. He'd betrayed her, but then he'd given his life to save her.

If he hadn't died, word of his involvement with Lear would have destroyed his reputation. Image was all he'd had left. Maybe he'd prefer it this way.

His bequest could never compensate for what she'd been through, but she respected his desire to make amends. She hoped his soul was at peace.

The death of Lear—identified in the media as George Sinclare—brought sheer relief.

Detective Garraway had said the drug ring scattered like roaches under a spotlight before their leader reached the morgue. So much for the carefully-assembled evidence.

While she'd have loved to see justice done, with Lear gone she and Paul were free.

Paul had sent Harry a letter after things settled down. She'd have to talk to Harry herself. Give him a chance to tell his side of the story, see if he'd truly changed. Someday.

For now, it was enough to be free.

The band's raw energy vibrated through the floor into her feet.

Free and in God's hands. God would do a better job shaping their lives than she had done alone. Look at Paul on stage, full of talent and potential.

She leaned into Joey's side. Who'd have thought she'd be learning to trust the heart of God—and the heart of an innocent man?

The song ended in a drawn-out chord rattling with reverb. When the applause died down, Paul gripped the microphone. "This next song's not in our usual lineup. For a special lady, Billy Joel's 'It's Still Rock and Roll to Me.' I love you, Mom."

~THE END~

~ ~ ~

Curious about what stopped Cousin Amy's wedding? Want to meet her and get to know Michael Stratton, the "Waters" painter?

Find out in *Without Proof,* Redemption's Edge book 3.

Keep reading for a peek at *Without Proof,* discussion questions for *Secrets and Lies,* and more.

~ ~ ~

And what exactly did Carol's brother Harry do? Could he have truly found redemption, despite his crimes? *Heaven's Prey,* Redemption's Edge 1, tells his story—and the story of Ruth Warner, the prayer warrior whose faith could have cost her life.

Find out more by reading *Heaven's Prey.* Because of the subject matter, this one's more intense. And it's not romantic, just suspense. Get your copy at books2read.com/heavens-prey-special.

~ ~ ~

Author's Note

Thank you for spending time with some of my imaginary friends. I hope you enjoyed *Secrets and Lies*.

You've finished the story, but you don't have to go yet.

Keep reading for a peek at the next Redemption's Edge novel, *Without Proof*. The following pages also include discussion questions for *Secrets and Lies*.

I hope you'll check out the rest of the Redemption's Edge series. You might also like my mystery/suspense Green Dory Inn series. For advance notice of new releases and any online discounts, be sure to subscribe to my mailing list at janetsketchley.ca/subscribe or follow me on Bookbub.

Finally, a favour if you're so inclined: Could you drop a brief review on Goodreads or your favourite online bookstore? Nothing fancy, just mention what you liked or didn't like, and why. No spoilers, please!

God bless you, and remember: trouble has a way of finding us, but God finds us too

Thanks for reading!

WITHOUT PROOF

(REDEMPTION'S EDGE, BOOK 3)

Prologue

ONE OF AMY'S spun glass Christmas angels twisted on its golden thread, sparkling in the tree lights. Of the original six, five remained, treasured links to her childhood.

Michael and his great-aunt had invited her to add a few ornaments to the bushy spruce he'd brought home this afternoon. Another thoughtful gesture in the string of kindnesses they'd shown her since the plane crash.

She inhaled the pungent sharpness of a live evergreen. Living alone, she'd had a tabletop artificial tree. This year, in the excitement of wedding plans, she and Gilles hadn't thought ahead to Christmas.

Now it was moot. Her fiancé lay in a frozen cemetery while she took refuge with his best friend.

Her injuries were healing. Her heart, not so much.

Adjusting the recliner's footrest, she repositioned the cold pack against her hip. She hadn't helped much with the decorating, but clearly she'd overdone something.

Aunt Bay returned to the living room carrying two china mugs. She set one on the table at Amy's elbow and carried the other to her seat. "Tired?"

"A little. Thanks for the tea."

"Orange spice. It's a good Christmas tea." Aunt Bay didn't look any more filled with seasonal joy than Amy felt.

Bare months since the tragedy, all three of them were still grieving. Yet Michael and his aunt claimed Christmas mattered more than ever in the middle of pain.

Amy picked up her tea and breathed the warm spices. The first sip was bitter, but her taste buds adjusted quickly.

Aunt Bay put on some quiet instrumental carols. "There's a candlelight concert at church this evening. You haven't been anywhere other than appointments. Come with us?"

Amy's chest tightened. "Thanks, but you know I don't do church."

"Christmas brings a lot of visitors who won't come other times."

"Let's just say God doesn't want me in His house."

The older woman's delicate eyebrows arched. "Why would you think that?"

Heat prickled Amy's hairline. "I'm an outsider."

"We're all outsiders until He brings us in."

Amy stared at the tree. "You and Michael go."

"Child, you're no better and no worse than the rest of the planet. That's the point of Christmas: Nobody's good enough to reach God, so God came to reach us. No matter who we've been or what we've done."

"Please—I can't—"

Aunt Bay's expression softened. "God does care. He'll show you, but you'll need to keep your eyes open to see it." A twinkle lit her pale blue eyes. "I can almost guarantee it won't be what you'd expect."

Holding her tea in both hands, Amy concentrated on the heat against her palms. With her heart in tatters, she didn't dare think about the other longings in her life.

The music seemed suddenly louder for "Joy to the World." Amy set her mug on the table and rammed the footrest back into place. Any more cheer and she might explode.

She grasped her cane and levered herself to her feet. Before she took a step, her cellphone rang. A perfect excuse to leave the room. "Excuse me."

Call display showed *L. Renaud.* The man who should have been her father-in-law. "Hello?" Pressing the phone to her ear, she kept walking.

"It's Luc. Are you free this evening? Could I see you?" Tension threaded his voice. Or perhaps it was the connection.

"Is there a problem?"

"I just picked up a rental car at the airport. Expect me in about forty-five minutes." He disconnected.

What now? She shoved the phone into her pocket and limped into the kitchen.

Not bothering with a light, she stared out the window at the darkness. She was stronger now. If Luc wanted more trouble, he wouldn't find her so easy to push around. Not that he'd done the pushing. He'd left that to his wife.

Footsteps sounded behind her. The under-cabinet lights flicked on. "Amy?" Michael's voice, gentle, tentative.

She pivoted on her cane.

He'd changed from his painting clothes into tan pants and a soft brown sweater a few shades darker than his hair. "Aunt Bay said she upset you."

"She didn't mean to."

"That doesn't make it better." He stepped nearer. "You don't mind being here by yourself tonight, do you?"

If only. "Luc just phoned. He's in town again and wants to see me."

His brows pulled together. "Do you want me to stay?"

317

"Go enjoy your concert. I don't expect him to be here long."

Michael's slow scrutiny seemed to satisfy his concern. "Say hello for me. And enjoy your space."

"I will."

When they left, Amy plugged her phone into the living room speaker dock and switched to mellow jazz. Anything but happy-peppy seasonal sounds.

Before long, engine vibrations indicated Luc's arrival.

She met him at the door.

Gilles' father wore his grief etched in his face. He seemed smaller somehow as if he were shrinking inside. He stood on the doorstep, shoulders hunched, and offered a smile. "How are you feeling?"

"I'm making progress. My therapist says I'll be able to lose the cane eventually." Trying her hardest not to limp, she led him into the living room and took a seat.

Luc walked to inspect the Christmas tree before turning to face her. "I arranged a meeting in Halifax tomorrow morning to have an excuse to be here. My wife—Amy, I'm beyond sorry."

He pulled an envelope from his coat, his hand shaking as he passed it to her.

What had Honore done now? The envelope was too small to be a legal document or other official paperwork. Holding her breath, Amy slit the seal and peeked inside.

A curve of metal lay tucked into one corner. "My engagement ring!"

Her fingertips caressed it, ached to return it to her hand. But those days were over.

Luc's face darkened. "I found it in the safe at home. I swear I didn't know she had it."

Amy pinned him with a hard stare. "The hospital staff gave Honore my jewellery for safekeeping. When she cleared all my things out of Gilles' apartment, she threw everything together in a mess and accused me of losing my ring in the bags."

"I'm sorry I wasn't there for you. I was—lost." Luc wiped a hand across the heavy lines in his face. He still looked lost.

Her heart twinged a tiny bit. Not enough to excuse him. "We were all devastated. At least you had the rest of your family. I had no one." Not that she'd wanted Honore's help.

Luc's sigh bordered on a moan. "Michael and his aunt are good people. They'll help you until you're ready to resume your career. I have nothing to offer you. I wish things could have been different." He walked to the door.

Amy pushed to her feet and followed him. "Luc? Thank you for my ring. For coming in person to return it."

"Goodbye, Amy. Stay safe."

The door opened, and he went out into the night.

Amy locked up behind him and climbed the stairs to her bedroom. She took the ring from its envelope and pressed the diamond to her lips.

So few connections to Gilles. A handful of photos on her phone and one or two gifts that his mother hadn't realized had come from him. Honore had taken everything else.

This ring couldn't bring him back, but it proved he'd loved her.

She opened her jewellery box and found a thin gold chain to hold her treasure. When she slipped the chain over her head and felt the weight of the ring against her chest, a shiver swept her shoulders.

Her mind replayed Aunt Bay's words. *It won't be what you'd expect.*

Amy narrowed her eyes at her reflection in the mirror. This couldn't be a sign of God's care.

There wouldn't be a sign. Not for her.

~~~

Eighteen months later

The man roamed the cramped apartment, phone to his ear. Nothing in the other's report could account for his disquiet.

His thoughts circled back to the heart of his concern. "You're certain she suspects nothing?"

"I'm telling you, she's not a threat to the organization. Even if she did start asking questions, there's no proof. Who's going to believe her? She's not worth the time to neutralize."

He spoke through clenched teeth. "I want to come out there."

"You'd blow it all sky high. We've invested too much in this plan to let you ruin it now. I'm here on the ground. Let me handle it."

"If she gets in the way..." A muscle spasm stole his breath.

If Amy Silver became a risk factor, he'd be on the next plane East. No matter the consequences.

~~~

Without Proof, Redemption's Edge book 3, is Carol's cousin Amy's story. It's another romantic suspense novel, available in ebook and print.

Order your copy at books2read/without-proof or at your favourite online retailer.

DISCUSSION QUESTIONS

1. Carol is afraid to pray for help, because last time she tried things got worse. How do our past experiences in prayer shape our present efforts?

2. Her praying friend blamed Carol's lack of faith for Keith's death. Have you encountered this type of toxic faith that blames a person for not getting what they pray for? How do you balance "whatever you ask for in prayer, believe that you have received it, and it will be yours" (Mark 11:24) with "Abba, Father... everything is possible for you... Yet not what I will, but what you will" (Mark 14:36)?

3. Carol loves her son Paul, but he feels trapped by the control she wants to have over his life. How can we give our children independence in stages as they grow while preparing them to make good adult choices?

4. To Paul, playing guitar is something he needs as much as breathing or eating. That doesn't excuse his disobedience, but what do you think might have happened to his easygoing nature if he'd denied his need? Is there another way he could have handled this?

5. What element of creativity is there in your life that's as essential as Paul's music? How does denying it affect you? What happens when you come back to it again?

6. The walls Carol puts up to protect herself keep out the good as well as the bad. And when she needs help, she doesn't necessarily turn to the best person. How can we discern whom to trust?

7. What do you think of Paul's reaction when Joey's church won't accept tainted money? Sincere Christians can find themselves on opposite sides of this emotionally charged issue. How do we deal with it while maintaining unity in the family of Christ?

8. Joey has a good understanding of God's grace. He doesn't judge others because he needed God to clean up his own problems. How can remembering where we've come from give us a non-judgmental acceptance of others?

9. What do you think of Joey's advice about not having to learn all the hard lessons ourselves? How have you learned from others' mistakes? How might your own help someone else? How might you share?

10. Joey encourages Carol to trust God's heart. What difference does knowing God's character and authority make when you're facing a crisis? What does walking with Him through a crisis do to your faith?

11. Patrick tried faith and gave up when it didn't bring the results he wanted. He asked for a good thing: healing for his wife. What could he have done instead of turning away? Is faith about us or about God?

12. Carol's convict brother claims God has forgiven him. Paul asks, does that make God amazingly weak or strong? Does forgiveness depend on what we've done or on the one doing the forgiving?

ACKNOWLEDGEMENTS

This is another novel that was years in the making, with too many bits of input along the way for me to safely remember them all.

For the first edition: Lyn Kublick and Eunice Matchett faithfully critiqued an early version, as did my patient husband, Russell. Thank you to my son, Matthew, for helping me better understand the character who Carol calls Creepy Voice. A shout-out to Janice Dick and Ramona Furst for the input in naming the character of Barry. Thank you to my early readers, Ruth Ann Adams, Heidi Newell, Russell Sketchley and Beverlee Wamboldt, and to everyone who contributed in any way, large or small.

I was greatly encouraged by Nicole O'Dell's positive words about this story. Thank you to Valerie Comer for allowing me to follow in her footsteps in this journey into the unknown territory of independent publishing. And thank you to Angela Breidenbach for her editing insights. Any mistakes are my own.

For this second edition, thank you to my patient early readers who followed me through this story once again: Ruth Ann Adams, Heidi Newell, and Russell Sketchley.

Above all, I thank God for allowing me to write and for giving me the ideas and the push I needed to use them.

BOOKS BY JANET SKETCHLEY

In the Redemption's Edge Series:

Heaven's Prey (book 1)

High octane Christian suspense meets women's fiction in this battle of wits between the prayer warrior and the fallen hero.

Ruth Warner is broken. Her adult niece's violent death at the hands of a serial rapist-murderer leaves her bitter. Tempted to reject her faith, Ruth instead finds healing through praying for the victims' families. But pray for the predator himself? Never. Until she does—and a botched kidnapping leaves her as his next victim.

Harry Silver is a champion race car driver gone wrong. His dark passions destroyed innocent lives, and now they've shattered the career he loved. Stuck with this middle-aged captive instead of the girl who fuelled his passions, Harry vows to make his prisoner pay. For being the wrong woman—and for being a Christian.

Harry has no idea he's stumbled into a battle for his soul—a soul he knows is not worth saving. Ruth has invested too many prayers and tears to give up now. Not when his coming to faith is the only way to save her life.

From the pulse-pounding tension to the grief and human drama, Heaven's Prey will keep you turning pages.

Order your copy at <u>books2read.com/heavens-prey-special</u> or from your favourite online retailer.

Without Proof (book 3)

"Asking questions could cost your life."

Two years after the plane crash that killed her fiancé, Amy Silver has fallen for his best friend, artist Michael Stratton. When a local reporter claims the small aircraft may have been sabotaged, it reopens Amy's grief.

Anonymous warnings and threats are her only proof that the tragedy was deliberate, and she has nowhere to turn. The authorities don't believe her, God is not an option, and Michael's protection is starting to feel like a cage.

How will Amy find the truth?

Order your copy at books2read.com/without-proof or from your favourite online retailer.

In the Green Dory Inn Mystery Series:

Unknown Enemy
Hidden Secrets
Bitter Truth
Deadly Burden
...and more TBA

For advance notice of when the next book releases, connect at janetsketchley.ca/subscribe or follow me on Bookbub.

Daily Devotions:

A Year of Tenacity
365 Daily Devotions to Warm Your Spirit and Encourage
Your Heart

Tenacity at Christmas
31 Daily Devotions for December

Readers' Journals (print only):

Reads to Remember
A book-lover's journal to track your next 100 reads

~~~

Janet Sketchley is an award-winning Atlantic Canadian writer who likes her fiction with a splash of mystery or adventure and a dash of Christianity. Why leave faith out of our stories if it's part of our lives?

She's the author of the Green Dory Inn mystery series, the Redemption's Edge Christian suspense series, and the daily devotional books, *A Year of Tenacity* and *Tenacity at Christmas*. She has also produced a fill-in reader's journal, *Reads to Remember: A book lover's journal to track your next 100 reads* (available in print only). Find her online at janetsketchley.ca.

Subscribe to Janet's newsletter at janetsketchley.ca/subscribe or follow her on Bookbub.